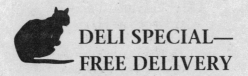

DELI SPECIAL—
FREE DELIVERY

"Joe, ever since you learned how to use the phone, my bill at Jolly's Deli has been unbelievable. Doesn't the delivery man get suspicious when you tell him to leave it on the porch?"

"Come on, Clyde, what am I supposed to tell him—shove it through the cat-door?"

Clyde picked up a wrapper. "What is this black smear? Caviar!?! And this pink—" He sniffed it and glared furiously at his cat. "Smoked salmon!!"

Joe Grey licked his whiskers. "They were having a special."

By Shirley Rousseau Murphy

Cat Under Fire

Shirley Rousseau Murphy

AVON BOOKS
An Imprint of HarperCollins*Publishers*

AVON BOOKS
An Imprint of HarperCollins*Publishers*
10 East 53rd Street
New York, New York 10022-5299

Copyright © 1996 by Shirley Rousseau Murphy
Cover illustration by Joe Burleson
ISBN: 0-06-105601-4
www.avonbooks.com

First Avon Books paperback printing: December 2000
First HarperPaperbacks printing: January 1997

Avon Trademark Reg. U.S. Pat. Off. and in Other Countries, Marca Registrada, Hecho en U.S.A.
HarperCollins® is a trademark of HarperCollins Publishers Inc.

Printed in the U.S.A.

20 19 18 17 16 15 14 13

For those who wonder about their cats.
And for the cats who don't need to wonder,
for the cats who know.
And, of course, for Joe Cat.

Cat
Under
Fire

1

The night was cool, and above the village hills the stars hurled down their ancient light-borne messages. High up on the open slopes where the grass blew tall and rank, a small hunter crouched hidden, his ears and whiskers flat to his sleek head, his yellow eyes burning. Slowly he edged forward, intent on the mouse which had crept shivering from its deep and earthen burrow.

He was a big cat, and powerful, his short gray coat sleek as velvet over his lean muscles; but he was not a pretty cat. The white, triangular marking down his nose made his eyes seem too close together, as if he viewed the world with a permanent frown. To observers he seemed always to be scowling.

Yet there also shone in his golden eyes a spark of wit, and a sly smile curved his mouth, a hint that perhaps his interests might embrace more of the world than simply the palpitating mouse which awaited his toothy caress— a clue that this big gray tom saw the world differently, perhaps, than another cat might see it.

Crouching low, he did his best to keep his white paws and white chest hidden, keep his white parts from shining out through the dark grassy jungle. He would have preferred to have been born solid gray in color—that would make hunting far easier—but one did not have a choice in these matters. And he did favor his neat white paws.

The mouse moved again, a quarter inch, watching warily for any presence within the blowing shadows.

Quivering, it stretched farther out from its shelter, its eyes gleaming black and quick as it strained to see any foreign movement. Its ears twitched, alert to any threatening sound upon the hushing wind, and constantly its body shivered with the habit of fear, every tiny muscle tensed for flight, ready to vanish again among the heavy roots.

The cat's eyes didn't leave his prey; they blazed with hunger and lust for the kill, bright as yellow coals. He drew back his lips over gleaming incisors as he tested the mouse's musty smell, his pink tongue just visible tasting that irresistible aroma. His shoulders rippled in anticipation, and he licked his nose as if he was already licking warm and succulent mouse flesh. The small rodent was damnably slow about leaving its cover. Joe remained still with great effort.

Below him down the grassy slopes the village of Molena Point slept snugly at this predawn hour, the cottages protected from the sea wind by the giant oaks among which they had been built, and by the surrounding hills into which the homes and shops were tucked like a tangle of kits snuggled against their mother. In the center of the village the courthouse tower rose tall against the dark sky, as pale and lonely as a tombstone. The Mediterranean building housed two courtrooms, various city offices, and, at the far end, the Molena Point Police Department. The ongoing murder trial which would resume this morning in the courtroom was, despite the tomcat's irritation about the matter, of great concern to him.

For weeks the quiet village had talked of nothing else but Janet Jeannot's murder and of the fire in which she had died. There was heavy speculation about the young man who had been indicted for her death. Prurient excitement about these events had transformed Molena Point's usual calm ambience into an emotional bedlam. Gossip and conjecture seethed through the village shops and cafés so that Joe, prowling the village streets catching snatches of conversation, was aware of little else. Though his own interest did not stem so much from village gossip as it did from a far more personal concern.

The mouse moved again, creeping farther from cover, half an inch, then an inch, bravely and foolishly leaving its grassy blind, drawing so close to Joe that Joe had to clamp his jaws to keep from chattering the age-old feline death murmur. He oozed lower, slipping silently toward it through the grass, disturbing no blade, every fiber of his being honed in on that sweet morsel.

The mouse froze.

Joe froze, his heart pounding with annoyance at his own clumsiness.

But no, it hadn't seen him. It had paused only to gather itself for a dash across the bare earth. It stared across, fixated, toward another stand of heavy grass, where a tiny path led away, a quarter-inch lane vanishing between the green stalks. Joe's muscles tightened, his lips drew back, his yellow eyes gleamed.

The mouse sped, streaking for its path, and Joe exploded across the little clearing. With one swipe of scimitar claws he raked the creature up into his waiting teeth, it fought and struggled as his fangs pierced the wriggling morsel.

The mouse knew a moment of apocalypse as it hung skewered and shrieking in the cage of teeth clamped through its body. Joe bit deeper into the warm, soft flesh, the sweet flesh. The mouse screamed and thrashed, and was still.

He crouched over it tearing away warm flesh, sucking up sweet, hot blood, crunching the mineral-rich bones, then the surprising little package of stomach contents. The stomach usually contained grass seed or vegetable matter, but this morning he was rewarded by a nice little hors d'oeuvre of cheese from the tiny mouse stomach. *Camembert*, he thought, as if the mouse had lunched on someone's picnic. Or maybe it had gotten into the kitchen of one of the houses that dotted the hills. He

could taste a bit of anchovy, too, and there was a trace of
caviar. Joe smiled. Its belly was full of party food.

How fitting. The mouse had taken its final repast
from the silver trays of a party table. Molena Point's
cocktail crowd had supplied, for the little beast, an elegant last meal, a veritable wealth of pre-execution deli-
cacies. Joe grinned, imagining the small rodent up in
mouse heaven, gorging for eternity on its memories of
anchovies, beluga, and Camembert.

He tried to eat slowly and enjoy every morsel, the
rich taste of the tiny liver, the so recently pulsing heart,
but the mouse was gone before he could slow himself.

When nothing was left but the tail, he licked a
whisker and settled down to wash. He never ate the tail.
His purr was deep and contented. This was living; this
was what life was about. Forget the complications of
that other life that had, some months ago, so rudely
infringed upon his normal feline pleasures. It was quite
enough at this moment to be no more than an ordinary
cat. Insolently he cleaned his paws and whiskers, then
gazed up at the star-strewn sky. Titillated by the vast
night and by the spinning universe, warmed by the rich,
nourishing mouse gracing the inside of his belly, he
savored the perfect moment. To be alive and healthy, to
roam the wild hills freely and take from the earth what
he wanted, this was life's answer to cat heaven.

The dawn wind rose stronger, tweaking his fur, teasing and exciting him. And from above him in the vast
sky came the far, high *chshee chshee* of a nighthawk
wheeling against the stars, diving and circling as it
sucked up insects invisible even to the tomcat's keen
eyes. Joe stretched and yawned.

Only one thing could improve the night, only one
presence could add to his pleasure.

Licking his whiskers, he rose on his hind legs to look
down the hill. Perusing the lower slopes, studying the
faintly lit gardens beneath the softly glowing streetlamps,
he watched for any quick flash of a small, swift creature

leaping up through the shadows, watched for one small cat racing up the dark hills beneath the sprawling oaks.

But the shadows lay unmoving. He looked and looked, and disappointment filled him. She wasn't coming. Maybe she'd overslept. She'd had some strange dreams lately, dreams that wakened her and made her prowl restlessly, destroying sleep.

He was about to turn away when he saw, far down between two cottage gardens, a large patch of darkness moving, and he stiffened, watching.

That was not his hunting companion; that shadow was too big. Now it was still again. Maybe it had been only dark bushes shaken by the wind. When he saw no sign of Dulcie he hunched down, feeling lost and lonely. She almost always joined him on such a perfect hunting night, with the wind not too fierce. And the sky, as she would say, as beautiful as black silk strewn with spilled diamonds. He reared again, searching disconsolately, studying the narrow village streets that wound and lost themselves and appeared again, climbing higher up the grassy hills. She could have spared a few moments to join him, even preoccupied as she was.

Though he did wish, if she came to hunt in the predawn dark, that she'd keep her mouth shut about the trial. *I'm sick of hearing about the damned trial.* These last weeks Dulcie had been interested in nothing else, she seemed able to think only of the fire in Janet Jeannot's studio and of Janet's terrible death—and of Rob Lake, who was being tried for the murder. Dulcie was so sure that Lake was innocent, and so damnably intent on proving she was right.

The day Janet died, they had come up the hills as soon as the fire was out, drawn by the activity of gathering police cars, by what appeared to be a full-blown investigation. Concealing themselves above the burn, where the ground wouldn't scorch their paws, watching the police working within the cordoned-off expanse of smoking, blackened rubble, Dulcie had been both repelled and fascinated. They had watched unmarked cars arrive, watched the forensics people examine Janet's body. But when forensics lifted Janet gently into a body bag, Dulcie had turned away shivering.

And then, when Rob Lake was arrested for Janet's murder, she had gone to watch him in his cell, seething with curiosity.

Observing Lake in his solitary confinement, slowly making friends with him as she crouched at the barred window above his cubicle, listening to him talk out his fears to her—baring his soul to a cat—she had become convinced of Lake's innocence. Soon she had completely bought Lake's story.

Lake has to be a strange dude, Joe thought. *What kind of guy spills his deepest thoughts to a cat—not even his own cat?* Sure Dulcie was charming, probably she'd given Lake that bright-eyed gaze that enchanted tourists and inspired shopkeepers to invite her right on in among their precious wares. *So she charmed him. So big deal.* But to let the accused charm her, to buy the idea that Lake was innocent was, in his opinion, stupid and dangerous. The grand jury wouldn't have indicted Lake if there hadn't been sufficient evidence. Anyway, this trial was not cat business; it was police business.

But Dulcie didn't see it that way.

And you can't tell her anything; she's going to go right on prying like some hotshot detective until she gets herself in trouble.

He hissed at the empty night and scratched a flea. She was only a cat, one small cat, but she thought she knew more than a court full of attorneys. Thought she was smarter than twelve court-selected jurors and a state judge. One small, defiant tabby whose arrogance was enough to make any sensible cat laugh.

He did not consider, in his assessment, that they had, together, already investigated one murder this summer and had helped police nail the killer. That case had been different.

Down the hills, wind scudded the grass in long waves,

rolling as the sea. Above him, riding the wind, the nighthawk dived suddenly, skimming straight at him swift as a crashing aircraft. He didn't duck from the bird, though another breed of hawk would have sent him scooting for cover. At the last instant it banked away, sucking up insects—the poor bird could eat nothing but bugs. Joe smiled. God had, in his wisdom, designed some mighty strange creatures.

As he turned, looking down the hill again, he started, then smiled. *There she is.* She came streaking up across a patch of lawn, a swift shadow so lithe and free she made his heart leap. He avidly watched her every move as she fled up across a narrow street and disappeared into the tall grass above, watched the grass ripple upward, stirred by her invisible flight.

She burst out of the grass high up the hill, racing up across a last flower bed, then an empty street, and into a tangle of weeds, steeply up, a dark bullet of speed. Halfway up the hill she stopped. Reared up. Stood looking up the hill searching for him. His heart trembled.

She saw him. She stood a minute on her hind legs, her front paws curved softly against her belly, then she sped up again, racing and leaping. When again she vanished, the grass tops heaved and swayed, as if shaken by a whirlwind.

She exploded out of the grass inches from his nose. She leaned into him warm and purring, tense from running, her heart pounding against him, her green eyes caressing him. She was all fire, switching her tail, licking his face. For weeks she'd been like this, a bundle of passion, her tempest generated not by love, though he knew she loved him, but by her fevered involvement with the murder, by the compulsion of purpose that blazed in her green eyes, and in her unexpected bouts of quick temper.

He liked her all keyed up, bright and vibrant, but she worried him. She visited the jail too regularly, listened too intently to Rob Lake, had become totally obsessed. Life had just begun to settle down after he and Dulcie solved Samuel Beckwhite's murder, and now Janet's death had thrown her into high gear all over again. The passion of her involvements tumbled and shook him like a dog shaking a rabbit. He was beginning to wonder if life with Dulcie would ever be anything but chaotic. He did not consider—did not choose to remember—his own intensity, once his own curiosity was aroused.

And Dulcie was possessed not only with the murder itself, but with trying to discover, as well, what made humans kill so wantonly.

Premeditated murder was quite beyond the normal feline experience. A coldly planned killing was totally different from the way a cat killed. Such destruction had nothing to do with hunger or survival or with practice training, or even with instinct. From a cat's view, Janet's death had been pointless. Insane. And Dulcie kept trying to understand, in one huge gulp, such human folly. Searching for answers scholars have been seeking for centuries.

Who could tell her that this was a task, for one small cat, as impossible as a gnat swallowing the sun?

But he couldn't stay angry with her, she was his love, his gamin, green-eyed charmer. Now, as she snuggled close, her gaze melting him, he licked the soft peach-tinted fur on her darkly striped face, licked her ears. She lifted a pale silken paw and smiled at him, then flopped down to roll in the grass, flirting.

But the next minute she leaped away again, feinting a run. As he raced after her, she paused to look back, wild-eyed, then ran again, light and swift as a bird in the wind. He chased her up the hill, careening up through the blowing grass, then crashing through a forest of Scotch broom, up toward the crest of the hills, climbing until at last they collapsed, panting, so high they could see nothing above them, and lay stretched close together, Dulcie limp and warm and silken.

"Needed to run," she said. "To get the kinks out. I got so cramped yesterday, crouched on that ledge above the courtroom, I thought I'd pitch a fit."

So don't stay there all day, he thought, but didn't say it.

"And then I kept going to sleep during the boring parts—in spite of those pigeons cooing and blathering all around me. And those attorneys aren't much better, dull as the drone of bees. That prosecuting attorney can put you right to sleep."

"You didn't have to waste all day there." He could never keep his mouth shut.

She lifted her head, her eyes widening. "I left an hour before they recessed. Don't you want to know what's happening?" She gave him a steady, green-eyed gaze, then rubbed her face against him. "Lake didn't kill her, Joe. I swear he didn't. We can't let them convict Rob Lake."

"You have no reason to be so sure. You're not . . . "

"There's not one shred of hard evidence. I told you this is how it would be—all circumstantial. That Detective Marritt didn't do a solid investigation, and he really isn't making a good case."

She flicked an ear. "But what can you expect? Captain Harper never wanted to hire Marritt. Marritt's nothing but a political appointee. I bet Harper didn't want to put him on this case; I bet the mayor had something to do with that. Marritt's so officious in court."

She saw she wasn't getting through. "Anyway, why are court trials so damnably slow? Every little legal glitch, and a million rules."

"They're slow, and have rules, because they're thorough." He looked irritably past her down the hill. "They're slow because they go by facts and logical procedures, and not by intuition."

She hissed at him and lashed her tail. "You might just try to keep an open mind."

He did not reply.

But at last she relaxed, yawning in his face, putting aside their differences—for the moment. Lying close together, warm upon the breast of the hill, they watched the village begin to waken. A few cottage lights had flicked on, and now, all over the village, as if a hundred alarms had gone off at once, little patches of lights began to blaze out. Above them, the sky grew pale, and soon the lifting wind carried the scent of coffee, then of frying sausages. They heard a child's distant laugh, and a dog barked.

And as dawn lightened the hills, a tangle of dark clouds began to sweep in from the sea, racing toward the north, probably carrying rain. Maybe it would blow on past, drench San Francisco instead of the village. Dulcie said, "Rob will be waking now, his breakfast tray will be shoved in under the bars."

Joe sighed.

"He needs me," she said stubbornly. "He talks to me like he doesn't have another friend in the world." She licked the tip of her tail. "And maybe it's easier for him to talk to a mute animal . . ." She smiled slyly. "Well, he thinks I'm mute. And why would he lie to a cat? As far as Rob Lake knows, he could tell me anything, and I wouldn't understand, couldn't repeat it."

Joe said nothing. Dulcie had an answer for everything. There was no diverting her. She was into the case of Janet Jeannot's murder with all four paws. Earlier this summer, when they'd searched for clues to Samuel Beckwhite's killer, they couldn't help being involved; their own lives were threatened. They'd both seen Beckwhite struck down, had heard the thud of the wrench against his head, had seen Beckwhite fall. They had seen the assailant clearly. And the killer, somehow, had known they could inform the police. From the moment the man saw them, he knew they could finger him, and if he could have caught them, he would have snuffed them both.

They had set out to solve the Beckwhite case because their own lives were at stake, but Janet Jeannot's murder was different.

Dulcie stared at him deeply, her dark pupils slowly constricting to reveal emerald green as the dawn light increased. "Don't you want to see the real killer caught? You liked Janet; Clyde used to date Janet. You can't want her murderer to go free, gloating all the rest of his life while she lies dead."

She nuzzled his face, licked his ear. "The first witness this morning is Janet's neighbor, that Elisa Trest. I really do want to hear what she'll say. Come on, Joe. Come on to the courthouse with me."

He just looked at her.

She sighed and started down the hill, pushing through the tall grass.

No point in trying to talk sense to her, she was going to do as she pleased. Grumbling, he trotted down beside her keeping pace, half-angry, half-amused.

But halfway down the first slope, she said, "There's a strange dog down there; I forgot. I don't see it now, but it followed me earlier, a huge dog."

"I didn't see any dog when I came up. Except the boxer and the golden, those two cream puffs." Those dogs were no threat—they'd chase a cat for sport but were terrified of claws. If no other cats taught the village dogs proper manners, he and Dulcie did. They'd had some interesting chases over these hills. Though a smart cat never let snapping teeth get too close. Even a playful dog, when excited, could turn innocent play into a killing bite. One mouthful of cat, and a harmless canine could become a killer, tearing and rending before he knew what happened.

"It was a big brown mutt," she said. "It stayed away from me, behind the bushes, but it watched and followed me. Well, it's probably harmless. After Mrs. Trest testifies I'm going up to Janet's burned studio again, and this time I mean to get inside even if it is boarded up."

"You can't be serious."

"Why not? Who knows what I'll find."

"Come on, Dulcie. You watched the police sort and sift and photograph. We've been up there enough, across that burn. That's the last place I want to spend the day." The burned hills were hell on the paws, and the rank fumes stung their noses and eyes. And of course there was no game up there among the ashes; the creatures that didn't die in the fire, that had escaped, would not return to that barren waste.

The fire had cut a half-mile swath through the lush green hillside, and had burned seven homes to the ground, leaving only two houses untouched. Dead, black trees stood bare against the sky, and the stink of burning was everywhere. The thought of padding through a half mile of cinders, broken glass, and sharp, twisted metal, did not appeal.

But the thought of Dulcie's going up there alone was less acceptable. He glanced at her sideways. "Come by the house for me. But you'd better hope we find something to make it worth the trip."

She gave him a sweet smile, and they moved on down through the tangled gardens, between comfortable little cottages, down across winding, residential streets. They crossed the narrow park that ran above Highway One where the road burrowed through its eight-block tunnel, then turned south two blocks to the wide green strip that divided Ocean Avenue. The parklike median marked the center of the village, running tree-shaded and cool along between the village shops toward the beach. Trotting down the springy, soft turf, they rustled through fallen leaves, scattering them with quick paws.

The shops weren't open yet, but Joe and Dulcie could smell raw meat from the butcher's, could smell fresh bread and cinnamon buns from the bakery. They basked in the aroma of fresh fish, where a truck was unloading cardboard boxes of halibut and salmon. The workmen saw them looking and hissed at them to chase them away. The cats hissed back and turned their tails. They didn't pause until they reached Joe's street.

There they touched noses, and Dulcie rubbed her face against his. "I'll come by later," she said, her green eyes catching the light. He watched her trot away toward the jail and courthouse, moving lightly as a little dancer, her tail waving, her curving stripes flashing dark and rich against the pale walls of the galleries and shops.

Glancing across at the bookstore, he could see the clock in its window. Seven-thirty. She'd go to the jail first, climb the big oak tree to the third-floor windowsill, and lie looking in at Rob Lake, maybe share his breakfast—he liked to feed her little bits of sausage and egg through the wide-mesh barrier. She'd hang around listening to him play on her sympathy until court convened at nine.

Turning away to his left, toward home, he raced across the grassy median to the northbound lane, gauged the slow-moving cars, and leaped across between them.

At least if Dulcie had to solve puzzles, the murder of Janet Jeannot was better than agonizing over the mystery of their own pasts. They'd done enough of that this summer. Their sudden onslaught of uncatlike thoughts, and their ability to speak human words had been a shocker. When Joe had first experienced his new and alarming talent, he had tried to remain cool and laid-back. Scared as he was, he'd attempted to handle the matter with some restraint. But not Dulcie. She had exploded into her new life with wild eagerness, embracing her sudden new talents with hot feline passion. Wanting to learn everything about the world all at once, trying to make sense of the entire universe, she'd just about driven him crazy. Even watching TV had become a challenge as she soaked up information

Ever since she had been a kitten, Dulcie had watched TV with her elderly housemate. Curled cozily on Wilma Getz's lap, she had basked in the music and motion of the programs, and in the incomprehensible but fascinating voices. Then suddenly this summer, when she had begun to understand human words, she'd fixed her attention on the programs, eagerly lapping up the smallest detail. Sitting rigid on Wilma's lap, like a little furry scholar, she had soaked up the daunting new experiences and ideas as if, her entire life, she had been waiting for this moment to learn and discover.

Good thing Wilma has some taste in what she watches. Though even Dulcie had better sense than to shape her total view of the world from TV.

Leaving Ocean behind him, Joe sped down the sidewalk the three blocks to his own front yard, to the small white Cape Cod that he shared with his own human housemate. Joe and Clyde's cottage, snuggled comfortably beneath the sheltering oaks, was a somewhat decrepit structure, mossy around the foundation, and with a green-tinged, mossy roof, the shingles loose where a reaching branch had been at them. Clyde grumbled hugely about having to replace a few shingles, though he wouldn't dream of trimming the trees. Nor did he do much else to pretty up the property, except mow the ragged grass. But the worn old place was home, cozy and safe.

Clyde Damen was thirty-eight, once married, before Joe's time. He was stocky and dark-haired. He liked professional boxing, liked all competitive sports. He worked out with weights regularly, an activity which he performed with much grunting in the spare bedroom, lying sandwiched between his battered desk and the guest bed. He loved his beer and his women; though he had grown far more selective, these last couple of years, in choosing the latter. Joe never could figure what women saw in Clyde, but they were always there, laughing, drinking beer with him, cooking his suppers.

Clyde had rescued Joe from the gutter as a half-grown kitten, where he lay fevered from a broken, infected tail. That was in San Francisco, and not in the best section of the city. One might say that Joe had been born on the wrong side of Market Street. Clyde had been driving up Mission when he saw Joe lying in the gutter. He said later Joe had looked like a bit of trash, and then like maybe a dead rat, but something had made him stop short, squealing his brakes.

Getting out, he had crouched over Joe, had touched him tentatively, then carefully examined him for broken bones.

When he found only the tail broken, he had gathered Joe up and taken him to the vet, then home to his small Sutter Street apartment. There Clyde had cared for him like a baby, had doctored him, spoon-fed him, and given him pills, talking baby talk to him. They had not been parted since.

They had moved from San Francisco to Molena Point a year later, and it was in the village, back in the summer, that Joe's strange metamorphosis occurred. Clyde had been surprisingly stoic about the matter.

Trotting across the ragged grass that Clyde euphemistically called a lawn, Joe leaped up the concrete steps and slid in through his cat door, wincing, as he always did, when the plastic flap dropped against his back. *If humans can go to the moon, can't they invent a more comfortable cat door? What's* with *human priorities?*

He crossed the living room, passing the dining room that Clyde seldom used. The instant he pawed open the kitchen door, the menagerie hit him like a kamikaze attack, the two big dogs pranced around, stepping on his toes, slobbering in his face, the three cats preening and pushing at him, inanely waving their tails.

The scent of fresh coffee filled the kitchen, and he could hear Clyde in the shower. Fending off the friendly, stupid dogs, he leaped up to the kitchen table. The old Lab and the elderly golden stood on their hind legs, staring at him, then at last resumed their pacing, waiting for Clyde to come out and fix their breakfasts. The three cats wound around the table legs, mewling as if Joe himself might open their cat food. The cats had treated him with great deference since the change in his life.

He gave them a patronizing stare and turned his back. They knew they weren't allowed on the table. And, while they didn't often mind Clyde, they minded him. The poor things never had figured out why, suddenly, he was so alarmingly different, but they respected that difference. *Well hell, I hardly know, myself, what's happened to me and Dulcie.*

All he and Dulcie knew was that their species seemed to go very far back into history, into Egypt and into the medieval Celtic villages. Clyde and Wilma had done enough research to turn up some spectacular and unsettling implications. In the Molena Point Library, they had found references to Irish burial mounds with doors opening down into them, doors carved with pictures of cats. Had found, in Egyptian and Celtic and Italian history, tales of people vanishing and cats suddenly appearing instead, tales that made Joe's whiskers bristle with unease.

He liked his new talents fine; he didn't need to go into some elusive background. He was what he was. A talking cat. Brighter than many humans, clever and talented. He didn't need all the hyperbole.

But Dulcie seemed fascinated that somewhere there were others like themselves, and she was intrigued by the further talents that they might yet discover in themselves—matters on which he would rather not speculate.

Now, atop the kitchen table, he sat down on the morning paper, reading quickly. The whole front page was given over to Rob Lake's trial. There might be famine, flood, and war in the rest of the world, millions dying, but you'd never see it in the Molena Point *Gazette*, not until this trial was resolved and Rob Lake was either convicted or released.

DAY THREE. AMES CALLS FOR DELAY. EVIDENCE SHAKY.

So the evidence was shaky. So, big deal. Couldn't the local reporters find anything else to write about?

But, he thought uneasily, *what if Dulcie's right? What if Lake didn't kill Janet? Could be, if Dulcie keeps poking around looking for the real killer, she's going to get herself hurt.*

Despite Dulcie's human perceptions, she was still a cat, small and delicate, heartbreakingly vulnerable. If she made too many waves, if she exhibited her strange talents too openly, she could end up in deep trouble.

Already one man in Molena Point had realized they weren't normal cats and had tried to kill them. And maybe other people knew.

Worrying about Dulcie, wishing she'd come to her senses, he sighed and stretched full-length across the newspaper. *So who can reason with her? She's going to keep on pressing until someone hurts her—or until she solves the damned murder.*

2

The Molena Point jail stood across a narrow alley from the police department and courthouse. Its ancient brick structure was well past its prime but solid as the proverbial brick outhouse, and Police Captain Harper fought each attempt to condemn the jail and tear it down. Its proximity to the station was convenient for new bookings and court case confinements, so his officers did not have to transport prisoners to and from the county lockup. The property, however, in the center of the village, was so valuable for commercial purposes that every year there was a battle. So far, Harper had prevailed. The back of the jail faced the police parking lot behind the station, and was shaded by a gnarled oak, its branches caressing the barred jailhouse windows.

Three stories above the alley, Dulcie crouched in the knotted, twisted tree, gazing intently across empty space to the window of Rob Lake's cell. On the brick windowsill two dozen pigeons strutted, dirtying the bars, eyeing her, and cooing inanely in their conviction that no cat could reach them across empty space. *Peabrains. Can't they remember I've leaped that chasm every day for a week?*

Gathering herself, fixing her attention on the narrow brick sill, she tightened down, flexed her haunches, lashed her tail, and sailed across. Pigeons exploded away loud as a clap of thunder.

Moving along the sill between pigeon droppings, she pressed against the bars and wire mesh. The high degree of security amused her. Max Harper took no chances with his prisoners. Below her in the dim cell, Rob sat hunched on his unmade bunk, his head in his hands, unaware of her. Hadn't even glanced up at the explosion of pigeon wings. He'd made no effort to clean himself up for the day, his brown hair was rumpled from sleep, his face stubbly, his prison blues wrinkled. His bedsheet and dingy blanket were in a tangle, his pillow fallen to the floor.

He was a young man, nice enough looking, though his soft face was perhaps a bit weak, a bit sullen. Maybe his very weakness drew her, stirred her pity—*my maternal instincts, Joe says*—and kept her coming back. He always seemed so happy to see her, as if she was perhaps the only visitor he had, besides his attorney.

And who could warm to that attorney? Deonne Baron might be a good defense lawyer, but she was abrupt and cold, and spoke with a harsh, precise voice that gave Dulcie a cat-sized headache. She could hardly bear to listen to Baron in court, had developed a deep, snarling dislike of the woman.

Now, she stared down into the cell at Rob's bent head, and mewled softly.

He looked up and grinned. The desolation, which showed for only an instant, left his face. He rose and came to the window, reaching up to press his fingers through the wire mesh and pet her. "Glad you're here, cat. I was getting the sweats real bad; the walls were closing in." He looked her over, reached a finger to rub her ear. "I don't know why, cat, but you always make me feel better. Somehow you take away the trapped feeling."

He frowned, scratched his stubbled cheek. "Another day in court. More endless testimony. And for what? They all think I killed her."

He looked at her deeply. "Why do you come here, cat? I'm sure glad you do, but hell, I don't even feed you, except a few scraps, sometimes. And I can't really pet you very well through all this metal. What brings you here, kitty? My sweet jailhouse smell?" He pressed his hand harder against the wire, seeking her warmth. She pressed back, rubbing her face against the cold wire, then winding back and forth on the narrow ledge, looking in at him inquiringly. Usually an inquiring look would get him to talk; this was how she had gotten him to tell her how he felt about Janet. He had sworn to her that he didn't kill Janet. And why would he lie to a cat?

Joe said maybe Rob was a pathological liar, maybe he'd rather lie than tell the truth, even to a cat, that maybe he lied to himself, too. Or maybe he liked to practice his lies on her, polishing them for his next court appearance.

But Joe was wrong. Rob Lake did not kill Janet.

She knew he felt trapped, trapped in the tiny cell, and trapped most of all by a legal system that should have protected him. Rob seemed, as the trial progressed, to grow more and more despondent. As if the whole world was against him, as if he didn't have a chance. And when he talked about Janet, Dulcie knew he had loved her, that he couldn't have hurt her.

Janet's death had shaken the whole village. The young artist had been such a bright part of Molena Point life, and so beautiful, her long pale hair, her slim build and easy stride, her cheerful, unassuming presence. She didn't fuss over her looks—she never wore makeup, and she usually dressed in old, worn jeans, which often had a welding burn or a paint stain. Of all their local artists, Molena Point had loved Janet best, and had loved her paintings best. Her big, splashy interpretations of the wind-driven rocky coves, her tiny cottages tucked between the huge and windy hills, were subjects which, treated by a lesser painter, would have been trite, but to which Janet brought a powerful vibrancy and magic. Dulcie had been deeply touched by her work. The transition Janet accomplished, turning an ordinary bit of the world into something new and wondrous, seemed to mirror exactly the transition in Dulcie's own life—from ordinary cat self into a world exploding with vistas and possibilities she'd never before guessed at.

She missed Janet, missed seeing her around the village, missed her casual visits to Wilma's when she would pop by for a cup of coffee and a few minutes of comfortable talk. The day of the fire, after Janet's body had been taken away, Dulcie came home and crept under the couch into the quiet dark and curled down into a little ball, her nose pressed to her flank, her tail tight around herself. No one but Wilma or Joe could understand how a cat could grieve for a human.

The night before Janet was killed, she had driven home alone from a long weekend in San Francisco, from the opening of the de Young Museum Annual, where she had accepted first prize for oils and second prize for sculpture. That was a heady night for any artist, to receive two top awards in one major show. That was Sunday night. She had left the reception around ten, driving south along the coast, the only direct route, arriving home near midnight. She had pulled the van into her hillside garage-studio, and in a few minutes, a neighbor said, her lights came on in her downstairs apartment. Half an hour later the lights went out, as if she had gone to bed.

She rose early Monday morning as was her habit—she was up by five. A neighbor leaving for his job on the Baytowne wharves saw her lights. She must have dressed, gone directly upstairs, and made coffee in the studio as she usually did. The newspaper said she was under a tight schedule, finishing up the last small touches on a metal sculpture commission to be delivered that week. The county fire investigators weren't sure whether, when she turned on her oxygen gauge, the tank exploded, or whether fire broke out first and caused the tank's explosion. She was hit in the head by flying metal.

The Molena Point police found a liberal smearing of oil on Janet's oxygen gauge and in the lines. Oil which, when the tank was turned on, could have caused the explosion. But that wasn't what killed her.

Traces of aspirin were found in her blood, and Janet

was deathly allergic to the medication; even a small dose would have dangerously slowed her breathing. The police had found traces of aspirin in the metal of the melted coffeemaker. The combination of aspirin and smoke inhalation had been sufficient to end Janet's life. And perhaps the explosion of her van had prevented her dazed escape.

Normally she did not weld with her van inside the studio complex, but she only had to do a little touch-up to the sculpture. When flames reached the van's gas tank the resulting explosion turned the fire into an inferno that leveled her studio and swept on across the hills. Fanned by the early-morning wind, it burned a wide swath of the residential hills, igniting a half-mile corridor of trees and houses to the south, but leaving Janet's apartment below the studio's concrete slab nearly untouched. The evidence soon pointed to Rob Lake. His old Chevy Suburban was seen in the drive just before the fire and his prints were recovered from the scene. Dulcie watched him now as he paced the cell, returning to her, reaching up again, then moving away. He could not be still.

Janet had broken up with Rob nearly a year before she died. They were not on good terms. They had parted when Lake began a professional relationship with Janet's ex-husband.

Onetime art critic Kendrick Mahl, now a gallery owner, had made a big name of Lake, though Lake's work wasn't much. Village gossip had it that Mahl took Lake into his stable to spite Janet. And who could blame Lake for jumping at the chance? Mahl was a big name in California art circles.

Mahl promoted one-man shows for Lake, pressed for articles in art publications, ran full-page, full-color ads in those same journals. Until the murder, Lake had been well on his way to becoming a big name. Now, except for the attention of sensation seekers, Lake's career was on hold. Rob Lake's world had shrunk overnight to the size of his jail cell.

Lake didn't have a solid alibi for the night Janet died. There was no witness to his movements once he left San Francisco. After the reception at the de Young, he had partied with friends. He returned home to Molena Point about 4 A.M. and went to bed. Two witnesses testified that he left San Francisco shortly after two in the morning. Lake had had keys to Janet's studio from the days when they were dating, as well as keys to her four-year-old Chevy van. He testified that for sentimental reasons he hadn't returned them, that he kept them in his dresser drawer.

But Janet's agent, Sicily Aronson, also had a set of keys, to both the studio and the van. And so had Kendrick Mahl at one time. Mahl, in court testimony, said he'd given them back and that he hadn't made copies.

Rob stroked Dulcie through the wire. "You know, cat, I never had pets. I always laughed at people with pets. I thought it was stupid, dogs fawning and whining, that having an animal was just a big bother.

"I figured cats were totally aloof, that cats just used a person. But you're not like that."

He looked at her intently. "I give you nothing, I can't even pet you properly, and still you come to see me. Why?"

Dulcie purred.

"Sometimes, cat, I don't think even my attorney gives a damn. I wish . . . But what the hell. Maybe all attorneys are like that." He was silent for a few moments, his gaze boyish and innocent. "Maybe if I could paint in here, if they'd let me have paints and some canvas, maybe I could relax." He pressed both hands against the mesh, his palms flat.

"But what good would it be to paint? Truth is, I'm not sure if I want to go on painting when I—if I get out of here."

She gave him a surprised look, then quickly she nibbled at her paw.

He studied her, frowning. "I'm not like Janet; I'm

not a passionate painter like Janet was." He grinned at the word. "But it's true. Janet painted because she had to, she was driven to paint. But me—I never had that kind of passion.

"And ever since she died, cat, I really don't give a damn."

He leaned his forehead against the concrete. "I envied her talent, cat. But you know I couldn't have killed her." He looked up at her searchingly. "I hope you know it. I guess you're the only one who does know it." He looked sheepish suddenly, then he laughed.

"I've really lost it, telling my troubles to a cat. But, I don't know . . ." He frowned, shook his head. "I feel like you really do care. Like you know I didn't kill her."

She purred louder, wishing she could speak to him, could comfort him.

That would really tear it—send Joe into complete orbit.

"Even when Mahl took me into his gallery, cat, when he made me a part of that exclusive stable, I knew I wasn't in the same league as Janet.

"Right from the start, I knew that Mahl did it to hurt her. I was ashamed of that," he said softly. "But not ashamed enough to stop him. I let him do it, and I didn't complain, I didn't have the guts. All I wanted was to be famous."

Lake turned away again to pace the cell, then whirled to Dulcie so suddenly she started and nearly fell off the narrow ledge.

"I wasn't ashamed enough to stop," he shouted. "Not ashamed enough to turn away from one big ego trip."

She stared at him until he calmed down. This guy could, without too much effort, become a real basket case.

"If I hadn't let Mahl build me into a big name, hadn't let him use me to hurt her, maybe she'd still be alive. Maybe we would never have broken up, maybe we'd still be together." He sat down on the rumpled bunk, looked up at Dulcie.

"Maybe we would have been together that night, and I might have prevented what happened." He stared up at her bleakly. "I didn't kill her, cat. But maybe it's my fault she died."

Dulcie was stricken with pity for him, but she was irritated, too. Right from the start he had stirred every ounce of her sympathy, yet his total lack of hope enraged her. He seemed to have given up already. Sometimes he was so negative she wondered why she bothered.

Maybe she *was* suffering from misguided mothering instincts, but one thing she knew for sure—Lake was innocent. He was in there because of Marritt's sloppy investigation. Captain Harper wouldn't keep Marritt on the force for a minute if the mayor and city council hadn't threatened Harper's own job. She thought Harper was biding his time, waiting for a good way to dump Marritt, one the city couldn't argue with.

And as for the prosecuting attorney, what could you say? The county attorney wanted a conviction.

But it was her dreams that had really convinced her of Rob's innocence. Three times she had dreamed of Janet's white cat, and he was trying to tell her something, show her something important.

Before the fire she and Joe had occasionally seen the white cat as they hunted the hills, and had glimpsed him leaping out through Janet's studio window, which the artist had kept open for him. They didn't see him often, and Dulcie thought he must have spent a lot of time in the house, sleeping. He was not a young cat.

After the fire, crews of villagers and SPCA volunteers had searched the hills for all the missing animals. They had found most of the dogs and cats, but they had found no trace of Janet's cat. Joe said he probably died in the fire; but no remains were found. It was a terrible thing to die in a fire; Dulcie was sickened to imagine such a death.

It was a week after the fire when she began to dream of the white cat. He was a longhaired tom, very elegant, with deep blue eyes. Her dreams were so clear that she could see the rabies tag fixed to his blue collar, and the small brass plate with Janet's name. In each dream he wanted her to follow him, he would turn looking back at her, giving a switch of his tail and a flick of his ears. But each time, when she tried to follow, she woke.

Rob stood looking out into the hall through his barred door, then returned to the window. "The police are going up to Janet's this morning; they're going to look for her diary. God knows what's in it, cat. God knows what she said about me."

She stared at him, puzzled, galvanized with interest. She'd heard nothing about a diary.

"Late yesterday a witness testified about the diary. That skinny old lady who said she saw my Suburban at Janet's the morning she was killed. She testified again, told the court that Janet had a diary."

The witness was Elisa Trest. Dulcie had thought Elisa wasn't going on the stand until this morning. If she'd known that, she would have stayed later yesterday afternoon.

"That Trest woman used to clean for Janet. I remember her up there poking around. Dried-up, nosy old biddy. She couldn't have seen my car. Why would she lie about it? She's saying Janet kept her diary on the shelf in the bedroom, but I never saw it. If there was a diary, I bet the old woman read every word, the way her face turned pink."

He sighed. "After we broke up, and I went with Mahl, I can imagine what Janet must have written about me. Well, it's out of my hands. But if the cops find it, that could mean another delay. Sometimes I think the delays are worse than a conviction; it's the delays that drain you, drag you down.

"But what do you care?" he said crossly. "What would a dumb cat care?"

Dulcie blinked.

He was like this sometimes, sweet and needing one minute, and angry the next. Well, the young man hurt;

and he was afraid. And she was the only one available to yell at. She narrowed her eyes, thinking about the diary, wondering if such evidence would help Rob or would strengthen the case against him. Wondering, if Detective Marritt found the journal, what he would do. And if Deonne Baron got hold of the diary, if she thought it would win the case, she was the kind of woman who would spread Janet's personal life all over the papers. Ms. Baron didn't care about Rob, Dulcie was convinced of that, but she was boldly aggressive about winning.

Dulcie lashed her tail, thinking. She wanted to see Janet's journal; she wanted a look at it before the police found it.

She turned, looking down into the police parking area. The officers' private cars were damp with overnight dew, the windshields fogged over. The shift hadn't changed. It wasn't yet eight o'clock, when the day watch came on, when Marritt would arrive at work and maybe head right up to Janet's to look for the diary.

She gave Rob a long look and left him, leaping across the three-story drop into the oak tree, scattering pigeons. Clinging to the branches, digging her claws deep into the rough bark, she backed down and took off, running.

3

A slash of morning sun careened across the kitchen table, warming Joe's fur where he lay sprawled on the morning paper. Below him Barney, the golden, and Rube, the Lab, fussed and paced waiting for their breakfasts. The cats had settled down, hunched, hungry, pretending patience. He glanced across through the wide window above the kitchen sink. A hummingbird flitted at the glass, then was gone. The neighborhood rooftops gleamed with slanting light as the sun lifted above the hills and far mountains. When he heard Clyde coming down the hall he stretched out more fully across the sports page, though he had already pretty much trashed it with his muddy feet, leaving long, satisfying streaks of soil and wet grass that obliterated portions of the text.

Clyde pushed open the kitchen door, carrying his empty coffee mug and a clean white lab coat. The dogs leaped at him, whining, and the three cats wound around his ankles, preening and purring. He dropped the lab coat over the back of a chair and knelt, hugging and baby talking the fawning beasts as if he hadn't seen them in months. Dressed in faded jeans and a red polo shirt, he was well scrubbed, freshly shaven, his cheeks still faintly damp. His black hair, handsomely blow-dried, would within an hour be wild as a squirrel's first try at nest building. Rising from his kneeling position, he straightened the pristine lab coat until it hung without a wrinkle. The starched white coat was a gross affectation—it would look fine on a doctor. Clyde had taken to wearing these garments only recently: Clyde Damen, Physician of Foreign Engines, resident M.D. to Molena Point's ailing Rolls Royces and Mercedeses. He even had the damned coats commercially laundered and starched.

Clyde acknowledged Joe with a soft shove to the shoulder and stood studying Joe's sprawled form draped across the sports page. "You have mud on your paws. Can't you wash before you come in the house? And why the hell do you always have to lie on the sports page? What's wrong with the editorials? You've left half the yard on it."

"Why should I lie on the editorials? You don't read the editorials. Your life would be incredibly dull without my little homey touches."

"My breakfast table would be cleaner, too." Clyde gave him a long look and set about opening cans of dog food and cat food and boxes of kibble. He filled five separate bowls, setting them down on the linoleum far enough apart to maintain a semblance of peace among the three cats and two dogs, to avoid unnecessary snapping. As the beasts ate, he propped open the door to the backyard so they could have a run when they were finished. He filled his coffee cup, pulled a box of cereal from the cupboard, dumped some into a bowl, and poured on milk. Every morning, watching him do this, Joe wondered what would happen if he absently dumped in dog kibble. But hey, add a little sugar, who would know? Clyde set the bowl on the table. "What do you want to eat?"

"Thanks, I've had breakfast."

"I can imagine. Blood and intestines." He sucked at his coffee, reaching for the front page. "'Baron's call for delay denied.' Damned lawyers would string it out forever." He looked up at Joe. "I suppose Dulcie's down there again this morning. Tell me why she's so determined. Where did she get this fixation that Lake's innocent?"

Joe sighed and rolled over, then sat up irritably, biting at a flea. "It's her dreams," he said uneasily. "Those dreams about Janet's white cat. I told you, she's convinced the cat is still alive, that he's trying to tell her something." He licked a whisker. "I wish those searchers had found the cat either dead or alive, then maybe she wouldn't be dreaming about him."

"The white cat's dead. He's dead or he'd have gone home—what's left of home. The neighbors would have seen him."

Joe preferred to think the cat was alive, that Dulcie was at least dreaming of a live cat and not a ghost.

The white cat's picture had been in the papers, as reporters dredged up every detail of Janet's life. If anyone in Molena Point had seen him, they would have taken him in, or notified the animal shelter, or called the *Gazette*.

"I find it interesting." Joe said, "that Janet's sister Beverly didn't make a fuss about the cat, that she didn't go out herself to look for him."

"The cat's dead," Clyde repeated.

"Maybe," Joe said uncomfortably.

"Dulcie's lost her head over this. Look at the evidence. Lake's Suburban was seen that morning in Janet's driveway—who could mistake that old heap. And after Janet and Lake broke up, Lake was so vindictive that Janet refused to talk to him. Don't you think that made him mad? These days, people kill for less."

Joe snorted. "If you murdered every woman you broke up with, Molena Point would be half-empty." He licked mud off his leg. "Anyway, the car is circumstantial. The witness only said it looked like Lake's Suburban—there are plenty of those old Chevys around. It was still dark, how much could she see?"

Clyde spooned more sugar onto his cereal. "Anyway the grand jury had to think there was sufficient evidence to indict Lake. They don't take a man to trial for nothing."

Joe shrugged. "Grand jury thinks he could be guilty. Dulcie swears he's not. What am I supposed to say to her? She won't listen."

"Just because she's gotten friendly with Lake, hanging out in his cell—just because Lake is a cat lover . . . "

"She doesn't go into the jail. She watches from his window," he said, hissing. He might be critical of Dulcie, but when Clyde started trashing her he got angry. "She doesn't think he's a cat lover; she just thinks he's innocent. And it's not only from listening to Lake," he said defensively. "It's from other stuff she's heard."

"Like what?"

Joe shrugged. "Like there might be another witness, who hasn't come forward."

"Who said?"

"Talk around the village."

"Well of course that's reliable. Village gossip is always . . . "

"Maybe it's not gossip. Maybe there's something to it. You can pick up a lot of information hanging around the restaurants and shops."

Clyde stopped eating. "What, exactly, do you mean by hanging around? Is that like the morning I caught you two cadging scraps under the table at Mollie's?" He fixed Joe with a hard look. "Have you two been in the shops again? Sneaking around into the restaurants? Don't you know there's a health law?"

"Dulcie and I are healthy. We won't catch anything."

Clyde sighed. "You two are lucky you live in Molena Point. Anywhere else, the shopkeepers would call the pound."

"Give it a rest. I've heard it a million times. 'Molena Point residents are good to you, you ought to return their thoughtfulness, try to act decent, remember your manners. Molena Point is cat heaven. You two don't know how lucky you are.' You tell me that every time I complain about any little thing. 'You live anywhere else, Joe, you wouldn't have half the freedom or half the perks.' "

"You better believe it. And you'd better stay out of the cafés."

"I thought we were talking about the trial."

"We were talking about the trial." Clyde's voice had risen. "And doesn't it mean anything to Dulcie that of the four suspects, Lake is the one the police arrested and charged with murder? And are you forgetting that Lake had a key to Janet's place?"

Joe licked a spill of milk from the table. "So he had a key. Kendrick Mahl had a key. And so did Sicily. Anyway, Janet had to be killed by someone who knew about welding equipment, and Kendrick Mahl gets the vote for that. Mahl has to know about gas welding—he handles the work of four metal sculptors."

"That doesn't make him a welder. And Mahl was questioned and released."

"Besides," Joe said, "everyone knows he hated Janet." It was common knowledge in the village that Mahl had never forgiven Janet for leaving him. "And what about sister Beverly? From the way people—including you— describe her, she sounds like a real piece of work. She didn't waste any love on Janet." Joe twitched an ear, flicked a whisker. "No, I wouldn't rule out Beverly."

"That doesn't make sense. If sister Beverly killed her, she wouldn't burn Janet's paintings. Beverly *inherited* Janet's work. Would have been over a million bucks' worth. Why would she set fire to a fortune?

"And why," Clyde continued, "would Sicily Aronson kill her? She made a bundle of money as Janet's agent. Now, with Janet dead, that's dried up. She'll sell the last few paintings, probably for huge prices, but that will finish it."

He looked at Joe bleakly. "Not only Janet, but most of her work is gone. Everything she hoped—that she cared about, gone.

"She said—told me once, if she never had children, at least her work would live after her. That generations down the line, maybe something of what she saw and loved might still have meaning for someone."

Joe said nothing. He'd seen villagers slip into the Aronson Gallery to spend a few minutes looking at Janet's paintings as if that pleasure turned a simple shopping trip into a special morning. He had seen villagers wave to Janet on the street and turn away smiling deeply, as if they were warmed just by the sight of her. Janet's death had generated such intense anger in the village that for a while the county had considered moving the trial to a more neutral town.

Before Lake was indicted, Detective Marritt and the Molena Point police and the county investigators had spent weeks sifting the ashes and debris of her burned studio, sorting and photographing bits of burned cloth, sorting through pieces of blackened metal and wood, bagging the charred debris for the county lab.

And the police had gone over Janet's apartment just as carefully. Sheltered beneath the concrete slab floor of the studio, the apartment had been left untouched by the fire. The police had fingerprinted, photographed, taken lint samples from every inch of Janet's home.

Clyde added more cereal to his bowl, and more milk. "Just suppose for a minute that Lake *didn't* kill her."

"So, suppose."

"So the killer's still free, Joe." Clyde gave him a long look. "So, is he going to take kindly to Dulcie snooping around looking for new evidence?"

Joe smirked. "I'm not sure I understand you. You're saying Janet's killer is going to be afraid of a kitty cat?"

Clyde didn't say a word. They both knew what he was thinking. At last Joe cut the bravado, his expression sobered. "You think someone besides you and Wilma knows about Dulcie and me—the way Lee Wark knew?"

"Wark was after you and Dulcie like a butcher after a side of beef. So why not someone else?"

"But Wark was a fluke. A Welshman who grew up knowing some pretty strange history. That won't happen again. How many Welshmen can there be in Molena Point."

Clyde rose and refilled his coffee mug. "I'm only saying, you and Dulcie keep nosing around, and there's going to be trouble."

My sentiments exactly, Joe thought. But he wasn't taking

sides against Dulcie. Shrugging, he began to clean his claws, stretching them wide and licking between, scattering dirt on the table.

"Do you always have to wash when you don't want to listen! Face it, Joe. Ever since you two got involved in Samuel Beckwhite's murder, you think you're some kind of detectives—feline Sam Spades." He sat down, digging fiercely at his cereal. "Don't you understand that cats don't solve murders, that cats . . ."

Joe leaped from the table to the kitchen sink, turning his back, staring sullenly out the window. "Who solved Beckwhite's murder? Who led the police to the auto agency, to where the money was hidden?"

"The police came because gunshots were reported."

"Sure gunshots were reported." He spun around staring at Clyde. "That nut nearly killed me and Dulcie before the cops got there. And who do you think saw Wark and Osborne change the VIN plates on the stolen cars? Who do you think saw them take the money out of the cars and stash it? Who made sure the cops found it?"

"All I'm saying is, you and Dulcie are . . ."

Joe flexed his claws, fixing Clyde with a narrow yellow gaze, his ears flat to his head.

Clyde sucked up coffee. "I know you two broke the Beckwhite murder, but that doesn't mean you need to spend the rest of your lives trying to solve murders that are already—that are . . . Why can't you just be happy? Why can't you two just enjoy life and leave this alone?" He got up and rinsed out his cereal bowl, brushing against Joe. "I understand why you and Dulcie were interested in Beckwhite—you saw Wark kill him. But this . . . Neither you nor Dulcie has any direct interest in Janet's murder."

Joe had said exactly the same thing to Dulcie, but he didn't like Clyde saying it. "Dulcie knew her just as well as I did. Dulcie was fond of Janet, and she loved Janet's work. That painting Janet traded to Wilma—Dulcie lies on the couch for hours, sprawled on her back, staring up at that painting."

Clyde set his bowl to drain on the counter. "The point is, if Lake didn't kill her, and if you two keep prodding at this, the real killer is going to find you just the way Wark did."

Joe examined his back claws.

"Oh hell. It's no good talking to you. Wait until Dulcie gets caught sneaking into the courtroom, and then see . . . "

"She doesn't sneak into the courtroom. She listens from the ledge—that ledge that runs along under the clerestory windows. It's October, Clyde. Balmy. All the windows are open. All she has to do is skin up one of the oak trees behind the courthouse and there she is, exclusive box seat." He grinned. "Box seat she has to share with about a hundred pigeons. The first day, it took her two hours to clean the pigeon crap off her paws and her behind. She said it tasted gross."

"Didn't you help her?"

Joe stared at him coldly. "I'm not licking pigeon crap off her. Now she carries a hand towel up with her, to sit on."

"That's cute. And when someone sees her going back there into the alley carrying a hand towel, what then? Sees her climb up the tree carrying the towel in her teeth, or sitting on the ledge on the damned towel. Don't you think they might wonder?"

"Cats do strange things. Everyone knows cats are weird. Read the cat magazines, they're full of stuff like that. Anyway, Dulcie says the trial is a farce. If she believed before that Lake was innocent, the shaky testimony has really convinced her." He lay down on the cool white tile of the countertop and patted at the tiny, intermittent drops of water falling from the leaky tap.

Clyde scowled at him and reached across him to turn off the tap. The dripping stopped. "What shaky evidence?"

"Lake's fingerprints in Janet's bedroom, for one thing." He lifted his head, staring at Clyde. "The guy lived with her for six months. Of course his prints were

all over. Don't you suppose the prints of every woman
you ever dated are plastered all over your bedroom?"

"I don't go to bed with them all."

"Name one."

"I didn't go to bed with Janet. I dated her but we
never . . . "

"Only because she wouldn't."

Clyde sighed. "You're off the subject. When Dulcie
didn't even know Lake, until after the murder, why is
she so hot to help him?"

*Female passions—feline passions—dreams of white cats—
who knows what runs Dulcie?* "You ever hear of justice?
Of wanting to see justice done?"

"Come off it."

Joe smoothed the fur on his chest with a rough tongue.
"She thinks Lake was set up. She thinks the evidence was
planted, that Lake's car was driven to the scene by someone else."

"Don't you think the cops checked that? Detective
Marritt . . . "

"You know what Captain Harper thinks of Marritt.
And sure they checked it out. That's the point—they
don't have any proof it was Lake's car, don't even have a
plate number." He sat up, admiring his muddy pawprints on the clean tile. "All the witness said was, it was
an old, dark Suburban like Lake's. What could that old
woman see, with her lousy eyesight?"

But as he watched Clyde, he was ashamed of arguing.
He knew perfectly well that much of Clyde's irritation
came from his pain over Janet. He seldom saw Clyde
hurting; it was a new experience. He told himself he
ought to be gentler. Clyde and Janet had been good
friends. They had dated heavily for a while, then had
remained friends afterward, casual and comfortable.

Feeling contrite, he rubbed his ear against Clyde's
hand, filled with an unaccustomed sympathy and ten-
derness. "Janet was special," he said quietly, pressing his
face against Clyde's knuckles. "She was a special lady."

They were silent for a moment, Clyde absently scratching Joe's head, both of them thinking about Janet.

At first, after Joe learned he could speak, he'd been uncomfortable about being petted. He and Clyde were equals now. He found himself weighing their relationship in a new light, and he hadn't been sure about this petting business. But then he'd decided. *It's okay; a little closeness is okay.*

Clyde had been shy about petting him, too. As if petting was no longer proper. But they were still pals, weren't they? Still human and cat, still crusty old bachelor housemates.

The faint sound of scratching from the front door brought him to sudden alert. He ducked out from under Clyde's hand, giving him a wide stare. "Gotta go." He leaped off the counter and trotted out through the living room.

Through the translucent cat door, he could see Dulcie's dark shadow pacing, could see her impatience in every quick line of her body. He pushed under the limber plastic, hating the feel of it. *If I live to be a hundred, I won't get used to that stupid door sliding down my spine.*

Before he was completely through, Dulcie pressed close to him, purring. Her green eyes were so huge they made him shiver. Every time he looked at her he fell deeper into joy. Just to be near her, just to know they were together, that was all he wanted from life. "What are you doing here so early? Has Elisa Trest already testified?"

She was strung tight, so wired, she couldn't be still. She wound around him, pacing, fidgeting.

"There's a diary, Joe. A journal. Janet kept a journal." She pressed against him, all green-eyed eagerness. "Mrs. Trest testified yesterday afternoon after I left. She said Janet kept a diary—Rob told me. The police are going up there this morning to look for it." She switched her tail impatiently, shifting from paw to paw.

He just stared at her.

"Well come on, before the police get there." And she whirled away, leaping down the steps.

"Hold it." He sat down on the porch, immobile as a stone. "You plan to snatch evidence out from under the cops' noses?"

"Just to have a look at it," she said innocently. "We don't have to *take* it."

Joe sighed. "Clyde's right. You're going to get into trouble. Besides, they've already searched her apartment. Why would . . ."

"Come on, Joe. Hurry." She spun around and ran, racing away up the sidewalk, her peach-colored paws hitting just the high spots, flashing above the concrete.

He remained sitting, looking after her. *The lady's nuts. No way we can reach Janet's place before the cops do.*

Or maybe she meant to go right on in, sniff out clues between the cops feet.

The fact that they had already pulled that kind of stuff, after the Beckwhite murder, didn't seem to matter. The fact that they had been right there under Captain Harper's boots, so much in the way that Harper had given them more than one puzzled look, didn't faze her.

Dulcie, you're crazy if you think we're going to push into the middle of another police investigation.

She stopped, up at the corner, looking back. He made no move to follow. Impatiently she raced back, leaped up the steps, and licked his nose. "We could just go up and see. If the police are there, we'll leave. Imagine it, imagine if Rob Lake is convicted and even put to death, and he's innocent and we could have helped and we didn't. Then how would you feel?"

Joe looked at her for a long moment, then laughed. "Oh, what the hell." He rose and followed her. "Who says we can't outsmart a few cops?"

And they ran, their paws pounding the pavement. Careening against her, he wished she wasn't so persuasive, so damned impetuous and stormy.

And he loved her stormy ways.

4

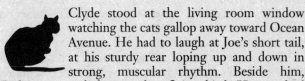Clyde stood at the living room window watching the cats gallop away toward Ocean Avenue. He had to laugh at Joe's short tail, at his sturdy rear loping up and down in strong, muscular rhythm. Beside him, Dulcie ran as light as a low-flying bird. He watched them worriedly. Their swift departure did not telegraph a casual, "let's go hunt." Crossing Ocean, zigzagging insanely between cars, they nearly made his heart stop.

When they were safely across, into the tree-shaded median, they turned north. Running through the lacy tree shadows, they were headed straight for the hills. And where else would they be going in such a hurry but to Janet's, to the burned remains of her studio. There was nothing else up in that direction to cause this degree of excitement. When they set out together simply to hunt, they stalked along, carefully looking around them, absorbing scents and sounds, working up slowly, he supposed, to the required intensity of concentration.

But now they were all fire, scorching away toward the hills like two little rockets.

They'd been up at Janet's before, returning with cinders on their coats and secretive but dissatisfied looks on their sly little faces.

Stepping out onto the porch, he watched them race out of sight, wishing they'd leave this alone.

So what was he going to do, follow them? Fetch them home?

Life had been simpler when Joe was just an ordinary tomcat, when Joe Grey had nothing to say but a demanding meow. When he had nothing on his mind but killing birds and screwing every female cat in Molena Point. Sometimes Clyde longed mightily for those days, when he had at least some control over the gray tomcat.

Now, face it, Joe and Dulcie were no longer little dough-headed beasties to be bossed and subjugated. Nor were they children to be guided and directed toward some faraway future when they could function on their own.

These two were already functioning in what, for them, was an entirely normal manner. The two cats were adult members of their own peculiar race: thinking creatures with free wills—though he didn't dare dwell on the historical convergences that had produced those two devious felines. The power of their heritage clung around the cats, the breath of dead civilizations shadowed them like phantom reflections, darkly. If he let himself think about it, he got shaky. When he dwelled too long on the subject, he experienced unsettling dreams and night sweats.

Whatever the cats' alarming background, the fact was that now he had little jurisdiction over Joe Grey. He could argue with Joe, but he was awed by the tomcat, too, and he was obliged to leave Joe pretty much to his own decisions.

And the tomcat, wallowing in his new powers, had grown far more hardheaded than ever he was before.

Joe Grey's own theory about his sudden new abilities was that the trauma of seeing Samuel Beckwhite murdered had triggered the change. That the shock had stirred his latent condition—much as shock might bring on latent diabetes, or propel a patient with high blood pressure to a stroke.

Whatever the cause, Joe's new persona was unsettling for them both. Clyde had to admit, Joe had had a lot to deal with, a lot to learn. He supposed the tomcat was still getting it sorted out. And as for himself, living with a talking cat demanded all the understanding a man could muster.

Wilma said much the same. That sometimes she wished Dulcie would just go back to her earlier vices of stealing the neighbors' clothes. Wilma had been used to Dulcie slipping in through the neighbors' windows, turning the knobs of their unlocked doors, trotting through neighbors' houses dragging away stockings, bed jackets, silk teddies.

He had known Wilma since he was eight, when she moved next door, a tall beautiful blond who soon was the object of his first pre-adolescent crush. She broke his heart each time she left to return to graduate school. She had not only been his first love, but his friend. She was fun, she was tolerant and good-natured, a gorgeous young woman who knew how to throw a baseball and when to keep her mouth shut.

Wilma was gray-haired now, and wrinkled, but she was still slim, a lithe and active woman. They had remained friends even after she finished her graduate degree, never losing touch, through his failed marriage and through Wilma's career as a parole officer, first in San Francisco, and then in Denver. She had retired, from the Denver office of Federal Probation five years ago. When she returned to Molena Point shortly after, they celebrated her retirement with dinner at the Windborne, lobster and champagne, sitting at a window table looking down the cliffs to the rolling sea.

Now, standing on his porch staring up the street where the cats had disappeared, he realized he was late for work. Maybe he'd go in at noon. How long since he'd given himself a half day off? He didn't have anything special this morning. In memory he could hear Janet saying, "Let the men run it for a day. Why bother with the headache of your own business if you can't play hooky?" She had loved to goad him into taking time off, though it meant that she had to abandon her own heavy schedule of sculpture commissions. Locking her studio, she had acted as if she were playing hooky. They would pick up a picnic basket at the deli and drive down to Otter Point, spend the day walking the sea cliffs, laughing, acting silly, getting sunburned.

He sat down on the steps, cold suddenly, hollow and used up. He saw Janet laughing at him, her blue eyes so alive, saw her standing on the wet black rocks of Otter Point, her pale hair whipping in the wind, saw the waves crashing up. Saw her at a little table at Mindy's, the candlelight sending shifting shadows across her golden hair, across her thin face and bare throat and shoulders in a low-cut summer dress.

He saw her burned studio, saw the fire trucks and police cars crowding the upper street behind the house and the street below.

Saw the tarp covering her body among the smoldering ashes.

They had started dating shortly after she left Kendrick Mahl. She was twenty-seven, slim, blond, with a devilish smile that drew him. They had hiked, gone to movies, gone swimming, spent days at the aquarium, driven up to the city just to go to the zoo. They both liked the outdoors, and Janet loved animals. But there the mutual interests ended. Janet's life lay in the world of art, a world that meant little to him.

He loved her paintings, but he had no interest in the art world, in the tangle of exhibits and awards and reviews, in the gallery gossip that occupied Janet. And she had no use for sports or for cars. She rated cars by how many paintings or how many tons of metal a vehicle could haul. Even though she was an artist, she had no interest in the skill that went into the design and manufacture of a fine Bughatti, an antique Rolls. He had taken her to one car show, and no more. She said she didn't have time to spend her day gawking at machine-made sex symbols. That was the only time they had fought. He didn't know why they had, over such a small thing.

During the months they had gone out she was dating several men, but she was committed to none. After they stopped dating they had dinner now and then, in between several heady romances for each of them. Janet had spent life as eagerly as if joy came in endless supply.

And maybe it did, if you knew how to look for it.

Or maybe, if you spent joy so brazenly, you died early. The thought shamed him. But the sense of waste, the knowledge of a vibrant life gone so suddenly, by someone's deliberate hand, the knowledge that Janet was no longer a part of the world, had left him perplexed, strangely weakened.

The morning of the fire he had waked at five-thirty, hearing sirens screaming. The room was filled with sweeps of red light and with the heavy rumbling of the village's four big fire trucks thundering up toward the hills. He had run for the kitchen to look out the back, had stood at the kitchen window watching the trucks' spiraling red lights sweeping up the hills, had seen the hills ablaze exactly where Janet's house stood, had seen the fire trucks converge, followed by an ambulance. He watched for a moment as the wind-fanned flames spread, licking at the dry hills, leaping toward the scattered houses, fingering roofs and walls. He heard the distant crack of a tree exploding, all this in an instant, and then he ran to the bedroom and pulled on pants and shoes and a sweatshirt.

He had propped the back door open, fearing for the animals, not wanting them to be trapped if the fire spread this far. He didn't know where Joe was. He knew the tomcat hunted up in those hills. He had grabbed a shovel from the carport and was just getting in the car when he saw Joe on the roof of their own house, watching the fire. He had wanted to tell Joe to stay away from the hills. But his motherly admonitions would only enrage the tomcat, goad him to do just the opposite. He had turned away, headed away up into the burning hills toward Janet's.

He had worked all morning in a line of volunteers, cutting breaks to keep the fire from spreading; trying not to think. When at nightfall he returned home, he was filled with despair, unable to stop seeing Janet covered by the police tarp.

He got up from the steps and went back in the house. Maybe he'd go on to work. Snatching up his lab coat, he let the animals in, kneeling to stroke them, giving the old dogs a hug.

But then in the car he didn't turn up Ocean toward the automotive shop; he drove on across the divided street, on through the village. This was Wilma's late day at the library, she didn't go in until one. Maybe she had the coffeepot on; maybe she was baking something. He was possessed by a sudden muzzy domestic craving, a yearning for company, for a warm, safe kitchen and the smells of something good cooking, yearning for the warm security he had known in his childhood.

He stopped at the cleaners and the grocers, the drugstore, took his time with his errands, then headed up San Carlos between the little cafés and galleries, between houses and shops pleasantly mixed, along with inconspicuous motels, all shaded by eucalyptus trees and sprawling oaks. The morning air was cool, smelled of the sea. The sidewalks were busy with people walking to work, jogging, walking their dogs. A few tourists were out, their walk more hesitant as they browsed, their clothes tourist-bright. The locals lived in jeans and faded sweatshirts, or, if business required, in easy, muted sport clothes.

He told himself he hadn't seen Wilma all week, that it would be nice to visit for a few minutes, but, watching for her stone house beneath its steeply peaked roof, he watched more intently the sidewalk in front, looking for a green van and a flash of red hair.

Wilma's niece had arrived from San Francisco three weeks ago, another disenchanted art school graduate who had found that she couldn't make a living at her chosen profession. Charlie had given herself two years to try, he had to hand her that. When she'd finally had enough she launched herself, no holds barred, into a hardheaded new venture.

Charleston Getz was an interesting mix, tall and lean like Wilma, but with big square hands, big joints despite her slim build. She wore no makeup—her redhead's delicate complexion and prominent bone structure didn't seem to require additional coloring. Her red hair, wild as a bird's nest, became her. He couldn't picture Charlie dressed up, had never seen her in anything but jeans.

But she knew how to behave in a nice restaurant. And, more to the point, she knew how to work. The day she arrived in Molena Point she had filed for a business permit and had bought a used van with most of her savings. By the end of the week she'd had business cards printed, had put an ad in the paper, and hired two employees. CHARLIE's FIX-IT, CLEAN-IT was off to a running start, and now three weeks later she had completed two jobs and taken on two more. It was just a small start, but she'd thrown herself wholeheartedly into a viable venture. The village badly needed the kinds of services she was providing.

It took, usually, about two years to get a business off the ground and established, turn it into a paying operation. But he thought Charlie would do fine. She liked the work, liked grubbing around spiffing up other people's houses and property, liked bringing beauty to something dull and faded.

Turning down Wilma's street, his spirits lifted. The van was there, the old green Chevy sitting at the curb. He parked behind it, smiling at the sight of Charlie's Levi-clad legs sticking out from underneath beside six cans of motor oil, a funnel, and a wad of dirty rags. Looked like the van was already giving her trouble. He hoped she wasn't dating him because he was a good mechanic. He swung out of the car, studying her dirty tennis shoes and her bony, bare ankles.

5

Where Charlie's ancient van stood two feet from the curb, Charlie's thin, denim-clad legs protruded from beneath, her feet in the dirty tennis shoes pressed against the curb to brace her as she worked. The six unopened cans of motor oil that stood on the curb beside a pile of clean rags were of a local discount brand, and the oil was fifty weight in deference to the vehicle's worn and floppy rings, oil thick enough to give those ragged rings something they could carry. Anything thinner would run right on through without ever touching the pistons. Clyde stood on the curb studying Charlie's bare, greasy ankles. He could smell coffee from the kitchen, and when he turned, Wilma waved at him from the kitchen window, framed by a tangle of red bougainvillea, which climbed the stone cottage wall, fingering toward the steeply peaked roof.

The cottage's angled dormers and bay windows gave it an intimate, cozy ambience. Because the house was tucked against a hill at the back, both the front and rear porches opened to the front garden, the porch leading to the kitchen set deep beneath the steep roof, the front porch sheltered by its own dormer. The house was surrounded not by lawn but by a lush English garden of varied textures and shades, deep green ajuga, pale gray dusty miller, orange gazanias. Wilma had taught him the names hoping he might be inspired to improve his own landscaping, but so far, it hadn't taken. He didn't like getting down on his hands and knees, didn't like grubbing in the dirt.

A muffled four-letter word exploded from beneath the van, and Charlie's legs changed position as she eased herself partially out, one hand groping for the rags.

He snatched up a rag and dropped it in her fingers. "Spill oil in your eye?" Kneeling beside the vehicle, he peered under.

She lifted her head from the asphalt, the rag pressed to her face. Beside her stood a bucket into which dripped heavy, sludgy motor oil. "Why aren't you at work? Run out of customers? They find out you're ripping them off?"

"I thought you had an appointment with Beverly Jeannot."

"I have. Thirty minutes to get up there." She took the rag away, selected a relatively clean corner, and dabbed at her eye again. "I didn't have to do this now, but the oil was way down, and I didn't want to add—oh you know."

"No, I don't know. All my cars run on thirty weight and are clean as a whistle. How's the Harder job going?"

"I have my two people working up there." She tossed out the oily rag, narrowly missing his face. "Thought I'd wash this heap, but I won't have time."

"What difference? Is clean rust better?"

Under the van she watched the last drops of oil ooze down into the bucket. Replacing the plug into the oil pan, she slid out from under, pulling the bucket with her. Kneeling on the curb, she opened a can of oil, stuck the spout in, then rose and inserted the spout beneath the open hood into the engine's oil receptacle.

"Better get a hustle on. Beverly Jeannot doesn't like the help to be late."

"Plenty of time. She's formidable, isn't she? How do you know her? I thought she lived in Seattle—came down just to settle the estate."

"I don't know her, I know of her. From what Janet told me."

She removed the can, punched another, and set it to emptying into the van's hungry maw.

"Like a suggestion?"

She looked up, her wild red hair catching the light, bright as if it could shoot sparks.

"Ride up to the shop with me, and take that old '61 Mercedes. It looks better than this thing, and it needs the exercise."

"You're being patronizing."

"Not at all. This is entirely in the interest of free enterprise—it will help your image. Beverly Jeannot's a prime snob. And I don't drive that car enough."

"And what's the tariff? How much?"

"You're so suspicious. It really needs driving. Scout's honor, no strings. Not even dinner—unless you do the asking." He watched her open the third can of oil, admiring her slim legs and her slim, denim-clad posterior. He liked Charlie, liked her bony face and her fierce green eyes, liked her unruly attitude. He was at one with her general distrust of the world; they were alike in that.

But beneath her brazen, redheaded shell she was amazingly tender and gentle. He'd seen her with the cats, kind and understanding, seen her playing with a shy neighborhood pup who usually didn't trust strangers.

Charlie had had a heavy crisis in her life when she realized she had wasted four years on a college degree that wouldn't help her make a living. He thought she was handling it all right. She would, when she met with Beverly Jeannot this morning up at Janet's burned studio, give Beverly a bid on the cleanup, the work to begin as soon as the police had released the premises. He thought that removing the burned debris, alone, would be a big job.

As she turned, he brushed dry leaves off the back of her sweatshirt. "There's a lot to do up there, cleaning up the burn rubble."

"I wouldn't bid on the job if I couldn't do it," she said irritably. Then she softened. "I'm going to have to

hustle. All I have is Mavity Flowers, and James Stamps."
She removed the last oil can and slammed the hood. "I
wish I could get a better fix on Stamps. But he'll do
until I can get someone I trust."

"Mavity, of course, is a whiz."

"Mavity has some years on her, but she's a hard
worker. She'll do just fine on the cleaning, and maybe
the painting. It's the other stuff, the repairs, that she
can't handle. That's my work." She picked up the oil
cans. "Beverly's in a big hurry, wants the work done
pronto, soon as the house is released." She tossed the
empty cans in a barrel inside the van. The Chevy's
bleached and oxidizing green paint was cracked, dim-
pled with small rusty dents. The accordioned front
fender was shedding paint, rust spreading underneath.

She looked the vehicle over as if really seeing it for the
first time, stood comparing it with Clyde's gleaming red
1938 Packard Twelve. "You serious about the Mercedes?"

"Sure I'm serious."

She grinned. "I'll just wash and change. Come on in,
Wilma's in the kitchen."

He followed her in, wondering why Beverly Jeannot
was in such a hurry to have the fire debris cleaned up.
Maybe she needed the money. He'd heard that she
meant to rebuild the upstairs and put the house on the
market. He thought she could make just as much profit
by selling the building in its present condition, with just
a good cleanup. Let the buyer design a new structure to
suit himself. He went on into the kitchen and sat down
at the table, where Wilma stood beating egg whites,
whipping the mixture to a white froth.

"Angel cake," she said.

He waited for the automatic coffeemaker to stop
dripping and poured himself a cup. From the kitchen he
could see through the dining room into the living room,
where Janet's landscape dominated the fireplace wall, a
big, splashy oil of the village and treetops as seen from
higher up the hills, lots of red rooftops and rich greens.

Wilma had paid for the painting in part by designing and planting Janet's hillside garden—she'd had some huge decorative boulders hauled in, and planted daylilies, poppies, ice plant, perennials she said were drought-resistant. She had done the garden the same week Janet moved in.

The house had suited Janet exactly. She had designed and had it built for the way she wanted to live. The big studio-garage space upstairs was connected to the upper, back street by a short drive. The studio was big enough for both a painting area and a welding shop, the east wall fitted with floor-to-ceiling storage racks for paintings and a few pieces of sculpture. And there was room to pull her van in, to load up work for exhibits. Wilma had admired Janet's planning and had loved the downstairs apartment. Both stories looked down over the village hills. The area Wilma had landscaped was below the house, between the apartment and the lower street.

He watched Wilma select an angel cake pan and pour in the batter. "Why don't you buy Janet's place? You've always liked it. It would be just right for you and Dulcie. You could build a great rental upstairs, where the studio was."

She looked at him, surprised. "I've thought about it." She set the cake in the oven. "But I'd feel too uncomfortable, living in the house where she died."

She poured coffee for herself, and sat down. "And it's too far from the village, I like being close to work." Wilma's cottage was only a few blocks from the library, where, since her retirement, she had served as a reference assistant. "I like being near the shops and galleries, I like walking down a few blocks for breakfast or dinner when I take the notion, and I like being near the shore.

"If I lived up there, it would be a mile climb home after work. Face it, the time will come when I couldn't even do that uphill mile."

"That'll never happen." He rose and refilled his coffee

cup. He didn't like to think about Wilma getting old, she was all the family he had. His mother had died of cancer eight years ago, his father was killed a year later in a wreck on the Santa Ana Freeway. He and Wilma were as close as brother and sister, always there for each other.

"Even though I still work out, and walk a lot, that climb up to Janet's can be a real artery buster.

"Besides, I enjoy my garden. Janet's hillside doesn't suit me. That was a landscape challenge, a minimum-care project, not a garden to potter around in. No, this place fits me better." She grinned. "It took me too long to dig out all that lawn, put in the flower beds. Now I want to enjoy it—I can potter around when I feel like it, leave it alone when I choose. I about wore out my knees planting ground cover and laying the stone walks.

"And Dulcie loves the garden. You know how she rolls among the flowers." She set a plate of warm chocolate cookies on the table. "I miss her, when she's not here for our midmorning snack. Lately, she's taken to eating a small piece of cake and a bowl of milk at midmorning—when she's home at that time of day.

"But this morning, she was gone when I got up. I wish I didn't worry so about her."

He restrained himself from eating half a dozen cookies at one gulp. "She came poking at Joe's cat door around nine. Looked like they were headed for Janet's."

"I wish she'd just torment the neighborhood dogs the way she used to. Spend her time stealing, and enjoy life." She gave him that puzzled look he had seen too often lately.

"But who can talk to cats? No matter how bizarre those two are, they're still feline. Still just as stubborn, still have the same maddening feline attitude."

He belched delicately.

She sampled a cookie. "Beverly Jeannot is meeting Charlie up at Janet's. If she finds those two in the apartment . . ."

"They'll stay out of her way. Do them good to get

booted out. Though I doubt they can get in—Harper boarded up the burned door with plywood."

"You don't think Beverly would hurt them?"

The idea surprised him and he thought about it. "I don't think she'd hurt an animal. And with Charlie there, she won't."

"Well, if the cats want to . . . "

They heard Charlie coming down the hall.

Wilma rose uneasily, turned her back, and busied herself at the stove. She had to be more careful. It was hard enough dealing with her own feelings about Dulcie's new talents. But having a houseguest, even if Charlie was her niece, didn't help. She'd barely recovered from the shock of Dulcie's eloquence when Charlie arrived. With Charlie in the house, she was terrified she'd say something to Dulcie and that Dulcie, in her boundless enthusiasm, would shoot back a sharp observation, come right out with it.

She'd talked to Dulcie ever since she'd brought her home as a small kitten. Cats were to talk to. She'd always talked to her cats. When Dulcie's replies had been a rub against her ankle, a purr, and a soft mewl, life was simple. But the first time Dulcie answered back in words, both their worlds had changed.

Now, of course, their conversations were hardly remarkable. Just relaxed remarks between friends.

Does the vacuum cleaner really bother you? . . .

Only when it jerks me out of a sound sleep; if you'll wake me up before you start it, that will help . . . I do love the scent of lavender in the sheets . . . Is there any more of that lovely canned albacore? . . .

Do you want to watch Lassie? *. . .*

No, Wilma. We both know Lassie *is stupid . . .*

You are a cat of impeccable taste. How about a Magnum *rerun? . . . Oh, I would much rather watch* Magnum. *And could we have a little snack of sardines . . . ?*

Charlie swept into the kitchen, dressed in fresh jeans and a pale yellow sweatshirt. She had tied back her hair with a yellow scarf, the curly red tendrils already escaping around her face, the effect fresh and electric. Snatching up a handful of cookies, she hugged Wilma and punched Clyde's shoulder to move him along.

Wilma stood at the kitchen window watching as they drove away in the Packard.

She had to be more careful around Charlie. In spite of her wariness, she had caught Charlie several times studying Dulcie too intently.

She told herself that was only the gaze of the artist. Charlie did have an artist's disturbing way of staring at a person or an animal as she memorized line and shadow, as she absorbed the bone structure and muscle, committing to memory some rhythm of line.

She hoped that was all Charlie was seeing when she studied Dulcie. She hoped Charlie wasn't observing something about the little tabby cat that would best go unnoticed.

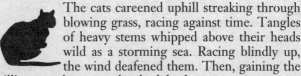The cats careened uphill streaking through blowing grass, racing against time. Tangles of heavy stems whipped above their heads wild as a storming sea. Racing blindly up, the wind deafened them. Then, gaining the hill's crest, they paused to look back.

Far down the falling land, the houses were toy-sized, and along the winding streets they still saw no police unit heading up from the village. They could not, from this vantage, see up across the black, burned hills to the streets that flanked Janet's house, to see if a police unit was already parked there. The buffeting wind tore at their fur, and they hunched down, flattening their ears against its onslaught.

But suddenly, below, something moved in the grass, a huge dark shape slipping upward, a quick, heavy animal shouldering closer. The wind picked up its scent as it lunged into a run.

They spun around, exploded apart, leaped away in opposite directions—the dog couldn't chase them both.

He chased Dulcie. She could feel the beast's heat on her backside, could hear it snapping at her hindquarters. She thought it had her, when she heard it yelp. She dodged to look, saw Joe riding its neck—he had doubled back. The dog bellowed with pain and rage, twisted to grab him, and she flew at its head, clawed its ears, clinging to its face, digging in. It ran blindly, bucking. They rode it uphill, twisting, and she could smell its blood.

Riding the beast, she began to laugh, heard Joe laughing, felt the dog tremble beneath them confused, terrified. It had never heard a cat laugh.

When it couldn't shake them and couldn't grab them, it bolted into a tangle of broom, trying to scrape them off. The rough branches tore at them, they were scraped and slapped by branches, hanging onto the beast, hunching low, ears down, eyes squeezed shut.

"Now!" Joe shouted.

They leaped clear, down through tangles of dark thorny limbs dense as basket weave. The dog thrashed after them, snapping branches, lunging, sniffing. They crouched below the dark tangles, creeping away, pulsing like the terrified rabbits they hunted. Listening.

He thrashed in circles, searching.

They fled away through the thorny forest, then again they went to ground, straining to hear, to feel his vibrations coursing beneath them through the earth. Maybe he would scent them and follow, maybe not. They dared not go into the open. Dulcie, hiding and frightened, knew he was the dog that had followed her down among the houses. He was the hunter now, and she the prey, and she didn't like the feeling.

He was quiet a long time, only a little hush of movement, as if he were trying to lick his wounds.

They heard him move again, hesitantly. They dared not rear up to look.

Then, poised to run, they heard him crashing away.

He was leaving. Joe reared up, watching, then laughed, dropped down, and strolled out of the bushes, lay down on the grass, grinned at her. "You raked him good."

"So did you." She stood up on her hind legs, to see the dog amble away downhill, making for the houses below, where, perhaps, he could find a friendlier world.

They lay down in the windy sun. "We should have stayed on his back," Joe said. "He would have carried us clear up to Janet's."

She spit out dog hair. "I smell like a dog, and I taste like a dog."

Far below, the dog had stopped in the yard of a scruffy gray house with a leaning picket fence. An added-on room jutted from the back, with a small, dirty window beneath the sloped roof.

The mutt lifted its leg against the picket fence, then began to twist in circles, trying to lick its wounded back while pawing at its face. But after a while it gave up, wandered to the curb, and leaped into the bed of an old black pickup.

That truck had been in the neighborhood for some time. Several weeks ago they had watched a thin, unkempt man moving into the back room, carrying in two scruffy suitcases and several paper bags. They had watched him, inside the lit room, moving around as if he was unpacking. They had not, then, seen the dog.

"Maybe it was in the cab of the truck," Joe said. "Or already in the room." He looked at her worriedly. "The mutt ought to be chained." He licked her ear. "That beast running loose really screws up the hunting."

"Maybe he'll lie low for a while, after the raking we gave him."

"Sure he will—about as long as it takes the blood to dry."

She smiled, rolled over in the warm sun. But a little ripple of fear touched her, thinking of the white cat somewhere among the hills, maybe hurt. If that dog found him . . .

She had dreamed about him again last night, but she hadn't told Joe—the dreams upset him. Joe Grey might be a big bruiser tomcat who could whip ten times his weight in bulldogs, but some things did scare him. The idea of prophetic dreams was a scenario he did not like to contemplate. When it came to spiritual matters, the tomcat grew defiant and short-tempered.

But her dreams were so real, every smell so intense, every sound so sharply defined. In the first dreams, when the white cat trotted away, wanting her to follow, he had vanished before she could follow. But in one dream, he stood on the surface of the sea. It was a painted sea, blue and green paint, and he had sunk into the painted waves, and the paint faded to white canvas so nothing remained but canvas.

And in her dream last night she had seen him wandering through twilight, walking with his head down as if burdened by a great sadness. He stepped delicately, lifting each paw hesitantly and with care, stepping among tangles of small white bones: the white cat walked among animal bones, little animal skulls.

But again when she tried to follow, he vanished.

He had been so real; he had even smelled stridently male. She longed to tell Joe the dream, but now, heading uphill again, running beside him, she still said nothing. Soon they had left the healthy wild grass and padded across burned grass, across the black waste, crossing the path of the fire, crossing its stink.

This was the shortest way to Janet's, but they trod with care through the gritty charcoal, watching for sharp fragments, for protruding nails and torn, ragged metal, for broken glass to cut an unwary paw. Skirting around fallen, burned walls, they crept beneath fire-gnawed timbers that stood like gigantic black ribs, angling over them.

A child's bedroom wall rose alone, like the remains of some dismantled stage set, its pink kangaroo wallpaper darkened from smoke. A baby crib stood broken, one rail crushed, its paint deeply scorched, blistered into a mass of brown bubbles. A sodden couch smelled of mildew, its springs and cotton stuffing spilling out. A burned license plate lay atop a heap of broken dishes and twisted silverware, a warped metal sink leaned against a bent and blackened car wheel. They trotted between melted cookpots lying whitened and twisted, between blobs of glass melted into bubbling new forms like artifacts from alien worlds.

The smell of wet ashes clung in their mouths and to their fur. They stopped frequently to clean their paws, to lick away the grit embedded in their tender skin and stuck between their claws. A cat's pads are delicate sensors in their own right, an important adjunct to his ears and eyes. His pads relay urgent messages of sharp or soft, of hot or cold. The feel of grit was as unwelcome as sand in one's eyes.

Higher up the hill, black trees stood naked, reaching to the sky in mute plea. And one lone, blackened chimney thrust up, an old solitary sentinel. The fire, after burning the top floor of Janet's house, had careened southward, leveling nearly all the dwellings within its half-mile swath.

But above Janet's burned house, on up the hill, the blaze had missed eight houses. They marched prim and untouched along the rising hill, along their narrow street. And, strangely, nearer to Janet's two houses had been spared, one up the hill behind her burned studio, one across the side street. And though Janet's studio was gone, flattened to ashes, the apartment beneath stood nearly untouched, held safe beneath the concrete slab which formed its roof, which had formed the studio floor. From the blackened slab rose three black girders, twisted against the clouds.

The garden below the house was largely undamaged, though its lush greens were dulled by ashes. The daylilies were blooming, their orange and yellow blossoms brilliant against the burn.

The front of Janet's apartment was all glass, the five huge windows dirtied by smoke, but unbroken. Behind the smoky glass, long white shutters had been closed across four of the windows, effectively blocking the view of the interior. The last wide window, down at the end, was uncovered—almost as if someone was there, as if someone had not been able to bear closing the house entirely. The sight of that window made Dulcie shiver—as if some presence within wanted sunshine, wanted to look out at the hills for a little while, look out at the village nestled below.

There was no police car parked below the apartment, and none above on the street behind, or in the drive which led to the studio slab. The little side street was empty, too, beyond the blackened vacant lot. There was no car at all parked along the side street before that untouched house. Strange that that ancient brown dwelling, among all the newer houses, would be left standing.

Steps ran up the hill. Halfway up, Janet's deck gave access to the front door. The cats avoided the steps, where charcoal and rubble had lodged. Trotting uphill they stirred clouds of ashes. Their eyes and noses were already gritty with ash, their coats thick with ash, Dulcie's stripes dulled, Joe's white markings nearly as dark as his coat. If they needed a disguise, they had it ready-made.

A fallen, burned oak tree lay across the entry deck. The front door was covered by plywood nailed across, affixed with yellow police notices warning against entry. They could see, beneath the plywood, the remains of the door, hanging ragged and charred. Dulcie dug at it, rasping deep into the burned wood, ripping away flakes and chunks of wood. She was nearly through when Joe hissed.

"Someone's watching—the house across the street."

She drew back, tried to look like she was searching for mice. Glancing across the empty lot she could see within the lone house a woman peering out, the lace curtain pulled aside, her face nearly flattened against the glass.

"Hope she gets an eyeful." Dulcie waited until the woman drew back and disappeared before she dug again, tearing at the charred wood. She had made a hole nearly two inches wide when a patrol car came up the side street.

The cats backed away as it parked directly below. Slipping up the hill to the concrete roof, they crouched at its edge among heaps of ashes, watching a lone officer emerge. Detective Marritt came quickly up the steps, carrying a crowbar and a hammer, his tightly lined face seeming far older than his shock of yellow hair and his lean, muscular body.

Metal screeched against wood as he pulled nails and pried away the barrier. Leaning the two sheets of plywood against the house, he unlocked the burned door, disappeared inside. Dulcie moved to follow, but Joe nipped her shoulder.

She turned back, her green eyes blazing. "What? Come on, can't you?"

"You're not going to push right in under his feet."

"Why not? He won't know what we're doing."

"Wait until he's finished."

"We can't. We won't know if he finds the diary. If he puts it in his pocket . . ." She started down the hill again, but Joe moved swiftly, blocking her, shouldering her into a heap of ashes and rubble.

She hissed and swatted him, but still he drove her back, snarling, his yellow glare fierce. She subsided unwillingly, ears back, tail lashing.

"The cops saw too much of us, Dulcie, when Beckwhite was killed. Captain Harper has too many questions."

"So?"

"Think about it. We've already made Harper plenty nervous. He's a cop, he's not given to believing weird stuff. This stuff upsets him. You force yourself on him, and you blow your cover."

She turned her back on him, lay down in the ashes at the edge of the roof, looking over the metal roof gutter watching the door below, sulking.

Joe growled softly "We can't find out anything if every time we show our faces around the police, they smell trouble and boot us out."

She sighed.

He lay down beside her. "We do fine when they don't know we're snooping. Don't push it."

She said nothing. She was not in a mood to admit he was right.

"We make Harper nervous, Dulcie. Give the man some slack." He moved closer, licked her ear. And they lay side by side, watching for Marritt to come out and waiting for their own turn to search the house. Hoping, if the diary was there, that Marritt came through in his typical sloppy style and missed it.

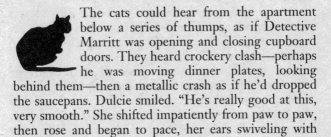The cats could hear from the apartment below a series of thumps, as if Detective Marritt was opening and closing cupboard doors. They heard crockery clash—perhaps he was moving dinner plates, looking behind them—then a metallic crash as if he'd dropped the saucepans. Dulcie smiled. "He's really good at this, very smooth." She shifted impatiently from paw to paw, then rose and began to pace, her ears swiveling with nerves.

"Settle down. He'll be gone soon."

"If he finds the diary, we'll never see it."

"It'll make a bulge in his pocket. So what's the alternative, go down there, snatch it out of his hand?"

She cut her eyes at him. "If I were alone, I'd charm him until he laid it down to pet me, then grab it and run like hell."

She shook herself, scattering ashes. Curving round, she tried to lick ashes off her coat, but that was like eating out of the fireplace. She spit out flecks of ashes and cinder. Beyond the heaps of ashes that had been raked up by the police, the charred garage door lay across the drive. The police had hauled away the remains of Janet's van.

"I wonder if her diary will have anything about museum opening," Dulcie said softly. "I wonder if she wrote in it that night when she got home from San Francisco. It would be interesting to know her version

of the weekend, after the testimony her friend Jeanne
Kale gave."

Janet's friend from San Francisco had testified that
Janet arrived in the city around seven Saturday morning, checked into the St. Francis, leaving her van in the
underground garage, and the two women had breakfast
in the hotel dining room.

"Imagine," Dulcie said, "breakfast at the St. Francis.
White tablecloths, cut glass bowls, lovely things to eat,
maybe French pancakes. And to have a beautiful hotel
room all to yourself, with a view of the city. Probably a
turn-down at night, with chocolates on the pillow."

He nuzzled her neck. "Maybe someday we'll figure
out how to do that."

She opened her mouth in a wide cat laugh. "Sure we
will. And figure out how to go to the moon."

Ms. Kale told the court that she and Janet had
shopped all day Saturday, using public transportation,
had ridden the cable car out to Fisherman's Wharf for
lunch. "Cracked crab," Dulcie said, "or maybe lobster
Thermidor." Her pink tongue licked delicately.

"I get the feeling your major interest here, is in the
gourmet aspects of the case."

"Doesn't hurt to dream. They must have had a lovely
weekend."

Late in the afternoon the two women had stopped at
an art supply store, where Janet bought oil paints, four
rolls of linen canvas, and a large supply of stretcher
bars. She had had the supplies delivered to the St.
Francis, where she gave a bellman her car keys, directing him to put the supplies in her van, in the underground garage. That night, Jeanne said, Janet had
dinner with Jeanne and her husband and with the couple for whom Janet was doing a huge sculpture of leaping fish, the sculpture she had meant to finish the
morning she died. They had eaten at an East Indian
restaurant on Grant, walking from the hotel, taking a
cab back to the St. Francis afterward.

Nancy and Tim Duncan had been friends of Janet and Kendrick Mahl before the divorce. Over dinner they talked primarily about the sculpture; Janet meant to deliver it to San Francisco early the following week. The Duncans owned a popular San Francisco restaurant, for which the ten-foot sculpture was commissioned. Janet had not taken her van from the parking garage that night, as far as Jeanne knew. After dinner she said she was tired, and had gone directly to her room.

Jeanne said that she and Janet spent Sunday sketching around San Francisco. Sunday night was the opening at the de Young, and Janet had dinner with three artist friends, not Jeanne. Jeanne had given their names. She said that Janet and her friends went directly from dinner to the de Young, in one car. There Janet received her two awards. They stayed at the reception until about ten, then drove back to the St. Francis. Janet changed clothes and checked out, put her suitcase in the van, and headed back to Molena Point. Jeanne said she saw Janet just before she left. That part of Jeanne's testimony was corroborated by the bell captain and several hotel employees. There was nothing in any of the testimonies to implicate Jeanne, or to imply that Janet had been worried about any aspect of her personal life, or that she was afraid to return home.

Dulcie tried again to wash off the ashes, but gave it up. The sounds from below were faint now—they could hear only an occasional thud, as if Marritt had retreated to the far end of the house. "We could slip in now, he'd never see us."

"Cops see everything."

"He's not a cop, he's a fraud. He shouldn't . . ."

"He's a cop. Good or bad. Cool it until he leaves."

She moved away among the burned rubble, pawing irritably at the ashes, nosing at pieces of burned wood and twisted metal. The police had gone over every inch of the site, had bagged every scrap that looked promising, even straining some of it through cheesecloth. They had taken Janet's burned welding tanks and gauges, Dulcie supposed those went to the police lab, too. The *Gazette* said the Molena Point police used the county lab for most of their work. The police had taken prints from the sculpture of leaping fish before Janet's agent took the piece away for safekeeping; it had been badly warped by the fire. The police photographer had shot at least a dozen rolls of film, must have recorded everything bigger than a cat hair.

Warily, she approached the hole in the center of the rubble-strewn slab, where the stairwell led down to the apartment. The steps, beneath fallen ashes and debris, were charred and eaten away, and the upper portions of the concrete wall were black. The lower part of the stair was relatively untouched, the door at the bottom hardly smoke-stained. She had investigated down there days before, finding nothing of interest. Now as she turned away, something sharp jabbed into her paw, causing a quick, burning pain. Mewling, she shook her hurt foot.

A blackened thumbtack protruded from her pad, with a bit of burned canvas clinging, the tack stuck so deep that when she pulled it out with her teeth, blood oozed.

She licked her pad, staring down at the tack and at the half-inch strip of blackened canvas, at all that was left of one of Janet's paintings, a pitiful fragment of burned metal and cloth. Dropping it, she crept back to Joe, to press forlornly against him, mourning Janet.

This summer, when she became aware for the first time of the riches of the human world, of music, painting, drama, and then when she discovered the Aronson Gallery, she had been so intrigued that she trotted right on in, and there were Janet's landscapes, a dozen huge works as exciting as the canvas that hung in Wilma's living room.

There had been only a few patrons in the gallery, and they were fully occupied looking at the exhibit and talking with Sicily, so no one noticed her. She prowled among the maze of angled walls, keeping out of sight, staring up at Janet's rich, windy scenes. She was thus occupied when a patron saw her. "Look at the little cat, why the cat's an art lover . . ." And the gallery had filled with rude laughter as others turned to stare. She had fled, frightened and embarrassed.

She didn't go into the gallery again for a long time, but she would slip up onto the low windowsill and lie looking in, pretending to be napping, but fascinated with the rich paintings. Strange, they gave her the same high as did the bright silks and velvets that she liked to steal. Until this summer, stealing had been her only indulgence; she'd had no notion that anything else in the world would so excite her.

She wasn't the only cat who stole; Wilma had saved a whole sheaf of clippings about thieving cats. Some cats stole objects inside their own homes—fountain pens, hair clasps—but others stole from the neighbors just as she did. Their owners said that stealing was a sign of intelligence. Maybe—all she knew was that from kitten-hood she loved *things*, and she stole them. Before she was six months old she had taught herself to leap up at a clothesline and slap off the clothespins, taking the brightest, silkiest garment, had taught herself to open the neighbors' unlocked screen doors, and she could turn almost any door knob. Once inside a house she headed directly for the master bedroom—unless there was a teenage daughter, then that room got top billing. Oh, the satin nighties and silk stockings and little lacy bras. Carrying her treasures home, she hid them beneath the furniture, where she could lie on them, purring. When Wilma found and returned the pur-loined items Dulcie felt incredibly sad, but she hadn't let Wilma know that.

Joe nudged her. "He's leaving. He doesn't have the diary. Not a lump in that tight uniform." Marritt's jacket and trousers fitted him as snugly as a second skin.

Bang, bang, bang. The concrete vibrated under their

paws as Marritt nailed up the plywood. The moment he was gone they fled down the hill and clawed their way underneath, ripping off hunks of the burned door, widening the hole Dulcie had started. She slipped under, flicking her tail through in a hurry though there was no one to grab her; her sense of helplessness at leaving her tail vulnerable was basic and powerful. Joe's short stub was not a problem.

Despite the bright sun outside, most of the room was dark. Blazing stripes of sunlight shone through the closed shutters, sharply illuminating a frosting of dust and ashes which coated the Mexican tile floor. The large living room must have been handsome before smoke and drenching water dirtied the white couch and white leather chairs, the white walls and white rugs. The floor was cold beneath their paws, but when Joe stepped onto a thick rug expecting a warm respite, he backed off fast; the rug was soaked with sour, stale water.

Marritt's footprints were everywhere incised into the dust, back and forth across the kitchen, and between the couch and chairs, as if he must have searched for the journal beneath the upholstered cushions. Six rectangles of clean white wall shone where Janet's paintings had been removed after the fire, the bare picture hooks clinging like dark grasshoppers.

The newspaper had said the paintings were being restored, that Janet's agent had taken them. Joe wasn't into the art scene, but he knew the monetary value of Janet's work. According to the Molena Point *Gazette* each of the forty-six paintings destroyed by fire was worth twenty to thirty thousand dollars. That added up to a nice, easy million.

He watched Dulcie sniff at the sodden chairs and couch, then leap to the counters of the open kitchen cube to paw at the cupboard doors. On the kitchen floor stood a bowl of cat kibble and a bowl of water, both scummed over with ashes and dust. Surely they hadn't

been touched since the fire. And how could they be,
unless Janet had had a cat door.

The stairwell door, just beyond the kitchen, had been
boarded up though it did not seem burned. From
beneath it came the smell of wet ashes, and a chill
breeze sucked down. Beyond the stairwell, the door on
the far wall was closed but not boarded over. Marritt's
intrusive footprints led to it, ripe with his scent, a combination of shoe polish and cigarette smoke. The crack
beneath the door was bright with sunlight. The smell
from within was not of ashes but of a woman's delicate
perfume. Dulcie sniffed deeply at the bright space, then
leaped up, grasping the knob between her paws.
Swinging, scrabbling with her hind feet against the
molding, she turned the knob, kicked against the door-
frame. The door swung in. They were struck in the face
by glaring sunlight, blinding them.

8

The cats narrowed their eyes, bombarded by sunlight. Sun blazed through treetops and bounced off burnished clouds. They stood at the edge of a terrace high above the hills, a tile expanse furnished with white wicker chairs, white wicker desk . . . a bed . . . bookcases . . .

Their eyes adjusted, their response focused, they saw clearly. They stood not on a terrace but on the threshold of Janet's bedroom, its two glass walls filled with trees and sky. To the left of the wide corner windows Janet's bed was tucked cozily into a wall of books. The white sheets had been tossed back in a tangle, the brightly flowered quilt lay half on the floor, as if Janet had just stepped away from the bed, had perhaps gone into the kitchen to make coffee; the sense of her presence was powerful. Her blue sweatshirt lay tossed across the wicker chair with a pair of jeans and a red windbreaker; beneath the chair lay a pair of jogging shoes leaning one atop the other, her white socks tucked neatly inside. Dulcie sniffed at the clothes of the dead woman and shivered; these would be the clothes she wore driving home from San Francisco that night after the opening at the de Young. The next morning she would have put on welding clothes, old scorched jeans, heavy leather boots, clothes that an accidental welding burn wouldn't hurt.

Three big white rugs softened the expanse of tile, thick and inviting and quite dry; the cats' paws sank deep, inscribing sooty prints. Dulcie sat down to clean her pink pads, but Joe stood, absorbing the warmth of the room, heat from the sun pressing in through the glass, absorbing the powerful sense of the dead woman. The feel of her presence was so strong he felt his fur tingle.

Beneath the white wicker desk was a tennis ball, and clinging to the desk legs and to the legs of the chair were fine white cat hairs. As Joe scented the tomcat, an involuntary growl rose in his throat; but it was an old scent, flat and faded.

He leaped to the bed, onto the rumpled sheets, leaving sooty pawprints, then belatedly he licked clean his own pads. The sun-warmed sheets smelled of human female, and of Janet's light perfume. He flopped down and rolled, purring.

The bookshelves above the bed had been recessed into the wall. The bottom shelf, at bed level, was bare. When he reared up to study the books, he could see the names of writers that Clyde liked to read, Cussler, Koontz, Steinbeck, Tolkien, Pasternak, an interesting mix. Half a dozen scrapbooks and photo albums were sandwiched between these, but he saw nothing that looked like a diary—unless Janet had made her journal in one of the big albums. As he clawed one down, Dulcie leaped up beside him.

"Strange that there's no nightstand. Where did she keep her night cream? Her facial tissues and clock? And Wilma keeps a bowl of mints by the bed. They're nice late at night."

Pawing open the album, they found newspaper clippings neatly taped to the pages, reviews of Janet's work and articles about awards she had won. Many had her picture, fuzzed and grainy, taken beside a painting or a piece of sculpture. There was a quarter-page article from the *L. A. Times* about Janet's top award in the Los Angeles Museum Annual, and another *Times* article gave her a big spread for a one-woman show at the

Biltmore. Northern California papers supplied clippings about an award at the Richmond Annual, and the San Francisco papers listed awards in Reno, San Diego, Sacramento. There seemed to be clippings for all the major exhibits, as well as for Janet's one-woman shows, many at the major museums.

"She's done—she did all right," Joe said. "It wasn't easy. She put herself through school working as a welder in San Francisco, lived in a cheap room in the commercial district. That's a rough part of the city. I was born in an alley just off Mission. That's where I got my tail broken, that's where Clyde found me.

"She didn't have any furniture at first, just an easel, and she slept on a mattress on the floor. She kept everything in cardboard boxes."

"How do you know all this?"

"From napping in the living room while she and Clyde drank beer and listened to Clyde's collection of old forties records." Joe grinned. "She liked the big bands as much as Clyde does." He'd loved those nights, just the three of them. He'd been comfortable with Janet, and, long before he'd discovered his super-cat talents, he had shared with Janet and Clyde a cat's normal pleasure in music. That heady forties beat seemed to get right under his skin, right in to where the purrs started.

"She was the only woman he ever dated who didn't pitch a fit about Clyde keeping my ratty, clawed-up chair in the living room. Janet called it a work of art." The covering of his personal chair, he had long ago shredded to ribbons. The chair was his alone: no cat, no dog, no human had better mess with it.

After graduation Janet had moved to Molena Point, to another cheap room, had picked up welding jobs around the docks to support herself. Every penny went into paint and canvas, into oxygen and acetylene for her sculpture, and into sheets of milled steel. She had taken her work to every juried show in the state, and in only two years she was picked up by the Aronson Gallery.

She had lived better then, had bought some used furniture and a used van. She had been in Molena Point less than a year when she started dating Kendrick Mahl. Mahl was the art critic for the *San Francisco Chronicle* then; he kept a weekend place in Molena Point. When they married, Janet moved in there, but she kept her old room for studio space. After the wedding, Mahl's reviews of her work were favorable but understandably restrained. After the divorce he called her paintings cheap trash. Months after she left Mahl, she started dating Clyde. Joe thought she'd needed that comfortable relationship.

He clawed down a second album, this one was filled with eight-by-ten glossies, publicity photos of Janet and of her work. In the first shot she stood turned away from a splashy landscape, a painting of the rocky sea cliff as seen from the level of the white, crashing waves. At the very top of the painting, just a hint of rooftops shone against a thin strip of sky. Janet stood before the painting looking directly at the camera, her grin mischievous, her hands paint-stained, her smock streaked with paint; her eyes were fixed directly on them, filled with power and life.

Shivering, Dulcie wrapped her tail close around herself and sat looking at the room where Janet had lived. Where Janet had waked that Monday morning with no idea that, within an hour, she would be dead.

Dead, Dulcie thought, *and with nothing else afterward?* Ever since Janet died, that question had troubled her.

They found in this album dated photographs of Janet's recent paintings, and at the back was a picture of the white cat, an eight-by-ten color shot. He sat on a blue backdrop, a carefully chosen fabric the color of his blue eyes and blue collar. His fur was long, well groomed, his tail a huge fluffed plume. His expression was intelligent and watchful, but imperious, too, coolly demanding.

There were shots of the white cat with Janet, one

where he sat in her lap, and one where he lay across her shoulder, his eyes slitted half-closed.

"*Can* he still be alive? Maybe he's hurt. Is that why I dream of him, because he needs our help?"

"The volunteers looked everywhere, Dulcie. There must have been twenty people combing the hills. Don't you think if he were alive, they would have found him? Don't you think that, even hurt, he would have tried to come home?"

"Maybe he's too badly hurt. Or maybe he did come home, maybe he found the studio gone, flattened, nothing but ashes—and Janet gone, no fresh scent of her. He would have been terrified. He might have just gone away again, frightened and confused. The fire itself must have been terrible for him. Maybe he was afraid even to come near the house."

"No matter how scared, if he were hungry, he'd go to the neighbors, at least to cadge a meal."

"There's some reason I dream of him." She gave him a clear green look. "The dreams have some purpose. They have to come from somewhere, not just from my own head. Before I dreamed of him, I didn't even know what he looked like, except from seeing him blocks away. I didn't know his eyes were blue, I didn't know that he wore a blue collar with a brass tag." She looked at him a long time. "Where did those bits of knowledge come from?"

"Maybe you saw his collar some time, saw him close up and don't remember."

"I didn't. I *would* remember."

But he didn't answer, and she let it drop. Maybe there was something in the male genes that wouldn't let him think about such mysteries.

The rest of the album contained snapshots of Janet at a picnic, and at a party, and several shots of her beside an overweight, overdressed woman. "Beverly," Dulcie said. "That has to be her sister Beverly—she's just the way Wilma described her. Looks like an overfed pug dog."

There were three shots of Janet in a wet suit beside a rocky shore, then pictures of a baseball game, where Janet stood tanned and grinning, ready to pitch, and there was a shot of her at bat.

They went through all the albums, pulling them off the shelves until the big, leather-bound books covered the rumpled bed. They found no diary. Dulcie prowled beneath the bed, under the fallen sheets and comforter, then searched the bookshelves again, thrusting her nose behind the disarranged books. When, balancing on the bottom shelf, she felt it shift beneath her paws she dropped down and dug at it.

They worried at the shelf, wiggling and clawing until it moved, then slid back.

The space beneath contained a box of tissues, face cream, a jar of hand cream, two small sketch pads, pencils, pens, and a small folding clock. Half-hidden beneath the jumble lay a small, leather-bound book.

Dulcie touched it with a hesitant paw. The scent of leather was mixed with Janet's scent. She took it in her teeth, dragged it out, dropped it on the bed. Gently she pawed it open.

The cats glanced at each other and smiled. This was it, this was Janet's diary.

Janet's handwriting was small and neat. She had written as much as she could on each page, leaving only thin margins, squeezing the lines close together as if she had felt frugal about the space, as if she had wanted to make the journal last over as many years as possible.

The last half of the diary was empty.

She had begun the journal during art school days, but had made only occasional entries then, mostly random notes of scenes she wanted to paint . . . *Corner Jones and Lombard, white Victorian towering behind shops . . . The top of Chestnut Street when the storm sky is low and dark, and the East Bay seems so close you could touch it . . . The light against Russian Hill when clouds break the sun. Who can put that light on canvas?*

She had made brief notes about her move to Molena Point, and some memos as to moving costs. There was a page of notes about apartment hunting, then a lapse of time. Then later, during her stormy marriage to Kendrick Mahl, the entries were long and painful, a montage of hurts from Mahl, his sarcasm about her work—and his involvement with other women, the details meant for no one else's eyes, as Janet set down her painful disappointment in Mahl, and then at last her resolve to leave him. Her notes about the divorce were raw and ugly, filled with her growing hatred.

Joe hadn't thought of Janet as one to hold on to hurts, but she had held on, clinging to her anger, and who could blame her? Kendrick Mahl was a vindictive man, hurtful and cold. Joe had no reason not to believe Janet; he thought Janet didn't lie easily. She had not talked to Clyde much about Mahl.

The journal entries were all tangled together, her personal life, her painting notes, brief reminders of when and where each painting was hung and if it had received an award, all the fragments of her life jumbled into one entity like the pieces of a jigsaw puzzle. In the occasional stilted notes about her sister Beverly, it was apparent that the two sisters did not get along. A year before Janet's death, Beverly had wanted to open a gallery and take Janet's work from Sicily, a proposal Janet had rejected. The entry reflected her anger with bold, dark handwriting. Not even when she was the most hurt by Mahl had she written in this little book with such obvious rage.

"How can they be sisters?" Dulcie said. "There's no love, there's no closeness at all between them." She stared at Joe with widening eyes. "I had three sisters and two brothers, and I never saw them again after Wilma took me away."

"And you're sorry she took you?"

She licked her whiskers. "If Wilma hadn't taken me, I probably would have died. I was the runt, they kept pushing me away from the milk. I didn't know what it felt like to be really, beautifully full of supper until I went to live with Wilma.

"But I do wonder what it would have been like to have someone to play with, when I was little."

"Maybe that's why you steal. You had a maladjusted kittenhood."

She gave him a gentle swat, and returned to Janet's diary. Scattered through the journal were brief passages that did not seem to be painting notes but were simply written for pleasure, little pleasing word pictures, a drift of clouds over the darkening hills, the sea heaving green against the rocks, vignettes more detailed than her painting notes. The entries where Janet broke off with Rob Lake were written shortly after Mahl became Rob's agent.

Anyone's head would be turned, Kendrick was the most powerful critic in Northern California before he left the Chronicle *to open his own gallery. He can make Rob's reputation, or prevent Rob from ever getting anywhere. Of course Rob's being used. Can't he see that? Or is he so eager that he doesn't care, that our relationship means nothing? I can't see him anymore, not when he belongs to Kendrick, I can't be comfortable with him now.*

Joe withheld comment. His remarks about Rob Lake only angered Dulcie. She would have to admit in her own time that Lake wasn't as pure as she'd imagined.

Near the end of the journal was a note about a Mrs. Blankenship, who seemed to be a neighbor. Janet described her as a harmless old dear who had nothing to do but watch other people from her bedroom window.

She has sent word by her daughter that she doesn't like me welding so near their house, that it isn't safe, and that the flashing light bothers her. I've put up heavy shutters in the studio, and started pulling my kitchen shade, too. Poor old woman doesn't have anything else to do with her time. Maybe she should get a dog.

"That's the woman we saw staring out the window across the street," Dulcie said. "It's the only house that looks right over to the studio." The houses on the street above were higher, farther away, and positioned so that probably no one cared what Janet did. But the house across the side street had a clear view. "I wonder," she said softly, "what that old woman saw, the morning of the fire. There hasn't been any witness named Blankenship."

"It was five in the morning. Why would an old woman be looking out her window at five in the morning?"

"Old people don't sleep well, they're up at all hours. Wilma wakes up in the middle of the night and reads. I have to burrow under the covers."

Her green eyes widened. "Maybe I can find out; maybe I can hang out there for a while. Play up to the old lady."

"Why not? You could do that. Get her to confide in you—tell her you're a talking cat, that you'd like to interview her. Like to ask her a few questions. Maybe you could borrow a press card, say you work for the *Gazette*."

"I could play lost kitty. Hungry lost kitty. Little old ladies are suckers for that stuff."

Silently he looked at her.

"It's worth a try. What harm?"

"That old woman might hate cats. Maybe she poisons cats."

"If she hates cats, I'll leave. If she puts poison out, I won't eat it. Do you think I can't smell poison?"

"Sometimes, Dulcie . . ." But he sighed. What was the use?

She smiled and returned to the journal. "Why does Janet say this about Sicily Aronson, that Sicily is admirably calculating? What does she . . . ?"

A sudden noise from the street startled them, the sound of a car door opening. They sprang to the window, looking down at the street.

A black Cadillac had parked at the curb. The driver's door was open, and, as they watched, a large woman began to extricate herself from beneath the steering wheel. Dulcie's eyes widened. "Beverly. That's Beverly Jeannot, has to be. Why would she come up here?"

"Why not? It's her house now. You know Janet left her the house."

"But the police tape is still up. I thought no one was supposed to come inside. I wonder if Captain Harper knows she's up here."

"Dulcie, it's her house. Don't you think she has a right to come in?"

Behind the Cadillac a pale cream Mercedes of antique vintage pulled up. Dulcie stared, her tail twitching with surprise. They could see the driver's red hair massed like a flame. "Where did Charlie get a pretty car like that? She can hardly afford a cup of coffee."

"That's Clyde's old Mercedes, the one he rebuilt. He must have loaned it to her. Maybe her old bus died. It wouldn't take much."

Charlie swung out of the Mercedes as Beverly emerged from the Cadillac. Beverly Jeannot was an overstuffed, soft-looking woman with large jowls, a wide stubby nose, and short brown hair set into such perfect marcel waves she might just have come from a 1920s beauty salon.

She was done up in something long and floating and color coordinated, all in shades of pink and burgundy, with high-heeled burgundy shoes and a natty little burgundy handbag. Her overdone outfit made a sharp contrast to Charlie's skinny jeans and faded yellow sweatshirt. The two women were as different as a jelly donut and a gnawed chicken bone. Charlie carried a clipboard, a claw hammer, and a wrecking bar.

As the mismatched pair started up the hill, moving out of sight along the far side of the house, Dulcie stared at the books scattered on the bed. There was no way to get them back on the shelves—that would take forever. She leaped to the bed, pawed the cubbyhole closed, and nosed Janet's diary to the floor; leaping down she pushed it under the bed. They slid under behind it, dragging it deeper beneath the fallen sheets as footsteps rang on the entry deck. They could hear the soft mumble of voices, then a wrenching screech as Charlie began to pull nails, releasing the boarded-over front door.

There were two thuds as Charlie leaned the plywood sheets against the house, then the soft, metallic click of the lock turning.

As Beverly Jeannot's high heels struck across the living room tiles, the cats backed into the far corner, pulling Janet's diary with them, shoving it under a fold of quilt. And, tucked warm beneath the quilt beside the leather-bound book, Joe found himself listening intently, surprised at his own sharp curiosity.

For the first time since Janet's death, his interest in her killer was intense, predatory. Determined. Now, suddenly, he meant to find out who killed Janet.

Maybe it was his immediate, instinctive dislike of Beverly Jeannot.

Or maybe his concern grew from the strong sense of Janet surrounding them, her scent, her pictures, her words—her deepest feelings shared.

9

Beverly stepped up onto Janet's deck, pulling her skirts around her, staying well away from the fallen, burned oak tree that had smashed half the deck and the rail. Looking helplessly at the plywood that had been nailed over the front door, she waited for Charlie to provide access.

Hiding an irritated smile, Charlie began to pull nails, wondering what Beverly would do if she had to get into Janet's apartment without assistance. She hoped she could work for this woman without, somewhere along the way, losing control of her temper. Their first meeting, three days before, had been strained.

Because she didn't yet have an office in which to talk with Beverly, she'd suggested meeting for coffee at the Bakery. Beverly kept the appointment, but let her know right off that meeting in a public restaurant was not the way in which she liked to conduct business. Charlie didn't know how much privacy Beverly required to discuss repair and janitorial services. Beverly had looked a mile down her nose at the little tables on the Bakery's charming covered porch; though when their tea was served she tied right into the pastries, devouring the apricot crescent rolls greedily.

Charlie pulled the last nails, slipped the two sheets of plywood out from under the police tape, and leaned them against the house. She didn't have to like Beverly Jeannot in order to work for her, and this was the biggest cleaning and repair job she'd bid on. Following Beverly up along the side of the house from the street below, she had hastily assessed the exterior damage. The smoke-stained siding would need pressure scrubbing, and that would mean covering the windows. She'd have to rent a pressure washer. It was too early on in the game to buy one— that would put her in debt for a year. The pump alone ran around eleven hundred, and the spray washer was probably more. A total of two to three thousand bucks.

Her profit from this job would go a long way toward paying for that kind of equipment—if she didn't lose her temper and blow it. Though it was more than Beverly's attitude that made her uncomfortable about this bid. She wasn't looking forward to cleaning the house where Janet Jeannot had been killed so brutally. She'd been a fan of Janet's, had admired Janet's work for years. She wasn't sure how she was going to feel, working there, where Janet had been murdered.

But that was childish, she was being childish. She couldn't help Janet; she couldn't change anything.

When she was still in art school, she had sometimes seen Janet at a gallery opening or a museum reception among a group of well-known painters. She had never had the nerve to approach the artist. Why should Janet Jeannot care that some gangling art student idolized her work?

But now she wished she had spoken to her. She hadn't learned until she moved to Molena Point three weeks ago, what a down-to-earth person Janet had been. Maybe a word of admiration, even from an art student, would have meant a little something.

Of course when she told Beverly, over coffee that day, how much she had admired Janet, she received only a haughty sniff. As if a common cleaning and repair person couldn't possibly distinguish an exciting painting from the Sunday comics. Now, following Beverly inside, she wondered if Beverly herself had appreciated Janet's work. Stepping over the burned threshold, Beverly gathered her skirts around her giving a little disgusted huff at the sour smell.

What did she expect, attar of lilies? There'd been a fire there: the white walls, the white rugs and furniture were dark from smoke, the rooms smelled of smoke and dampness, and strongly of mildew. There were drip lines running down the smoke-darkened paint where water had leaked in from the fire hoses.

"I will want all the food removed from the cupboards, and that cat stuff thrown out." Beverly directed her glance to the dusty water and food bowls on the floor by the kitchen sink. "She kept a cat, but I suppose it's dead or has found somewhere else to live.

"I want you to clean the refrigerator thoroughly, and pack up all the dishes and cookware. Those will go to the Goodwill—there's nothing here worth keeping. I want the house completely emptied except for the rugs and furniture. You will see to having those properly cleaned, so that I can sell them." Beverly stood waiting, as if to be sure that Charlie understood.

Charlie dutifully noted the details on the pad inserted in her clipboard, then picked up the wet throw rugs and carried them out to the deck. Wringing them out, she hung them over the undamaged portion of rail. She'd drop them off later for cleaning—a good professional would do a better job than she ever could with a rented steam cleaner. Straightening the rugs, looking down the hill, she admired the view. Maybe someday she'd have a place like this. She wondered where the cat was, the one that belonged to the dusty water and food bowls. That would be the white cat that Wilma had helped to search for. Wilma thought the poor thing had died in the fire; they'd found no sign of him.

She stood in the big living room for a few moments, assessing the smoke-stained walls. They'd need a heavy scrubbing before she painted. The floors would be fine with a good mopping; nothing could hurt that Mexican clay tile.

"I'm in here," Beverly called imperiously.

Out of sight, Charlie stuck out her tongue, then moved obediently toward the bedroom.

This room was huge, too, and so bright it took her breath. It would make a wonderful studio. She'd kill for that view down the hills. Beverly stood beside the unmade bed, shuffling through a tangle of scrapbooks scattered across the rumpled sheets. The sheets were streaked with black dirt, too, and when she looked more closely she realized they were pawprints.

So Janet's cat had survived, had been in the house—or some cat had. Must have slipped in through the charred hole under the front door. Beverly seemed not to see the prints or was ignoring them, caring nothing about the cat.

Before she left, Charlie thought, she'd put out fresh water, food if she could find any, maybe leave the bowls under the entry deck where Beverly wouldn't notice.

"I'll want her clothes boxed up for charity. She had no valuable jewelry, only junk. Please look through the closet and dresser now, so you will know how many containers you will require. I will want a complete and detailed list for tax purposes." Beverly flipped through each album, left them in an untidy pile, and turned to inspecting the bookshelves, moving books and glancing behind them. It occurred to Charlie to wonder if Beverly Jeannot really ought to be in there. Maybe she hadn't any more right to be in this house than the general public, until the police cordon was removed and the trial was finished.

Opening the dresser drawers, she found them half-empty. Not as if Janet's clothes had been removed, rather as if Janet hadn't had much, as if perhaps the artist saw no need for an abundance of clothing. Her few jeans and sweatshirts lay neatly folded. There was one nice sweater, in a plastic storage bag, a dozen pairs of socks, two pairs of panty hose. Janet had worn plain cotton panties. She didn't seem overly fond of brassieres—she had only one.

Beverly, preoccupied and intent, moved from the bookshelves to the desk, opening drawers, shuffling through the contents. Charlie watched her, then checked the closet. It was half-empty, too. Janet must have unpacked from her San Francisco trip before she went to bed. There was a small, empty suitcase on the top shelf beside a folded garment bag. The clothes on the chair must be what she took off that night, as if she'd been too tired to put them away. The closet contained a wide, transparent storage bag with three dress-up outfits: a beige silk suit, a print dress, and a gold, low-cut cocktail dress. Two more pairs of jeans hung neatly beside a second windbreaker and some cotton shirts. This completed the wardrobe. She heard Beverly pick up the phone and punch in a number, listened to her asking for Police Captain Harper.

She could imagine how that imperious tone would go over if she used it on Harper.

She had met Max Harper only once, but she knew enough about him from Clyde to know the dry, lean man didn't tolerate being patronized. What cop did? Listening, she returned to the dresser and pretended to inventory jeans and sweatshirts.

Beverly must have pull, in spite of her rudeness, because within seconds she had Harper on the line.

Though likely it wasn't pull at all but Beverly's connection to Janet. For all she knew, Beverly herself might be suspect in some way.

"Captain Harper, the man you sent up here to search this house has left an unacceptable mess. I can't imagine why he would do this—he has pulled nearly all the books off the shelves for no apparent reason, has, in fact, trashed the entire bedroom."

Charlie didn't see anything trashed. She could imagine the chief of police raising an amused eyebrow, puffing away on a cigarette while Beverly ranted.

"What do you mean, I'm not allowed in the house? This is my house now. Have you forgotten that Janet left the house to me? Surely your police rules apply simply to the general public. I don't . . . "

Abruptly Beverly stopped talking, was quiet for some minutes, then, "Captain Harper, I came up here on legitimate business. I would remind you that I don't live in Molena Point, and that my time here is limited. I came up here to assess the interior damage and to arrange for much-needed repairs—once you have released the premises. I'm sure you know that much of the damage was caused by your police officers and city firemen. I am, in fact, facing monumental cleaning and repair costs, thanks to you city workers."

There was another long silence, then Beverly gave a sharp huff of exasperation and hung up, banging the receiver. Charlie pretended to be absorbed in noting the number of moving boxes she'd want. She paced off the size of the rooms in preparation for ordering paint, then went down to the Mercedes to retrieve a box of paint chips from her canvas tote. Beverly wanted a perfect match to the existing white walls. This seemed a needless expense, to have the paint specially mixed, when the woman was going to sell the house. Particularly when she was in such a hurry.

But what does a simple cleaning person know?

Returning from the car, she looked up at the house with a stab of longing, dreaming how it would be to have that lovely apartment. The studio above could be rebuilt, with plenty of space for tool storage and building supplies, maybe room left over for a small rental.

Sure, just whip out the checkbook and plunk down half a million or maybe more, and it's mine. Molena Point property was incredibly expensive.

Back in the house again, she sorted through paint chips, *India Ivory, Rich Almond, Pagan White, Winter Snow, Narcissus.* She chose *Pale Bone,* matching it to a little patch of wall down behind the couch that seemed to have escaped smoke damage.

But when she checked the color with Beverly, Beverly huffed and had to try a dozen samples. She returned to the *Pale Bone* as if she had just discovered it. In a few minutes she was back in the bedroom. Charlie could hear her still rummaging, heard her open the closet door, heard the hangers slide, heard her unzip the suitcase, zip it up again. Whatever the woman was looking for, she hadn't found it yet.

Well at least the police knew she was there. If Harper didn't want her nosing around, he'd send a squad car.

In the kitchen cupboard she found a supply of cat kibble and a dozen small cans of gourmet cat food. Reluctant to move the bowls on the floor and generate questions, she dug out an aluminum pie tin and a chipped china bowl. Filling the bowl with water, she carried it all outside, poured kibble into the pie tin, placed it and the kibble box and bowl of water just under the deck. She could see, down the hill, the house she was now working on, just a few blocks south. She could run up to this house easily to replenish the food and water. If the cat did come back, she could see if it was hurt and take care of it.

Returning to the bedroom, she startled Beverly. The woman turned abruptly from the empty bookshelves. Having pulled off all the remaining books, she looked cross and frustrated.

"When you get Janet's clothes packed, get them off at once to the Junior League or the Goodwill, then take these albums and scrapbooks to her agent. It is the Aronson Gallery, on San Carlos."

Charlie nodded and held her tongue.

"Any of Janet's sketches, or sketchbooks—or any journals, are to be given to me. Pack them carefully in a large, suitably flat box. Don't fold the sketches, please. Anything drawn or written by Janet's hand must come to me. Bring them to my motel. Don't leave them in the house while you are working.

"The bedding and towels can go with the clothes and kitchen things. In short, everything to charity except albums, scrapbooks, diaries, or journals, and any remaining artwork. And of course the rugs and furniture, which I will sell."

For a woman whose sister had died so recently, and

so horribly, Beverly Jeannot was maintaining a remarkable strength of spirit. Charlie pretended to take notes, but they weren't needed. Beverly's sharp instructions had etched themselves on each individual brain cell.

"You understand that you cannot start any work until the police legally remove the barrier," Beverly said. "I have no idea how long this trial will take. Once it ends, beginning the day it ends, when the premises are released, I want the work started immediately and done with dispatch. The living room cleaned and painted, the outside of the house scrubbed, the windows washed. The remains of the studio fire must be removed and the area swept clean so the builders can start, and the entire yard must be cleaned and raked." She looked Charlie over. "How long will that require? I hope no more than two or three days. Can you assure me that you have sufficient crew to handle the job expeditiously? If you cannot, I would like to know at once."

"My crews will be on the job the moment the police allow us to enter. I'll do the bid this evening, fax it to your motel. Will that be satisfactory?"

No other repair and cleaning service would put their jobs on hold in this way—a customer waited his turn. She wouldn't make this arrangement either, to be available at any time without notice, if she wasn't just getting started.

She hadn't told Beverly how short a time she'd been in business, and Beverly hadn't asked. She reminded herself again that she had better not lose her sense of humor. She prayed that she'd be able to find additional help for the job. One fifty-year-old, addle-brained cleaning lady and one male handyman of questionable skills were not going to cut it.

Under the bed, the cats glanced at each other. There was only one place Beverly hadn't searched. Her footsteps tapping across the tile were bold and solid.

She stopped beside the bed, her shoes inches from

Dulcie's nose. Thick ankles in thick, pale stockings, burgundy high heels with wide straps across the instep. The springs squeaked and one burgundy foot disappeared upward, then the other, as Beverly climbed to kneel on the bed.

She had already pulled all the books out. Now a dry, sliding sound suggested that she was running her hand down the wall, maybe pressing along the moving shelf beneath which Janet had kept her tissues and clock and the missing journal. The springs complained as she shifted her weight.

They heard the movable panel rattle. Heard her suck in her breath, heard the shelf slide open.

They listened to her rummaging among the contents, but soon she closed the little niche again and eased herself down and off the bed.

When Beverly began to pull the sheets off, Dulcie snatched the diary in her teeth and they slipped out behind her, staying between the comforter and the wall. As she tugged at the bedding, jerking sheets and comforter onto the rug, they fled, streaking for the closet.

They peered out, ready to run again.

But she didn't turn, hadn't seen them. They watched her shake the bedclothes, drop them on the rug, then roll the bed away from the wall. As she searched behind it, her posterior bulged in the plum-colored skirt. At last she straightened up, brushed dust from her suit, and returned empty-handed to the living room.

The cats did not leave their shelter until they heard the front door close, heard the lock slide home, heard Charlie nailing up the plywood.

When an engine started down below they left the closet, trotted to the window, and watched Beverly drive away. Charlie left directly behind her, the Mercedes softly purring.

The apartment was still again, empty.

Crouching together on the rug with the diary lying between them, they pawed it open to the last pages.

Here were entries about the de Young opening, notes which Janet must have made only days before she died. *Ironic that Kendrick is on the museum board which is giving me two awards. A jury with Kendrick on it wouldn't even have hung my work, so I guess he didn't have any say in the matter, it's the jury that decides, bless them.*

She had tucked a clipping between the pages, a group photo of the board, taken a week before the opening. She had drawn beside Mahl's picture an owl that looked so like Mahl, Dulcie rolled over laughing. The dowdy bird had Mahl's hunched shoulders, Mahl's beaklike nose. Its eyes closely resembled Mahl's round, rimless glasses.

In the photo Mahl had his suit coat off and was holding a piece of clay sculpture, his white shirt cuff revealing, where it had pulled back, an expensive-looking watch, heavy and ostentatious.

Joe stared at it. "What kind of man would wear a watch decorated with cupids and those heavy wings sticking out. Pretty pretentious, for someone who's supposed to have the tastes of an artist."

"Where did you learn about the tastes of an artist?"

"Not from Clyde, you can bet."

The last entry in Janet's diary had been made the night before she died, a one-line comment which perhaps she had written just before she went to sleep.

Lovely night at the de Young. Two awards. Euphoria. All perfect. Except K. was there.

Behind that page she had tucked a newspaper review of the exhibit, her hotel bill, a charge slip for gas, and a plain slip of paper with some numbers jotted on it.

"Could be the van's mileage," Joe said. "For her tax records. Mileage when she left, and again when she got home." Janet had crossed out the beginning mileage and penciled in a new one, two hundred miles larger.

"Guess she wrote the original number wrong, then corrected it—put a three hundred where she should have had a five."

"She must have been in a hurry," Dulcie said. "What

should we do with the diary? We can't let Beverly—or the police—come back and find it."

"We have to get it to the police, Dulcie. It could be evidence."

"But there are personal things in here. She wouldn't want this read in court."

"We don't have any choice, if it's evidence. And there are things in here about Rob Lake."

She laid a soft paw on the pages, on Janet's small, neat handwriting. "Would they read it out loud in court? If the papers get hold of this, they'll print everything—all the things she said about Mahl." She licked her chest, smoothing her fur. "Janet wouldn't want this made public, plastered all over the newspaper."

"It belongs with the police. Max Harper won't let the papers have it."

"Detective Marritt would, behind Harper's back."

"You think Harper would let anything happen behind his back?"

"Marritt messed up the investigation, didn't he?"

Joe sighed. "You're not really sure of that. We'll hide it for tonight, until we decide what to do." He rose and headed for the kitchen.

Pawing open the lower cupboard doors, he prowled among the pans until he found a supply of plastic grocery bags rolled neatly and stuffed in an empty coffee can.

· Within minutes they had bagged the diary to protect it from the damp and rain, and had dragged it outside and hidden it beneath the deck, pushing it deeper under than the bowls which Charlie had left for the white cat.

"That was nice of her," Dulcie said. "I guess *Charlie* believes in the white cat."

"I didn't say I don't believe in him. I just think he's— Oh, what the hell. Maybe he'll show up and eat the damned kibble."

She gave him a long green stare, but then she snuggled close. "Come on, let's go con that old Mrs. Blankenship, see what we can find out."

10

"Suck in your stomach, try to look hungry."

"I am sucking it in, I can hardly breathe." She let her ears go limp and forlorn, let her tail droop until it dragged the ground.

"Yeah. That's better, that's pitiful. You really look like hell."

"Thanks so much."

"A starving stray, not a friend in the world."

The plan was, she'd approach the old woman alone as this was definitely a one-cat job. One starving, pitiful little kitty could turn the hardest heart, while two cats tramping the neighborhood would give the impression of mutual support, of perhaps greater hunting options. A pair of cats could never achieve the same high degree of helplessness and neglect, elicit the same pity.

"She's still watching," Joe said, peering out at the old woman. "And even if she didn't see us come into the bushes, she's already seen us together, up at Janet's house. She knows you're not alone. I don't think this is going to work."

"It'll work." Dulcie studied Mrs. Blankenship. The soft, elderly woman looked a perfect mark, like some old grandmother there behind the curtain, her nose pressed to the glass. "But before I go into my half-starved act, we need a little drama, a little pathos. How about a cat fight? Before you nip out of here, how about you beat the stuffings out of me."

Joe smiled. "A screaming frenzy of a fight."

"Exactly. Poor little kitty torn apart by the big ugly bully."

"So who's ugly!" He lit into her, kicking and clawing, knocking her out onto the lawn. She screamed, yowled. He was all over her, they rolled clear of the bushes tearing at each other, raking and kicking, tearing divots from the grass—but not a bit of fur flew. They didn't lay a claw on each other. Dulcie's screams were loud enough to have drowned out all the fire engines in Molena Point, her voice ululating in crescendos of terror and rage.

Mrs. Blankenship's troubled face remained pressed against the glass for only an instant, then the old woman's window banged open. "Stop it! Stop it! Leave her alone!"

They gave it a few more licks for good measure, then Dulcie escaped into the bushes. The old woman yelled again, and Joe fled, hissing and snarling.

He paused behind a rhododendron bush out of sight. *I'm pretty good at this acting stuff, a regular Robert Redford—or maybe Charles Bronson.* He pictured himself bashing skulls, leaping atop runaway cars.

Mrs. Blankenship had opened the screen and was leaning out, beckoning to Dulcie. "Kitty? Oh you poor, poor kitty." She reached out as if Dulcie would come to her outstretched hand. She was dressed in a flowered bathrobe, her gray hair confined beneath a thick, old-fashioned net.

Dulcie crept out from her shelter, staring up.

"Come on, kitty. Oh you poor, pretty kitty."

Dulcie mewled pitifully, her voice unsteady and weak.

"Oh, you poor little thing. Come on, kitty. Are you hurt? Did the bad tomcat hurt you?"

At least, Joe thought, *the woman knows how to tell a tomcat. Broad shoulders, thick neck. It doesn't take a look at your private parts, necessarily, to know you're a stud.* He watched Dulcie creep across the lawn, walking slowly, managing to limp. Shyly, warily, she approached the window. This cat was no slouch, either, as an actor—she could play Scarlett to his Rhett.

"Oh, you poor, poor kitty. Come on up here to Mama. Can you jump? Are you hurt too bad, or can you jump up?" The old woman tapped on the sill with a shaky finger.

But Dulcie lay down on the grass, trying for the wan, coy effect. Lying upside down, widening her green eyes with longing, she let her little peach-colored paws fold over her poor empty tummy.

Yes, that did it. Mrs. Blankenship leaned farther, her lumpy bosom pressed down over the sill. Her body in the flowered robe was round and soft, the robe bleached out from numerous washings, baggy and wrinkled. Her eyes were a faded brown. And her hair was not gray, but the color of old, dried summer grass.

"Oh, you poor, sweet little girl. That terrible tomcat. Come on, sweet kitty. Come on, dear. I'll take care of you."

Dulcie remained shy and frightened.

"I can't come out to get you, dear, Frances will see me, she'll have a fit." Her face wrinkled up, petulant and cross. "She doesn't like animals—doesn't like much of anything. Come on, kitty, you'll have to come up on the sill—if you're not too hurt to jump. Oh, dear . . ."

Dulcie played coy for another few minutes, wondering about this Frances, thinking maybe she ought to cut out of there while she had the chance. But at last she rose haltingly and approached the window.

"Come on, poor baby. Poor sweet baby, I won't hurt you."

She stood looking up, then gathered herself both in spirit and in body, and leaped, exploding onto the sill, their faces inches from each other.

"Come on, pretty kitty. Come and let me see. Did that old tomcat hurt you?" Old Mrs. Blankenship's wrinkles were covered with a thick layer of powder. Her brown eyes were faded. She had fuzz on her face and little hairs in her ears.

Standing on the sill halfway in through the window,

Dulcie let the old woman stroke her. Mrs. Blankenship's hands were very fat, very wrinkled, laced with thick, dark veins like little wriggly garden snakes. But they were surprisingly strong-looking hands.

And the lady did know how to stroke a cat. She rubbed gently behind Dulcie's ears, then held out her fingers so Dulcie could rub her whiskers against them. Next came a nice massage down the back, her strong hands rubbing in all the right places. With this, Dulcie abandoned her shyness, purred extravagantly, and padded right on in over the sill and onto the dressing table, stepping carefully to avoid the clutter of little china animals, small framed photographs, medicine bottles, and half-empty juice glasses. She could hardly find room to set a paw. She just hoped she was doing the right thing. Hoped this old lady didn't turn out to be some kind of serial cat killer.

The table had been dusted without moving anything, so that around each little china dog and pill bottle shone a thick circle of grime. The stuffy, too-warm room smelled of Vicks VapoRub. Mrs. Blankenship did not close the window. The old lady seemed to understand that a cat with an escape route open behind her was far braver than a cat locked suddenly in a strange house. Dulcie smiled, giving her a dazzling green gaze and another loud purr.

"That's it, pretty kitty. Come on, sweet kitty." The old woman patted her lap by way of invitation. As Dulcie oozed down off the dressing table onto that ample resting place, Mrs. Blankenship's round wrinkled face broke into a smile of delight. "Did that old tomcat hurt you? Let me see, kitty. Let me have a look."

Dulcie lay limp and cooperative as the old woman examined her, her fingers exploring carefully for battle wounds inflicted by the tomcat, her mumbles of endearment meaningless and soothing, words which she had perhaps employed one time or another with countless other cats.

"I can't find a scratch, kitty. Not a sign of blood." She looked so puzzled that when she touched Dulcie's shoulder, Dulcie deliberately flinched.

She examined Dulcie's shoulder, but, "Nope, no blood. Maybe a bruise or two. Otherwise, you look just fine, kitty. I think you were only scared." She settled back comfortably, with Dulcie curled in her lap, Dulcie taking care to keep her claws in. Mrs. Blankenship petted her, and dozed, and woke to mumble, then dozed again, seeming truly content to have a little cat in her lap.

But after some time in the hot room, pressed against Mrs. Blankenship's round stomach, Dulcie began to pant. The room was not only hot, but the smell of Vicks made her nauseous. Maybe she should have encouraged Joe do the spying.

Not that he had volunteered.

Mrs. Blankenship's sweet talk and little snoozes were interrupted only when a younger, dark-haired woman entered the room carrying a neatly folded stack of clean towels and sheets.

She stopped in the middle of the room, stared at Dulcie, stared at the open screen. "Oh, Mama. Not a cat. You haven't brought a cat in here."

"It's hurt, Frances. And starving. Go get it something to eat."

"Mama, this is a stray. Why would you let a stray cat in the house? It'll be full of fleas. It could have rabies, ringworm, anything. Why did you let it inside?"

"Where else would I bring a hurt and starving cat but inside? The poor thing needs food. Go get it some of that steak from last night."

"It doesn't look starving. It looks like a mangy freeloader."

Dulcie lifted a soft paw, gave Frances an innocent smile, her green eyes demure. The woman stared back at her with no change of expression.

Well the same to you, lady. Go stuff it.

Frances Blankenship was sleekly groomed, her short dark hair perfectly coiffed. She was dressed in tailored white pants and a pink silk blouse, and pale lizard pumps, probably Gucci's, over sheer hose. Dulcie let her gaze travel down the woman's length, and up again to that smooth, unsmiling face. Very sleek. But not likable. This was a woman who would throw a sick cat out in the freezing rain and laugh about it.

"Go get the steak, Frances."

Sighing, Frances went. Dulcie watched her retreat, wondering what power the old woman had over that cold piece of work?

She could hear Frances in the kitchen, heard the refrigerator open, then a *thunk, thunk*, as of a knife on a cutting board. In a few minutes Frances returned carrying a small portion of cold steak cut up on a paper napkin. Dulcie hoped she hadn't seen fit to lace it with oven cleaner or some equally caustic substance. Frances put the little paper with its offering down on the floor, stood studying Dulcie with a new degree of interest.

"Give me the napkin, Frances. I'll feed her. Couldn't you have managed a plate?"

Frances passed over the napkin. Dulcie, in the old woman's lap, sniffed at the meat but could smell only the rare steak and the scent of what was probably Frances's hand cream.

Mama held out a little piece of good red steak.

Here goes nothing. Dulcie snatched it from her fingers as if she were truly starving. And as she wolfed the meat, Frances watched her with what Dulcie now read as a definite increase of attention.

The steak was lovely, nice and red in the middle. Obviously the Blankenships had a good butcher; probably the same meat market Wilma frequented, the small butcher shop up on Ocean. The little repast could only have been improved by privacy. She didn't mind the old woman's presence as she ate, but Frances's intent stare made her nervous. When she had finished eating,

Frances wadded the napkin, threw it in the wastebasket, and looked down benevolently at Dulcie. "I guess you can keep the cat, Mama. If it makes you happy."

Dulcie watched her warily.

But maybe Frances was only considering what a nice diversion a cat would afford. If Frances was Mama's only caregiver, maybe she was thinking that if Mama had a cat to entertain her, Frances herself could enjoy more freedom. Hoping that was the answer, Dulcie settled back again, against Mrs. Blankenship's stomach.

She remained in the Blankenship household for four days, missed four days of the trial, and endured increasing claustrophobia in the hot, crowded dwelling. Four days can go by in a blink or they can drag interminably. She soon learned that Frances was Mrs. Blankenship's daughter-in-law. The first thing she learned about the old woman's son, Varnie, when he came shouldering in from work the first night, was that he did not like cats.

Varnie Blankenship was a short, square man, sandy-haired, with peculiarly dry, pale skin reminiscent of old yellowed newsprint. He worked at the nearby harbor, at a pleasure boat rental, tending the small craft. He arrived home smelling of grease, sweat, and gasoline.

Varnie was fond of a large, heavy supper. Frances cooked his meals, but she ate little. During the time Dulcie was in residence, Varnie read no books. He read only the daily newspaper, then folded it up into a small packet and stuffed it in the magazine stand. His spare time was taken up with television, with some activity which he performed out in the garage, and with submissively dusting his mother's curio collection, his broad hands clumsy but patient.

The entire house was crammed full of bookcases and little shelves and tables, and every surface, shelf, and table-top and cabinet top were crowded with china animals and other assorted knickknacks. The china shop atmosphere did not fit Frances, and certainly it didn't fit Varnie. Yet Varnie seemed resigned to caring for the clutter, moving among his mother's curios and dusting away like an uneasy and oversized servant. Maybe Frances and Varnie had moved in with his mother, not the other way around. Maybe the old woman had willed the house to them, provided they cared for her collection. Who knew? Maybe Varnie's subservience was generated by some propensity in the old woman to abrupt changes of mind.

Whatever the Blankenship family arrangement, the crowded house made Dulcie feel increasingly trapped. She didn't dare jump up onto any surface for fear of sending hundreds of little beasties shattering to the floor; she padded around the rooms as earthbound as any dog. She was unable even to rub her face against a table leg for fear of tipping it, of knocking down an armload of china and porcelain curios in a huge landslide. The rooms were a fireman's nightmare, and a mouse hunter's paradise. There were a thousand places for mice to hide, and their scent was heavy and fresh.

But she didn't dare. Who could chase a mouse in this maze without incurring major damage? *Good thing Joe isn't here, he'd lose patience and send the entire clutter crashing.*

In the evenings, moving warily among the crowded rooms, trying to eavesdrop but stay out of Varnie's way, listening to their every conversation and idle remark, she heard nothing about Janet, nothing about the murder or the fire. And so far, the old woman's monologues were confined to baby talk. It would be really too bad if she'd gone to all this trouble for nothing.

But Mama did spend all day at her window, as Dulcie had guessed. And she did wake up well before dawn, often to draw on her robe and return to her window, to her unrewarding vigil over the neighborhood. It seemed to Dulcie a very good chance that the old woman had seen something that morning, the morning of the fire. *It's worth a try, worth a few more days of suffocation.*

Varnie talked very little on any subject, except to say

that he didn't want a cat in the kitchen when he was eating, and didn't want a cat in the living room while he was watching the news. And Varnie was inclined to throw things: cushions, his slippers, the hard, folded-up newspaper. She decided, if she was going to pull this off, she'd better leave Varnie alone and hang out with the old lady.

But she did follow Varnie out to the garage, on that first night, before he started throwing things. He had an old truck out there that he was working on, doing something to the engine. The truck and the garage smelled strongly of stale fish, and there were fishing poles slung across the rafters. She wanted to jump up on the fender and see what he was doing, and see if she could make friends. She approached him. He looked down at her. She rolled over on the garage floor, smiling up at him.

He reached down to pet her. For a moment she thought she'd made a conquest.

Then she saw the look in his eyes.

She flipped over and backed away.

Since that moment she had kept her distance. She investigated the unfamiliar parts of the house secretly, slipping behind tables and crouching in the dark corners and beneath the beds, ignoring the smell of mice. She was still convinced that it was Mama who would spill something of interest, but she was resolved to miss nothing from any source.

Though when she crept under Varnie's easy chair to listen, or into the conjugal bedroom, she remained tense and wary. She had the distinct impression that Varnie wouldn't hesitate to snuff a little cat—and that Frances would enjoy watching. She was in this house strictly under the sponsorship of Mama—and for whatever selfish reason Frances might entertain. She was there to find out what Mama knew, and she'd hang in there until she had an answer.

But in the end, it wasn't Mama who supplied the telling clue. As it turned out, Dulcie would have learned nothing if it hadn't been for Varnie and his love of beer and stud poker.

11

ART DEALER ON STAND

Defense attorney Deonne Baron today called three additional witnesses in the murder of artist Janet Jeannot. The first to take the stand was art dealer Sicily Aronson, owner of Molena Point's Aronson Gallery, and victim Janet Jeannot's agent . . . Aronson testified that there had been bitterness between Ms. Jeannot and the accused, Rob Lake. Under detailed questioning she told the court that Ms. Jeannot was not happy over Mr. Lake's gallery association with her ex-husband Kendrick Mahl. Ms. Aronson also told the court that since Janet Jeannot's death, and the destruction of most of the artist's work in the fire that burned her studio, the remaining canvases have doubled in price. The Aronson Gallery . . .

Wilma scanned the lead story with mild interest, standing in her front garden. The *Gazette* articles were getting tedious. Much of this story was a rehashing of Janet's personal life, which the reporters seemed to find fascinating; newspaper reporters were not conditioned to let the dead rest, not as long as there was any hint of story to be milked from a tragedy. She folded the evening paper again, tucked it under her arm, and bent to pluck some spent blooms from the daylilies. A cool little breeze played through the oak tree, rattling the leaves. Above her, above the neighbors' rooftops, the sky flamed red, so blazing a sunset that she considered hurrying the five blocks to the shore to enjoy its full effect spreading like fire over the sea. But she had dinner cooking, and she'd pulled that trick before, turning the stove low, nipping down to the beach for a few moments—and returning home to find her supper burned.

She wished Dulcie was home. She grew upset when the little cat was gone for more than a night and a day. Even with Clyde's reassurrances that the cats were all right, Dulcie's absence was unsettling. Clyde would say little, only that they were perfectly safe. Turning from the daylilies she headed for the house, moved on through the kitchen, where she'd left the noodles boiling, and into the dining room to have another look at the drawings Charlie had left propped on the buffet.

She'd discovered them when she got home from work, had stood looking at the little exhibit, amazed. She'd had no idea that Charlie was drawing Dulcie, and she'd had no idea, no hint that Charlie could draw animals with such power. Until that moment she'd thought of Charlie's artistic efforts as mediocre, dull and unremarkable. The work which she had watched over the years consisted mostly of uninspired landscapes bland as porridge, studies so lacking in passion that she was convinced an art career was not the best use of Charlie's talents. She had felt a deep relief when Charlie gave up on making a living in the field of either fine or commercial art. Had felt that Charlie, in making a break from the art world, could at last throw herself into something which would fit her far better.

But these drawings were totally different, very skilled and sure, it was obvious that Charlie loved doing animals; strange that she'd never seen anything like this before. Always it was the landscapes or Charlie's hackneyed commercial assignments from class. But these showed real caring—the work was bold and commanding, revealing true delight in her feline subject.

The three portraits of Dulcie were life-size, done in a combination of charcoal and rust red Conte crayon on rough white paper. They brought Dulcie fully alive; the little cat shone out at her as insouciant and as filled with deviltry as Dulcie herself. In one drawing she lay stretched full-length, looking up and smiling, her dark, curving stripes gleaming, her expression bright and eager. In the second study she was leaping at a moth, her action so liquid and swift that Wilma could feel the weightless pull of Dulcie's long, powerful muscles. The third drawing had caught Dulcie poised on the edge of the bookshelf ready to leap down, her four feet together, her eyes wild with play.

This work was, in fact, stronger and far more knowledgeable than any animal drawings Wilma could remember. The cat's muscle and bone structure were well understood and clearly defined beneath her sleek fur, the little cat's liquid movement balanced and true. There was nothing cute about this cat, nothing sentimental. These studies created for the viewer a living and complicated animal.

Leonardo da Vinci said the smallest feline is a masterpiece. These drawings certainly reflected that reverence. She couldn't wait for Dulcie to see these.

To an ordinary cat, such drawings would read simply as paper with dark smudges smelling of charcoal and fixative. A drawing would communicate nothing alive to the ordinary feline, no smell of cat, no warmth or movement. A normal cat had no capacity to understand graphic images.

An ordinary cat could recognize animal life on TV primarily by sounds, such as barking, or birdsong, and by the uniqueness of movement: feline action sleek and lithe and deeply familiar, birds fluttering and hopping. Action was what most cats saw. She had no doubt about this, Dulcie had told her this was so.

But Dulcie would see every detail of these drawings of herself, and she would be thrilled.

Returning to the kitchen, dropping the evening *Gazette* on the table, she turned to finishing up her dinner preparations. Her cheerful blue-and-white kitchen was warm from the oven, and smelled of the garlic and herbs and wine with which she'd basted the well-browned pot roast. Removing the noodles from the stove, she drained them in a colander then pulled the roaster from the oven, releasing a cloud of deliciously scented steam. She basted the roast, put the lid back, put the noodles in a bowl and buttered them, set them on the back of the stove to keep warm. It was nice having company; she was pleased to have Charlie staying with her. She deeply enjoyed her solitude, but a change was delightful, and Charlie was just about all the family she had since her younger brother, Charlie's father, had died. There were a couple of second cousins on the East Coast but they seldom were in touch. Her niece was the closest thing she had to a child of her own, and she valued Charlie.

She laid silverware and napkins on the table, meaning to set them around later. Beyond the window the sunset had deepened to a shade as vivid as the red bougainvillea which clung outside the diamond panes, the red so penetrating it stained the blue tile counter to a ruddy glow, sent a rosy sheen over the blue-and-white floral wallpaper. She set out the salt and pepper, then returned to the dining room for another look. She couldn't leave the drawings alone. Now, suddenly, it seemed to her a great waste for Charlie to be starting a cleaning and repair business. Why had she hidden such work?

Charlie had mentioned once there wasn't any money in drawing animals, and maybe she was right. Certainly animal drawings weren't big in juried shows; one would have to build a reputation in some other way than Janet had done. Charlie said Janet was truly talented, and that she herself was not. Wilma wondered how much of that came from the narrow view of the particular art school she had attended.

She returned to the kitchen, moving restlessly. She was tearing up endive and spinach leaves for a salad when Charlie's van pulled up at the curb, parking up toward the neighbors' to leave room behind. The red sky was darkening, streaked with gray, the wild kind of sky Dulcie loved. She tried to put away her worries about Dulcie; it did no good to worry. Clyde had said, on the phone, that the cats were fine.

So where are they?

At Janet's. Joe is at Janet's.

Then where is Dulcie?

She's nearby—gathering some information, Joe said.

What does that mean? Snooping somewhere? She can't . . . Those cats can't . . .

Joe says not to worry, and what good does it do to worry? He'd let me know if anything—if they . . .

She had hung up, shaken, and no wiser.

She shook the salad dressing, fussed with the salad. Standing at the window, she watched Charlie come up the walk dragging, looking hot and irritable.

Charlie dropped her jacket in the entry and came on through the dining room into the kitchen, slumped into a chair. Her red hair was damp with sweat, curling around her face, her limp, sweaty shirt was streaked with white paint and rust.

"Not a good day," Wilma said tentatively.

Charlie reached for a leaf of spinach to nibble. "Not too bad. Mavity got a lot done. She's a good worker, and a dear person." Mavity Flowers was an old school friend of Wilma's. She had gone to work cleaning houses when the small pension left by her husband began to dwindle under rising prices. She'd be in fair financial shape if she'd sell her Molena Point cottage and move to a less expensive area, but Mavity loved Molena Point. She would rather stay in the village and scrub for a living.

Charlie rose and got two beers from the refrigerator.

"Cold glasses in the freezer," Wilma said. "I guess Mavity can be a bit vague at times."

"Aren't we all?" Charlie fetched two iced glasses, opened the bottles, and poured the dark brew down the frosted sides with care. "Mavity works right along, she doesn't grouse, and she doesn't stop every five minutes for a smoke the way Stamps does. I don't think James Stamps will be with me long."

Charlie had hired Stamps from an ad she'd put in the paper. He hadn't been in Molena Point for more than a week or two. He told Charlie he'd moved to the coast because Salinas was too dry. He was renting a room somewhere up in the hills, near to the house Charlie was cleaning, the Hansen house; she was getting it ready for new owners.

"I got all the little repairs done. Replaced the cabinet door hinges in the kitchen, fixed the leak in the garage roof. Fixed the gate latches." She sighed and settled back, taking a long swallow of beer. "Mavity and I painted the bedroom, and Stamps picked up the shelving units for the closets."

"Sounds like more than a full day."

"I had to tell Stamps twice, no smoking in the house. He said, 'What difference? They won't be moving in for a week.' I told him that stink stays in a house forever. But how can he smell anything when he reeks of smoke himself."

"Did he do any work besides picking up the shelving?"

"Under my prodding. Got the front yard cleaned up, the lawn trimmed, and the new flowers planted. But my God, I have to tell him everything. Mix the manure and conditioner in before you plant, James. Treat the flowers tenderly, don't jam them in the ground.

"It's not that Stamps is dumb," Charlie continued. "He's bright enough, but he doesn't keep his mind on the job. Who knows where his thoughts are. The cleaning and repair business is definitely not James Stamps's line of work."

Charlie glanced idly at the paper. "One day I'll find the right people. Meantime I keep on baby-sitting him. I had to tell him twice to tie up his dog. It sleeps in his truck; I guess the people he rents from don't want it in his room. I don't blame them, the beast is a monster. I didn't want it tramping around in the clean house, getting dog hairs stuck in the fresh paint."

"I thought you loved dogs."

"I can hardly wait to get a dog. A big dog. But not a beast like Stamps's mutt. I want a nice, clean, well-mannered animal. That creature won't mind, and it's mean." She grinned. "At least Stamps didn't eat lunch with Mavity and me, that was a pleasure. It was real nice to be rid of him.

"But then he was twenty minutes late getting back, and when I made him work the extra twenty, he got mad." She finished her beer and got up. "I'm heading for the shower; I smell like a locker room."

Wilma hadn't mentioned the drawings. She wanted to wait for Clyde—and wait until Charlie had cleaned up and didn't feel so hot and irritable. Charlie could be testy—if she was in a bad mood, anything you said could be taken wrong. Patiently, sipping her beer, she sat reading the rest of the lead article and a second, longer story.

Ms. Aronson was unable to produce witnesses to her whereabouts the early morning of Ms. Jeannot's death. She claimed that she was alone in her Molena Point condominium. Neighbors testified that lights were on that morning in her living room and bedroom, but no witness saw her white Dodge van parked on the street. Ms. Aronson told the court she had parked on a side street, that there had been no empty parking places in front of her building.

She testified that she did not leave her apartment until nearly 7 A.M., when police phoned to notify her that Janet's studio had burned and that Janet had died in the fire. She said she dressed and drove directly to Ms. Jeannot's studio. Under questioning, Ms. Aronson admitted that she had a set of keys for Jeannot's studio and apartment. She claimed that Jeannot had given them to her so she could pick up and deliver work for exhibitions.

The second witness was Jeannot's sister, Beverly Jeannot, who also admitted to having a set of keys. Police said that on

the day Janet was murdered they were not able to reach Ms.
Jeannot at her home in Seattle until noon, though they made
several attempts by phone to notify her of her sister's death.
Ms. Jeannot claimed she had not been feeling well, and that
she had unplugged her phone the night before. She said she
slept until 11:45 the morning of the fire, that once she was
notified she booked the next flight to San Francisco, with a
commuter connection to Molena Point. She arrived in the
village at three that afternoon.

Scheduled to testify later in the week is San Francisco art
agent and former critic Kendrick Mahl, a name of national
stature. Mahl is Janet Jeannot's ex-husband and is also the
representing art agent for the accused. A partial transcript of
today's court proceedings follows.

Wilma was scanning the transcript when Clyde
knocked at the back door and pushed on in. He was well
scrubbed, his dark hair neatly combed. He smelled faintly
of Royal Lime, a nonsweet scent from Bermuda that
Wilma liked, though she detested the heavy and too-sweet
scents that most men applied. He was wearing a new shirt.
The store creases spoiled only slightly the fresh look of
the red madras plaid. He got a beer from the refrigerator
and pulled out a chair, scowling at the headlines. "Don't
they have anything else to write about?"

"Good color on you. Don't sit down. Go in the dining room."

"What? Are we eating formal?"

"Just go."

He gave her a puzzled look and swung away into the
dining room, carrying his beer.

He was silent for a long time, she could hear the soft
scuff of his loafers as he moved about the room, as if he
were viewing the work from different angles and from a
distance. When he returned to the kitchen he was grinning. "I thought, from the way you talked and from
what Charlie said, that her work was really bad, that art
school was a waste of time."

"It was a bust," Charlie said, coming in. She was dressed in a pale blue T-shirt with SAVE THE MALES stenciled across the front, and clean, faded jeans and sandals. She had blow-dried her sweaty hair and it blazed around her face as wild as the vanished sunset. "I should have gone to business school. Or maybe engineering, I've always been good at math. I'm sorry I didn't do that, maybe civil engineering. It was a big waste of time, that four years in art school. Big waste of my folks' money."

Clyde shook his head. "Those drawings are strong. They're damned good."

Charlie shrugged. "I enjoy doing animals, but it's nothing that will make me a living."

Clyde raised an eyebrow. "Don't put yourself down. Who told you that?"

"The fine arts department. My drawings—any animal drawings—are way too commercial, they have no real meaning. Just a waste of time."

"But you took commercial art, too," Clyde said. "You got a BS in both. So what did the commercial people say?"

Charlie gave him a twisted, humorless smile. "That there is no market for animal sketches, that this is not commercial art. That you have to use the computer, have to understand how to sell, have sales knowledge and a strong sense of layout. Have to be a real professional, understand the real world of advertising, bring yourself up into the electronic age. That this—drawing animals—is hobby work."

"Rubbish," Clyde said.

"Trouble is, I don't give a damn about commercial work." She got another beer from the refrigerator and picked up the silver flatware that Wilma had dropped in the center of the table. As she folded the paper napkins neatly in half, she gave Clyde a long look. "They know what they're talking about. I can draw for my own pleasure, but as for making a living, right now my best bet is CHARLIE's FIX-IT, CLEAN-IT. And I like that just fine." She tossed back her hair and grinned. "I'm my own boss, no one telling me what to do." Reaching across the table, she arranged the silver at their three places and set the napkins around. At Clyde's angry look, she laughed. "My illustration instructor said I can draw kitties as a hobby."

"Who the hell do they think they are?"

"They," Wilma said, "are our rarefied and venerable art critics, those specially anointed among us with the intelligence to understand true art."

Clyde made a rude noise.

Wilma studied Charlie. "I'll admit I didn't like your landscapes. But these—these are strong. More than strong, they're knowledgeable, very sure. Do you have more?"

"Some horses," Charlie said. "Lots of cats, all my friends in San Francisco had cats. A dog or two."

"Did you bring them with you?"

"They're in the storage locker with my cleaning stuff and tools."

"Will you bring them home?" Wilma said patiently. "I'd like to see them all."

Charlie shrugged and nodded. "The sketches of Dulcie are yours, if you want them."

"You bet I want them. Dulcie will be . . . is immortalized," Wilma stumbled. She caught Clyde's eye, and felt her face heating. "I'll take them down right away, to be framed." She rose and began to fuss at the sink, her back to Charlie, and hastily began final preparations for dinner, again checking the roast, making sure the noodles were still warm.

She was going to have to be more careful what she said to Charlie, and in front of Charlie.

And, she'd have to get those drawings out of the house before Dulcie saw them. The little cat could be as careless as she. If Dulcie came on those drawings unprepared, she would be so pleased she'd very likely forget herself, let out a cry of astonishment and delight that, if Charlie heard her, would be difficult to explain.

12

It was poker night at the Blankenships'. Frances served an early supper of canned spaghetti and a limp salad, then hustled Mama off to bed. Returning to the kitchen, she made a stack of baloney and salami sandwiches, wiped the counters, and dutifully removed from the round kitchen table its collection of animal-shaped salt and pepper shakers, pig-shaped sugar bowl, the cream pitcher made in the image of a cow, and the potted fern. Varnie slapped a new unopened deck of cards and a rack of poker chips on the table, and checked the refrigerator to assess once again his stock of cold beer. Dulcie watched the preparations from a dark little space between the end of the stove and the kitchen wall.

But, crouching in the shadows, she was tempted to nip out the open laundry window or return to Mama's room before the kitchen filled up with boisterous jokes and cigarette smoke. She expected Frances would retire to her own secluded part of the house, to the pristine little lair at the back, which Dulcie had investigated just this morning.

When Frances had made a quick trip into the village for groceries, Dulcie had been able for the first time to inspect closely Frances's small office. Heretofore she had only looked in from the hall. Certainly the room was off-limits to both Mama and Varnie; neither seemed welcome there. This morning she had slipped in quickly, padding across the bare wood floor, staring up at the unadorned white walls. The plain white desk was bare, except for Frances's computer. White desk chair, white worktable, low white file cabinets. No clutter anywhere. She could see nothing on any surface, certainly no china beastie or tatty fern plants. Leaping up onto the desk she paced its bare surface, brushing by the computer. And she could not resist the slick surface, it was perfect for tail chasing—she'd spun, snatching at her tail, whirling until she fell over the side, landing hard on the oak floor.

She tested the white leather typing chair, found it soft and inviting, and then atop the white filing cabinets she had investigated the copier. It was very like Wilma's copier at the library. Next to it stood a state-of-the art white telephone with answering machine and fax.

A fax still unnerved her. Though she had watched the library's fax, she couldn't get used to it spitting out pages suddenly without any apparent human input—as if the messages were generated by nothing living.

But she had felt that way about the telephone, at first, shivering with fear. As Joe pushed the headset off, punched in a number, and talked into the little perforated speaker, she had deeply distrusted the disembodied voice which answered him.

She felt easier with a copier. She had played with Wilma's copier, and that machine seemed to her more direct. You pressed a paw into the sand and created a pawprint. You put a page in the copier and got a copy. No invisible, offstage presences.

Even computers seemed more straightforward. You punch in CAT, you get CAT on the screen. She considered a computer to be a glorified typewriter—until you got into modems. Then the ghosts returned.

Frances had a modem; Dulcie had watched her from the doorway and knew that she received many pages via modem. These she edited, making changes, putting in appropriate punctuation, then sent the material away again to some mysterious, unnamed destination.

Mama, complaining that Frances neglected her for
the computer, said Frances typed some kind of medical
report. Mama had even less notion than Dulcie herself
about the workings of a modem. And Dulcie had no
idea whether Frances did this work to help support the
household or to get away from the old woman. Maybe
both. Whatever the reason, she spent a good part of the
day in there. And who could blame her. Anything to get
away from the oppressive clutter in the rest of the
house—there was nowhere to go in this house that
didn't make Dulcie herself feel trapped.

Last night, her second as a secret agent, in the old
woman's lap she had waked in a panic of confinement,
kicking and fighting, trying to free herself. In her
dream, dark walls pressed in at her, threatening to crush
her. She was with the white cat, pushing along beside
him between damp, muddy walls that pressed in too
close and dark, she was wild with fear; she woke with
the old woman's hands pressing against her, trying to
calm her. "Kitty? Oh, dear, what a dream you must have
had. Were you chasing mice—or was a bad dog chasing
you?"

She had leaped off the old woman's lap and raced
away, totally frustrated.

She'd been with the Blankenships three days, waiting
for some pearl of information about Janet's murder, and
all she got was bad dreams and cuddled to death by
Mama and yelled at by Varnie.

She'd made herself as accommodating to Mama as
she could, obligingly eating string beans and mashed
potatoes and even Jell-O, whatever the old woman
saved from her own meals. She should feel flattered that
Mrs. Blankenship put aside part of her supper despite
Varnie's sarcastic comments.

Now, even the dark little space between the stove
and wall was beginning to get to her, to give her the jit-
ters. It was cramped, too warm, and smelled of grease.
Peering out, she watched Varnie open a beer, stand

looking out the window, then prowl the kitchen, opening cupboards, maybe looking for additional snacks. She longed to be with Joe out on the cool hills, running free. The brightest moments in her day were when she leaped to Mama's window and looked across the street. If Joe was sitting in Janet's window watching for her, immediately she felt free again and loved, didn't feel like a prisoner anymore.

This morning when he saw her, he had stood up against the glass, his mouth open in a toothy laugh, then disappeared. In a moment he came slipping out beneath the burned door, grinned at her, and, assured that she was safe, trotted away up the hill to hunt, cocky and self-possessed. She had looked after him feeling painfully lonely. She didn't remind herself that this little visit with the Blankenships had been her own idea. And she'd been tempted to go hunt with him; there was nothing to prevent her. The first night, Frances had propped open a window in the laundry and slid back the screen, leaving a six-inch opening through which she could come and go. Frances hadn't done it out of thoughtfulness but was saving herself the trouble of letting the cat in and out, or of cleaning up a sand box.

But if she went to hunt with Joe, began nipping back and forth between the two houses, the old lady was going to get curious. And she would find it harder, each time, to return. No, she had come for information. She'd stay until she got it. When she went outdoors she remained close to the house, returning quickly. But by the third night she was ready to pitch a fit of boredom, wanted to claw the furniture and climb the drapes.

Yesterday, when she looked out Mama's window, she'd seen Charlie's van parked below Janet's, and seen Charlie kneeling beside the porch checking the cat bowls. Strangely, that made her lonely, too.

The crackle of cellophane and cardboard echoed in the kitchen as Varnie opened chips and pretzels. He snatched up a handful and began to munch. She stiffened at the sound of footsteps on the back porch, then loud knocking. As Varnie headed for the door, she heard a dog bark.

She knew that bellowing. She slipped out from behind the stove and leaped to the counter, pressing against the window to look. Behind her, the two men's voices thundered in jocular greeting. Staring into the night, she couldn't see the dog, but she could smell him. It was the beast that had chased her and Joe, the dog with a mouth like a bear trap.

Looking across the street to Janet's, she couldn't see Joe at the window—the black glass was unbroken by the tomcat's white markings. She prayed he hadn't been outside when the dog came, prayed that he was safe.

"Get the hell down from there." Varnie shoved her, knocked her off the counter, and she hit the linoleum with a thud, jarring all four paws. "Frances, get this cat out of here."

She ran, fled into the hall. But when he turned his back she eased into the kitchen again and hid behind the stove. She didn't want to miss anything. Varnie might talk more to his friends than he did to Mama or Frances.

The two men popped open beers and sat at the table spraddle-legged, eating pretzels, obviously waiting for the rest of the group. She studied the newcomer with interest. Varnie called him Stamps. There was a James Stamps who worked for Charlie, and this guy fit Charlie's description, thin face, thin, round shoulders. Long sleazy brown hair and little, scraggly brown beard. Long, limp hands. And the same whiny voice that Charlie had mimicked.

The same sullen attitude, too. When he began to talk about his boss, he was not complimentary. Belching, stretching out his long skinny legs, he chomped a handful of pretzels. "Don't know how long I can keep that job."

"What's so hard about it? It's a dumb-head job. You didn't blow it already?"

"Didn't blow it. Don't know how long I can stand that woman. Pick, pick, pick at a man. Redheaded women are so damn pushy, and who wants to work for a woman. This one is hard-nosed like you wouldn't believe—worse than my parole officer, and that guy is a real hard-ass."

Stamps aimed a belch into his beer can; it echoed hollowly. "Never saw a woman didn't have a thing about getting to work right on the damn minute. And you don't dare think about leaving early. You come back from lunch two minutes late, they want you to work overtime—for straight pay. Make up every friggin' minute."

Behind the stove, Dulcie smiled. Too bad she couldn't repeat Stamps's remarks to Charlie. Soon Stamps began talking about the trial.

"That art agent, the one that testified this morning. That's another hard-assed woman. She had a set of keys to that place, did you know that? Had keys to the woman's van, too." Stamps settled back, tilting his chair, crossing his legs. "Made herself look bad, talking about those keys. But she don't know nothing. And the dead woman's sister, that Beverly Jeannot, they had her on the stand."

"So?"

"So there's a lot of action there, all these people testifying. We better get on with it."

"I told you, James. Cool it. We get greedy now, we end up with mud on our faces."

"But that just don't make sense. Why would . . . ?"

The dog began to bark. Roaring deep and wildly agitated, it sounded like something had disturbed it. She felt her fur stand up, her heart quicken. Where was Joe?

Stamps rose, swearing, and went outside. She wanted to bolt out behind him, but then she heard him scolding the beast. It sounded like it was still there on the porch. Stamps muttered something angry, then a low growl cut the night, followed by a surprised yelp. She was bunched to bolt through the open door when Stamps returned.

"Tied him to the porch rail. Don't know what he saw. Nothing out there now. He don't like that rope; he snapped at me." Stamps laughed.

Dulcie settled back against the faintly warm stove.

Varnie said, "Should've tied him up the other time. Damn dog barking was what woke the old woman. Frances is still trying to make her go to the cops, and who can shut Frances up?"

"That's one more reason to get what we can, before those two women spill to the cops. Get it and get out. If we wait . . ."

"I said, no. You keep pushing, James, and you'll blow it."

Stamps ducked his head, cleared his throat, and took a swig of beer. "What about the other?"

"That's all right. You still casing?"

"I don't see why I have to make notes. I can remember that stuff."

"Make the notes. You can't remember your own name. Only way to get our timing right so we can hit all seven places the same morning. No one pays attention to the street in the morning, they're too busy getting to work, getting their kids on the bus, but we got to have the timing right or we blow it. Piece of cake, if you keep good notes. Let me see the list."

"It's back in the room."

"Very smart. So someone goes in there—the landlord."

"They got no business in my room, I pay my rent. And those jerks wouldn't know what that paper is—but I got it all down, times people leave for work, everything. It's a damn bore, walking the dog there every morning."

"Just keep doing it, James. And make sure you keep your mouth shut when Ed and Melvin get here."

"What the hell. You think I . . ."

The dog barked again, then screamed a high yip—as if he had been scratched. This time when Stamps pushed open the door Dulcie streaked out past him. Pausing in the shadows, she couldn't see Joe. But the dog was on the porch, it had got its rope wrapped around the post and around its ear—must pinch like hell. Stamps stood in the doorway, looking disgusted and yelling. And before she could slip back inside he turned away, slamming the door nearly in her face. She leaped back. The dog wasn't four feet from her, and, without warning, it lunged at her. She flew off the porch, running, terrified he'd break the rope.

She hit the street—and the dog hit the end of the rope. But he was jerked back—the rope held. He fought and roared as she bolted across, straight for Janet's door.

She met Joe coming out. He grinned and licked her ear. "I thought he had you. That's the dog that chased us, I can smell him clear over here."

"It's James Stamps's dog, the Stamps who works for Charlie. He's the one who rented that room down the hill, the room behind the gray house."

He glanced down the hill. "Interesting. What are they doing in there?"

"Big poker night."

"What did you find out from the old lady? Come on in, supper's on." He slid in under the door, and she followed. This was lovely, just the two of them. She'd missed him.

Inside, he grinned down at her from atop the kitchen counter. Leaping up beside him, she regarded his supper layout with amazement. He had a regular feast prepared. "Is this all for you?"

"It was until you got here. You don't think I'm entertaining other ladies?"

She didn't smell another cat in the house, only Joe. "You got the refrigerator open."

"Just practicing what you taught me," he said modestly. "Front paws in the handle, hind feet against the counter. Quick push, and *voilà*! Sorry, the Brie is gone. It was a bit old, it made me belch."

He had found half a brick of Cheddar cheese and a tub of sour cream, rather ripe but still edible. Toothmarks dented the plastic where he'd pulled the lid off. He had unearthed a pack of stale crackers, too. Beside it lay a warm, freshly killed chipmunk.

They dined.

Chewing off a hunk of Cheddar, Dulcie dipped it in the sour cream. "Has Beverly been back? Or the police?"

"No one. The night you left I brought Janet's diary in, read it again, then put it back. I thought maybe we'd missed something, some clue, but I guess not. Slept on her bed, that comforter's nice and warm."

"No sign of the white cat?"

"None. And what did you find out? What's with the old woman? I've been watching Varnie come and go; he's a real piece of work. I looked in their garage window. That old truck smells like a warehouse full of stale fish. What's he doing to it?"

She shrugged. "Some kind of repairs. Varnie and this James Stamps—I'm wondering if they killed Janet."

He stared at her.

"They're into something. Somehow it has to do with the murder." She licked sour cream from her whiskers. "They mean to make money from it, whatever it is. Varnie said, 'If we get greedy now, we end up with mud on our faces.' And Stamps said they should get all they can before Varnie's mother spills to the cops. I told you she knows something."

She pushed a morsel of chipmunk onto a cracker. "And they're into something else, too. Stamps is keeping a list, I think of when people are home and when they leave for work."

"Planning burglaries?"

"Sounds like it. Early-morning burglaries. Varnie said, 'Hit and clear out.'"

"You think the burglaries, if that's what they're doing, are connected to Janet's murder?"

"I don't know. Those two seem to me like a couple

of small-time hoods, just snatching at opportunities. I'm not sure they're the kind to have killed Janet."

They shared out the last of the chipmunk, Dulcie eating delicately. "I want to see Stamps's list." But she could see he was not receptive to the idea.

"If they're planning burglaries, the police need to know."

"But we don't know *when*, or where. What good is it to tell the police and not give them any facts? If we could get Stamps's list . . ." But she could see he was not receptive to the idea.

"Anyway," she said, "now I know Mama did see something, and that she's afraid to testify. Frances is trying to get her to testify. And Varnie's afraid she will."

"If Varnie did kill Janet, why would Frances want his mother to testify against him?"

"Who knows what Frances wants? There's more to Frances Blankenship than is apparent."

She licked her paws and whiskers. "Frances and the old lady have midmorning coffee in the kitchen. They talk more then, when Varnie's away at work." She licked blood and cracker crumbs from the counter. "Most of their talk is about relatives, they have more cousins than the pound has dogs. But maybe I'll get lucky—hear something." She gave him a long look. "I'm getting stir-crazy over there."

"Maybe I can help."

"How?" Her eyes widened at his sly leer. "What are you thinking?"

"I'll have to work it out. Just be ready." He twitched an ear.

"How can I be ready, if I don't know what you're up to?"

"Don't miss morning coffee," he said softly.

She gave him a puzzled look. "I'd better go, before they untie the monster."

Joe trotted across the tile counter and looked out the kitchen window. "He's still on the front porch, sitting under the light. I can see the rope. Stupid thing has himself wrapped up again."

She trotted over to look. The dog was a black lump, huddled miserably against the porch rail. "Let him rot." She gave Joe a long, loving look. "Thanks for the supper. It sure was better than Mama's leftover carrots."

"Take care." He licked her ear. "I'll be watching. Don't forget, morning coffee."

She gave him a whisker kiss, jumped down, and slid out beneath the door. She was back at the Blankenships' and through the laundry window before the dog knew she had passed. When belatedly he scented her, he fought his shortened rope, roaring. Inside, she dropped to the laundry room floor. Padding toward the kitchen, she paused in the shadows of the hall.

In her absence two more poker players had arrived, the room stank of cigarettes and beer and reverberated with loud voices. Hurrying on past, she headed for the old woman's room. She'd hear no more secrets now.

Another night in this house didn't thrill her, but maybe, if Joe did have a plan, tomorrow she'd hit pay dirt.

13

As Frances opened the back door, airing the kitchen of stale beer and cigarette smoke, Dulcie trotted out to crouch on the threshold. Sniffing the fresh morning air, she was just getting comfortable when Frances nudged her with her an impatient toe.

"Go on out, cat. You're in the way."

She hunkered down, gluing herself to the floor, then leaped over Frances's offending foot, back into the kitchen. She had no intention of going out; she wasn't going to miss a lick this morning. Whatever plot Joe had hatched for Mama and Frances's coffee hour, she meant to be right there, cat on the spot.

Impatiently Frances returned to the table, fussing around, restoring the salt and pepper shakers and potted fern, the pig sugar bowl and cow-shaped cream pitcher to their rightful places, her movements abrupt, sharply agitated. Maybe her anger was the result of Varnie's loud poker party. Dulcie watched her with interest.

Last night, as Dulcie crouched behind the stove listening to Varnie and Stamps, Frances had been listening, too. Dulcie had been so intent on the conversation, she'd hardly paid attention, thinking that Frances was just passing.

But she hadn't been passing, she'd been standing in the hall, very still. Then, in a moment, she had turned away again, back to her office.

Now, as Mama came wandering into the kitchen,

shuffling along in her soft slippers, Frances poured the coffee and set the pot on the table beside a plate of day-old cookies. Mama sighed and settled into her chair. The room had begun to smell of baking, the hot, peachy scent of turnovers from the oven soon overpowering the barroom stench. Dulcie sniffed appreciatively and leaped up to Mama's lap, prepared for a little snack. Whoever said cats didn't like sweets didn't know much.

Curled up against Mama's fat tummy, watching Mama nibble a cookie, she shuttered her eyes against the likely event of spilled crumbs. Interesting that Frances seemed to have no compunction about loading the old lady up on sugar and fat—but maybe Frances had her reasons.

She curled into a little ball, hoping Mama wouldn't spill hot coffee. Mama herself seemed irritable this morning. She nibbled her cookie, sipped her coffee, but said little. Dulcie was drifting into sleep when Frances said, "Mama, you're going to have to make up your mind."

"About what?"

"You know about what, about what I told you at breakfast."

Dulcie was wide-awake. She *had* missed something when she went out earlier.

"I have made up my mind. Made it up long ago."

"Mama, all you've done is avoid the issue. You know the right thing to do."

"Not going to the police."

"You have to go, Mama. You know the police think someone is withholding evidence. They'll search until they find out who."

"Nonsense. Where would they get such an idea?"

"It was on the local news, I told you. The seven o'clock news."

Mama sat up straighter, jamming Dulcie against the edge of the table, forcing her to change position. "You're making that up."

"They think one of the neighbors saw something that weekend—didn't report it."

"What would make them think such a thing?"

"I don't know, Mama. I don't know how the police get their information."

"This is rubbish." Mama stiffened. "Or else you told them," Mama said warily.

The timer made a small ding, and Frances rose. Standing at the warm stove, she removed the baking sheet of bubbling turnovers, placing two on a plate for her mother-in-law, totally unconcerned that she was feeding Mama enough calories to keep a young hippo. She took one for herself, setting the rest by the window to cool. Dulcie wondered if that rich smell of baking would waft across the street to Joe. Frances sat down again and refilled their cups. She cut a small bite of turnover, taking it on her fork. "If the police think you saw something and withheld evidence, they're going to make trouble."

Mama tried to eat a turnover with her fingers, but it was too hot. She kept juggling it from one hand to the other. At last she broke it in two, dribbling hot peach down Dulcie's ear.

Dulcie licked her paw and swiped at her scorched ear. The hazards of investigative work. Hungrily she licked her paw, making Mama smile. Mama blew on the half turnover, broke off a small piece, and held it for Dulcie to nibble.

"Mama, don't feed the cat and then handle your own food—you don't what diseases it has."

Ignoring Frances, Mama broke off a bite for herself with the same hand, gobbled it greedily, and offered the last crumb to Dulcie.

"Mama, you never listen. About hygiene, about that cat—about the police . . . "

"Varnie says I don't need to go to the police. Varnie says I don't need to go through such indignity at my age, going down to that police station and being cross-examined and then up in front of everyone in that courtroom. I'm too old and frail to get up in front of all those people; my bad heart would never stand it."

"It will be far worse for your heart, Mama, if the police arrest you."

"Why would they arrest me?"

Frances sighed. "For withholding evidence," she said patiently.

The old woman snorted, scattering crumbs.

"They put people in jail every day for less than that, Mama. It won't help your bad heart if they put you in jail."

"Put an old woman with heart trouble in jail? Don't be silly. Varnie wouldn't let them do that."

"Varnie can't . . . "

The ringing phone startled them. Mama gave a little jump, unsettling Dulcie so she nearly scratched Mama as she tried to hang on. Hastily she retracted her claws, watched Frances reach to the counter, pick up the phone and set it on the table.

"Blankenship residence." Her voice was cool, impersonal.

She listened a moment, frowning, then put her hand over the mouthpiece, looked at Mama for a long moment. She started to hand Mama the phone, then seemed to change her mind.

Speaking into the phone again, her voice was pure ice. "Mrs. Blankenship isn't feeling well. I'll speak with her. May she return your call?"

She reached for a pad and pencil, and jotted down a number. She repeated it back, then hung up. She looked helplessly at Mama.

"It was an attorney, Mama. I told you this would happen. He's connected with the trial, and he wants to talk with you."

"I don't know any attorneys. I don't have to talk with anyone."

"You will if he gets a subpoena; you won't have any choice."

"Call him back," Mama told her. "Tell him I'm too sick. He can't get a subpoena for a sick old woman."

"You want to tell him that, here's the phone." Frances pushed it across the table.

"You have to tell him, Frances. I'm not calling anyone. Who is this lawyer—what's his name? What business does he have calling me?"

Dulcie could feel her paws gripping at Mama's leg.

"I don't know anything about him, Mama. His name is Grey—Joseph Grey. Grey, Stern, and Starbuck. I don't recognize the firm, but that doesn't mean anything. He . . ."

Dulcie's claws went in before she could stop herself; Mama yelped and shoved her to the floor.

She crawled contritely under the table, trying not to laugh. Attorney Joseph Grey. Grey, Stern, and Starbuck. She wanted to roll over screaming with laughter.

"*I* never heard of him," Mama said. "You're making all this up. Why would you lie to an old woman?"

Frances rose and came around the table to stand beside Mama's chair, putting her arm around Mrs. Blankenship's shoulders. "I wouldn't make up that phone call, Mama." She looked pale, her thin face was drawn. "I told you, you should have gone to the police."

Mama just looked at her.

Dulcie sat under the table grinning. Joseph Grey, Attorney at Law. Joseph Grey, Feline Jurisprudence. She could just picture Joe sitting in the window over at Janet's, laughing his head off.

Frances pulled out a chair and sat down close to Mama. "We have to call him back, Mama. We have no choice."

As Dulcie leaped up into Mama's lap, Mama began to cry, her soft flesh shaking. Oh, this was too bad. This was really too bad. The poor old thing was coming all apart. Gazing up at the frightened old face, she reached up a soft paw and patted the old lady's cheek.

Mrs. Blankenship clutched her close, hugging her, squeezing her hard, burying her face in Dulcie's fur. "I don't know what to do, Frances. Tell him I'm not here. Call him back and tell him I'm in the hospital."

"He knows you're not in the hospital. You have to talk to him, Mama."

"Anyway, it's too late now. They've already put that young man on trial," Mama said. "How could it make any difference what I say? No, it's too late for that."

"No, Mama. That's just the point. If Rob Lake is innocent, you could save him. Hadn't you thought that you might save his life?"

Frances rose, fetched the pan of turnovers from beside the window, and shoved them across the table where Mama could reach them. "Without you, Mama, Rob Lake could be sentenced to death. If he's innocent, Mama, his death would be your fault."

"But that white van the night before the fire could have belonged to anyone. I don't know that it was Janet's. Maybe if I told the police, that would just confuse everyone."

"The police will sort that out. That's their job. You can't choose what the court should know, Mama, and what it shouldn't be told."

Frances sipped her coffee. "Trust me, Mama. The sooner you go to the police, the gentler the court will be with you. Just tell this Mr. Grey what you saw. Tell him you're not sure the van was Janet's. Tell him what time it was—2:00 A.M. Saturday night when the van pulled into her garage and shut the door. Two-thirty when it left again."

"He'll want to come up here, want me to sign papers. Want me to go to court. I told you, Frances, my heart won't stand that."

"I'll explain to him, Mama, that with your heart so bad you're afraid to testify. I'm sure they'll make special arrangements."

Dulcie was so wired she couldn't keep still. She started to fidget, then began to wash, trying to calm herself. She might get annoyed at Joe sometimes, might call him an unimaginative tomcat, but this—this was a stroke of genius.

Mama reached for a turnover and crumbled it between her fat fingers. "I wish that young woman had never moved over there; I knew she'd cause trouble. Who in their right mind would build a welding shop in a residential neighborhood, and right on top of their own house? The city should never have allowed it. All that fire flashing around, it's no wonder . . . And that bang, bang, bang of gunfire going on for hours. Probably one of those indoor target things. Why would a young woman want one of those things. I don't . . . "

"It wasn't gunfire, Mama. I told you, it was just a staple gun. One of those big commercial staple guns. You know she used it to stretch her canvases. You know what she said, that putting in thumbtacks made her thumbs ache for days. Please, Mama, I've got to return this attorney's call."

"You've got a stapler right in there on your desk, Frances. It don't sound like that. You know I'm right. That crazy artist set the whole hillside on fire. I always knew she'd do that. Burn up the whole neighborhood. If not for my prayers to save this house, we would have burned up, too."

"Oh, Mama, she didn't . . . "

"Anyway, you don't need to argue. I won't do it. I don't want to be a part of it."

"But Mama, don't you see? You *are* a part of it. If you don't testify, they could convict the wrong person."

Dulcie crouched, very still. The morning was full of surprises.

A staple gun.

Janet had stapled her canvases. She hadn't used thumbtacks.

Then what was that thumbtack that had gotten stuck in her paw? That thumbtack with the burned wood and blackened canvas sticking to it? What were all those thumbtacks scattered among the ashes? There were hundreds of them, many with scraps of canvas clinging. Hundreds of fragments of paintings . . .

She caught her breath. Mama stared down at her. She

pretended to scratch at a flea. Those tacks were not from Janet's paintings they were from someone else's canvases.

Those were not Janet's paintings that had burned. Janet's paintings had not been in the studio when it burned.

"It wouldn't hurt your heart, Mama, just to talk to Joseph Grey. If I call him back, won't you just speak to him? He could take your deposition right here. And even if you did have to go to court, they'd make it easy for you. A special car, probably a limo with a driver. Get you right in and right out, not make you wait. I'll bet it wouldn't take forty-five minutes. We could stop for ice cream afterward."

"Don't you patronize me, young lady. Besides, someone else must have seen her van besides me. Why don't they go to the police?"

"It was two in the morning, Mama."

"It was Saturday night. Young people stay up late."

"Our neighbors aren't that young, Mama. At two in the morning they're asleep."

"Yes, and no one cares if an old sick woman can't sleep. No one cares about an old woman sitting alone in the night—except to get information out of her." She stroked Dulcie so hard that static sparks flew, alarming them both. "Call him back," Mama said. "Tell him I won't."

But when Frances tried, she had the wrong number. It was not an attorney's office, and no one had ever heard of Joseph Grey.

Frances looked totally puzzled. "I know I wrote it down right. You heard me, I repeated it back to him." Frances was not the kind of woman to record a phone number wrong. As she dialed again, Dulcie jumped down, trotted into the laundry room, and leaped to the open window.

And she was out of there. Racing across the yard straight for Janet's house. She could see Joe in Janet's window: Felis at Law Joseph Grey, his ears sharply forward, his white markings bright behind the glass, his mouth open in a toothy cat laugh.

14

The cats fled down the black, burned hills, down into the tall green grass careening together, exploding apart, wild with their sudden freedom. Four days hanging around the Blankenships' had left them stir-crazy, dangerously close to the insane release people called a cat fit. Flying down, dropping steeply down, they collapsed at last, rolling and laughing beneath the wide blue sky. Dulcie leaped at a butterfly, at insects that keened and rustled around them in the blowing grass; racing in circles she terrorized a thousand minute little presences singing their tiny songs and munching on their bits of greenery, sent them scurrying or crushed them. "I wonder if Mama gave in—if she let Frances call the police." She grinned. "I wonder if Frances tried again to phone Attorney Joseph Grey."

She stood switching her tail. "If that was Janet's van that Mama saw, the Saturday night before the fire, what was she doing? She drove up to San Francisco that morning. Why would she come home again in the middle of the night, load up her own paintings? Take them where? If there'd been a show, her agent would have said."

She looked at him intently. "Those weren't Janet's paintings burned in the fire, so whose paintings were they?"

"Could Janet have hidden her own paintings, to collect the insurance?"

"Janet wouldn't do that. And there wasn't any insurance." She lay down, thinking.

"Of course there would be insurance," he said. "Those paintings were worth . . . "

Dulcie twitched her ear. "Janet didn't insure her work."

"That's crazy. Why wouldn't she? How do you know that?"

"Insurance on paintings is horribly expensive. She told Wilma it costs nearly as much as the price of the work. The rates were so high she decided against it, said she tried three insurance agents and they all gave the same high rates. Wilma says a lot of artists don't insure."

"But Wilma . . . "

"Wilma has that one painting insured, with a rider on her homeowner's. That's a lot different."

She was quiet a moment, then flipped over and sat up, her eyes widening. "Sicily Aronson has a white van. Don't you remember? She parks it behind the gallery beside the loading door."

"So Sicily took the paintings, at two in the morning? Killed Janet and took her paintings, to sell? Come on, Dulcie. Why would she kill Janet? Janet was her best painter, her meal ticket."

"Maybe Janet planned to leave her. Maybe they had a falling-out. If Janet took all her work away . . . "

"You've been seeing too many TV movies. If Sicily tried to sell those paintings, if they came on the market, Max Harper would have her behind bars in a second.

"And Beverly wouldn't take them, she inherited Janet's paintings." He licked his paw. "And if there wasn't any insurance, Beverly had nothing to gain." He nibbled his shoulder, pursuing a flea. Even with the amazing changes in his life, he still couldn't shake the fleas. And he hated flea spray.

"Maybe," she said, "Sicily could sell them easier than Beverly. If she did, she'd keep all the money, not have to split with Beverly. With Janet dead, and with so many paintings supposedly destroyed, each canvas is worth a bundle."

"Whoever has them could sell them. Beverly. Sicily. Kendrick Mahl."

"But Mahl had witnesses to everything he did in San Francisco."

Mahl had gone out to dinner with friends both Saturday and Sunday nights, leaving his car in the hotel parking garage. Mahl lived in Marin County across the Golden Gate Bridge. He had driven into the city Saturday afternoon and checked into the St. Francis; the hotel was full of artists and critics. In the city he had taken cabs or ridden with friends.

Dulcie scowled. "I guess anyone could have rented a van. When we know who was in that van, we'll know who killed her. I'll bet Detective Marritt didn't take one thumb-tack, one scrap of the burned paintings as evidence."

"Or maybe Marritt took thumbtacks but didn't bother to find out how Janet stretched her canvases. You'd think someone would have told him. Wouldn't Sicily?"

"Unless she didn't want the police to know." Dulcie examined her claws. "It'll take a lot of phoning, calling all the rental places, to find who rented a white van that night."

"Dulcie, the police will check out the rental places, as soon as they know about the van, and about the missing paintings."

"Where would someone hide that many paintings?" she said speculatively.

He sat up, staring at her. "You think *we're* going to look for those canvases? You think *we're* going to find two million dollars' worth of paintings? Those paintings could be anywhere, a private home, an apartment, another gallery . . . What do you plan to do, go tooling up and down the coast maybe in your BMW, searching through warehouses?"

She smiled sweetly, cutting her eyes at him. "We could try Sicily's gallery."

"Sure, Sicily's going to have those big canvases right there under the cops' noses. And don't you think Captain Harper deserves to know that the paintings are gone, that they weren't burned?"

"It would take only a few minutes, just nip into the gallery and have a look. If we find them, we'll be giving Captain Harper not just a tip, but the whole big, damning story." She grinned. "Not just a sniff of the rabbit but the whole delicious cottontail." Her eyes gleamed green as jewels. "We can slip in through the front door just before Sicily closes, stay out of sight until she locks up."

His eyes gleamed with the challenge. But his better judgment—some latent natural wariness—made his belly twitch. "If we do that and get caught, I hope it's the cops and not Sicily."

"Why ever not? She wouldn't know what we're doing. And Sicily likes cats."

He couldn't, in his wildest imagination, picture Sicily Aronson liking cats. The woman put him off totally. With her dangling bracelets and jiggling earrings and tangles of clanking chains and necklaces and her blowing, layered clothes, she was like a walking boutique. Dulcie practically drooled over the expensive fabrics Sicily wore, the imported hand-dyed prints, the layers of hand-painted cottons drooping over her long, hand-woven skirts. Her handmade sandals or tall slim boots smelled of the animals they came from; and her dark hair, bound up in intricate twists secured with strands of silver or jewels, was just too much. She did not look like Molena Point; she looked like San Francisco's bordello district, like some leftover from Sally Stanford days, when that madam was the toast of the city.

And the fact that Sicily could amortize interest in her head, so Clyde had told him, and could accurately compute every possible tax write-off while making light banter or a sales pitch, made her all the more formidable.

"She only dresses like that for PR. It's part of the gallery image." She reached a soft paw to him. "She's really nice. If she catches us in the gallery, she'll probably treat us to a late supper."

"Sure she will. Braised rat poison."

She looked at him, amused. "I've been in the gallery a lot lately, and she's been nice to me." And suddenly she looked stricken. "Oh dear. I guess . . . I hope we don't find the paintings there, I hope she didn't do it. I was thinking only of proving Rob innocent. But she has been kind to me."

"I didn't know you went in there."

"I've done it for weeks, sometimes at noon when court breaks for lunch, just to listen."

"You suspected her?"

"No, I just wanted to find out what I could. After all, she is Janet's agent."

"So what did you learn?"

"Nothing." She licked her paw. "Except she's a sucker for cats. But I guess most people in the art world like cats. Last week she fed me little sandwiches left over from an opening, and twice she's shared her lunch with me; and she folded a handwoven wool scarf on her desk for me to nap on."

"With that kind of treatment, Wilma may lose her housemate."

Dulcie smiled. "Not a chance. Anyway, if Sicily catches us in the gallery, just roll over, curl your paws sweetly, and smile."

"Sure I will. And nail her with twenty sharp ones when she reaches down to grab me."

She turned away, snorting with disgust.

But in a moment, she said, "I wish we knew what to do about Janet's journal."

"It's evidence, Dulcie. We have to tell the police where to find it. We've been over this."

She sighed.

He moved close against her, licking her ear. "The diary is Captain Harper's business."

"But her diary is so private, it's all that's left to speak

for her—except her paintings." She looked at him bleakly. "Why did that terrible thing have to happen? Why did she have to die?"

"At least Janet left her work. That's more than most people leave behind them—something to bring pleasure to others."

"I guess," she said, touching her paw to his, half-amused. Joe did have his tender side, when it suited him. "I guess that's better than poor Mrs. Blankenship. She won't leave the world anything but a house full of china beasties."

Earlier, when she and Joe departed Janet's house, slipping away in the shadows so Mama wouldn't see them, she had looked back across the street and seen Mama sitting at her window eagerly waiting for her.

"It was cruel to make her think I loved her, then to leave. Now she'll be more lonely than ever."

Joe brushed his whiskers against hers. "You could get her a cat. An ordinary little cat who would love her. A kitten maybe."

"Yes," she said, brightening. "A little cat that will stay with her." Her mouth curved with pleasure. "A sweet little cat. Yes, maybe a kitten. Or maybe the white cat. He'll need a home when we find him."

He did not reply. In his opinion, the white cat was long dead—except, if he was dead, then what were these strange dreams? Did the dreams arise, as he hoped, only from Dulcie's active imagination?

They headed down again watching the hills for Stamps's dog. The wild rye and oats on the open slopes was so tall and thick that the animal could easily crouch unseen. They did not see it on the streets below, among the gardens and cottages, did not see it near the gray house, or around the old black pickup. Dulcie studied the ragged house with narrowed eyes, and a little smile curved her pink mouth.

"What?" he said.

"Looks to me like Stamps's window is open."

He said nothing. As they drew near where the pickup was parked, they saw the dog, a shadow among shadows, asleep in the truck bed.

But even as they looked, the beast came awake and sat up and shook himself. Staring up the hill, he either saw them or smelled them, and he suddenly exploded, leaping from the truck straight up the hill . . .

. . . and was jerked to a stop by a chain attached to the bumper.

The cats relaxed, their hearts pounding. The dog fought the chain, rattling and jerking the truck, lunging so violently they thought he'd tear off the bumper and come clanging after them.

But the chain held. The bumper didn't give; it seemed to be solidly bolted. "Come on," Dulcie said, "he can't get loose. If we can get in, get the list, we can be out again before the beast stops bellowing."

"What makes you think he isn't home? His truck's there. And why would he leave the list?"

"He left it the other night. And he'll be at work. Charlie told him if he took any more time off, he was through."

"Why would he leave the truck and dog?"

"She told him to lose the dog. She hates that dog. Maybe he had nowhere else to leave it but tied to the truck. He can walk to the job, it's only a few blocks. Look at the window, Joe. It's cracked open. What more do you want? It's a first-class invitation."

Joe grinned. "Sometimes, Dulcie . . . "

"It won't take a minute. Snatch up the list and out again, home in time for breakfast."

He stood, studying the house, then took off running, a gray streak. They fled past the truck and the dog, straight for Stamps's open window.

15

The back lawn of the decrepit old house was brown and moth-eaten. Two dented garbage cans leaned against the step beside the sunken, unpainted picket fence. The cats, slipping along through the weeds beside the added-on wing, crouched below Stamps's window, then reared up to look.

They could see no movement beyond the black screen and dirty glass, only the warped reflection of hills and trees. Leaping to the sill, they pressed their faces against the wire mesh, looking in.

"No one," Joe said.

"He can't be known for his housekeeping. What a mess."

The bed was unmade, sheets drooping off a stained mattress. Stamps had left most of his clothes discarded in little piles across the floor. One could imagine him undressing at night dropping garments where he stood, stepping away from them. The open closet revealed only two hanging shirts and a lone shoe. A bath towel hung over the doorknob. The stink beneath the double-hung window was of stale cigarette smoke, dog, and Stamps's laundry. Probably Stamps had sneaked the dog inside when the landlord wasn't looking. The dog himself, behind them on the street, rattled and clanged and bellowed, his pea-sized brain fixated on dreams of cat flesh. The window screen was securely latched.

Tensing her claws into little knives, Dulcie ripped

down the screen, efficiently opening a twelve-inch gash. Joe pushed through the hole and shouldered the window higher, and they slipped through, leaping from the sill to the back of an upholstered chair. Its ragged, greasy cover smelled of hair oil. One could imagine him sitting there all evening, smoking and drinking beer among the heaps of clothes. Dulcie made a rude face, ears down, eyes crossed. "Can't he even drive to the laundromat?"

An open bag of potato chips stood on the floor beside a muddy boot. Wrinkled jeans and T-shirts hung out of an open dresser drawer, and the top of the dresser was a tangle of junk. Joe, leaping up, met his reflection charging at him from within the dusty glass.

The refuse dumped on the dresser must have come from Stamps's pockets, emptied out each night over a long period. He could envision the pile growing until it overwhelmed the dresser, cascaded to the floor, and eventually filled the room. He nosed among half-empty matchbooks, odd nails and screws, a broken pocketknife, dirty handkerchiefs, two crushed beer cans, a rusty hinge, bits of paper, a folding beer opener, a broken shoelace, and a scattering of coins. He pawed open each folded paper, but most were gas receipts, or store receipts, or hastily scribbled nearly illegible lists for hardware supplies and plumbing supplies. At the bottom of the pile lay several wrinkled fast-food bags and flattened, nearly empty packs of cigarettes.

"Why would he leave the list in this mess? What's in the nightstand?"

She stepped around a full ashtray wrinkling her nose. "Greasy baseball cap, a sock with a hole in it. Three candy bars, some half-empty cigarette packs, a paperback book with no cover. Lurid stuff. Just what you'd expect from Stamps."

She jumped down to nose beneath the mattress. She was pawing the sheets away when Joe said softly, "Come look." He stood poised very still, staring at a wrinkled white paper. She leaped up beside him.

Beneath the nails and coins, beneath the tangle of gas receipts and McDonald's bags and wadded paper napkins, lay Stamps's list. Joe smoothed the wrinkled paper and fold marks where he had pawed it open. They crouched side by side, reading Stamps's nearly illegible script.

He had recorded the addresses of the targeted houses, how many people lived in each, the times of normal departure for each individual, and whether they left the house walking or by car. The list might be messy and hard to read, but Stamps's information was admirably detailed. He noted the make and model of each car in each household, noted whether the car was kept in the garage or on the street. He recorded whether there were children to be gotten off to school, underlining the fact that the school bus stopped at the corner of Ridgeview and Valley, at five after eight. He identified any regular cleaning or gardening services, and what days they would appear, and he noted whether there were barking dogs in residence at each address. He had listed what kinds of door locks, what kinds of windows, and whether there was any indication of an alarm system.

"Nice," Joe said. "Messy but very complete." He shook dust from his whiskers. "Too bad we can't take it with us."

She got that stubborn look.

"Dulcie, if he finds it missing, they'll scrap their plan or change it. We'll have to memorize it; we can each take half."

"We really need a copy for Captain Harper, not just another anonymous phone call. Don't you get the feeling that telephone tips make Harper nervous?"

"Of course they make him nervous. They drive him nuts. They have also supplied him with some very valuable information. And we don't have any choice. What're you going to do, type up a copy?"

"Even better. We'll take it up to Frances's office, it's only a few blocks. Run it through her copier and return the original, put it back under the junk."

"And of course Frances will invite us right on in to use her copier. After all, look at the comfort you've given Mama."

She hissed at him and cuffed his ear. "You can distract her. Fall out of a tree or something. While she's busy watching you, I'll nip inside through the laundry window, it won't take a minute. Her copier's pretty much like Wilma's."

"She's sure to have left the window open, thinking you'll be back."

"Of course she's left the window open. Mama's probably fit to be tied, waiting for me. It's nearly noon, and I've been gone since ten-thirty. I'm always there for lunch, so she'll be nattering at Frances to make sure the window's open."

He just looked at her. "Dulcie, sometimes . . ."

She gave him a sweet smile and nuzzled his cheek. Nosing the list closed along its folds, she took it carefully in her teeth, leaped to the chair, and slid out through the partially open window. Joe followed, keeping an eye on the dog. They scorched past him as he bellowed and streaked away up the hill.

"Maybe he'll hang himself on the chain."

He glanced at her. "You're drooling on the list."

She cut her eyes at him and sped faster. It was impossible, carrying the paper in her mouth, not to drool on it. She held her head up, sucked in her spit, but despite her efforts, by the time they neared the Blankenships' the paper was soaked. She was thankful Stamps had written in pencil and not water-soluble ink. The Blankenships' brown frame house stood above them plain and homely. They approached from the side yard, where the spreading fig tree sheltered the back porch.

At the tree they parted, and, as Dulcie slipped around to the laundry room window, Joe swarmed up into the branches. Situating himself as high among the sticky fig leaves as he could, he looked down between them, straight into the kitchen window. He could see Mama sitting at the cluttered table, sipping coffee. Frances stood at the counter, and she seemed to be making lunch. He could smell canned vegetable soup. He could hear them talking, but their voices were just mumbles; he could not make out the thrust of the conversation. Clinging among the twiggy little branches, he took a deep breath.

Filling his lungs so full of air he felt like a bagpipe, he let it out in a yowling bellow. His screams hit the quiet street loud as a siren. He hadn't sung like this since adolescence, when he fought over lady cats in the San Francisco alleys. He sang and squalled and warbled inventive improvisations. He was really belting it out, giving it his full range, when Frances burst out the kitchen door.

She stared up at him, incredulous, and tried to shake the tree, then looked for something to throw. Joe yowled louder. She snatched up a clod of garden earth, heaved it straight at him. She had pretty good aim—the dirt spattered against the branch inches from him. He ducked but continued to scream. The next instant the back door swung open, and old Mrs. Blankenship pushed out, waddling down the steps in her robe.

"Oh, poor kitty. My poor kitty, my kitty's up there. Oh, Frances, she . . ."

When Mama saw that it wasn't her kitty, she sat down on the steps, made herself comfortable. As if prepared to watch a good show. She seemed highly entertained by Frances's rage, and it occurred to Joe that Frances might have reached her limit with stray cats.

Frances heaved another clod. "Shut up, you stupid beast. Shut up, or I'm getting Varnie's shotgun."

"He's frightened, Frances. The poor thing can't get down."

"Mama, the cat can get down when it wants down."

"Then why would he be crying like that? He's terrified."

Joe tried to look frightened, warbling another chorus of off-key wails but watching Frances warily. *Come on,*

Dulcie, get on with it. I'll have to skin out of here damn fast if Frances goes for a gun. In order to hold her attention, he pretended to lose his balance. When he nearly fell the old woman yelped. But Frances smiled, and threw another clod.

The moment Joe began to yowl, Dulcie leaped in through the laundry window. Streaking down the hall for Frances's office, she sailed to the top of the file cabinet and hit the on switch of the copier.

She hoped it wasn't out of paper, she didn't think she could manage a ream of paper. She was greatly cheered when the machine's sweet hum filled the room and no panic lights came on. How long did it take to warm up? Seemed like the ready light would never turn green.

But at last the little bulb flashed. She lifted the lid, laid the list inside, and smoothed it with her paw.

Lowering the lid, she pressed the copy button and prayed a beseeching cat prayer.

The machine hummed louder. The copy light ran along under the lid. In a moment the fresh copy eased out into the bin, and she slid it out with a careful paw. Joe was still singing, his cries muffled by the house walls. She thought she heard Frances shout.

Stamps's handwriting looked better on the copy than in the original. The oily stains and the wrinkles had not reproduced. She retrieved his own list from inside the machine and managed to fold the clean sheet of paper with it, using teeth and claws.

Joe's cries rose higher, bold and reassuring. She patted the little packet flat, gripped it firmly between her teeth, and switched off the machine.

Trotting back down the hall, she was almost to the laundry when she heard footsteps hit the back porch and the door open. She started to swerve into the bathroom, but there would be no way out. That window was seldom opened. She bolted down the hall for the laundry as Frances's footsteps crossed the kitchen.

Frances loomed in the doorway, saw her. "The cat . . . What's it got?" She ran, tried to grab Dulcie. "Something in its mouth . . ." The look on her face was incredulous.

Dulcie sailed to the sill and out.

"Damn cat's taken something . . . "

She dropped to the side yard, crunching dry leaves as Frances shouted and banged down the window. Scorching away from the house, Dulcie prayed Joe would see her and follow, but as she hit the curb and dived beneath a neighbor's parked car, he was still yowling.

16

Late-afternoon sun slanted into the Damen backyard, warming the chaise lounge, and warming Joe where he slept sprawled across its soft cushions. He did not feel the gentle breeze that caressed his fur. He was so deep under that the term *catnap* could not apply—he slept like the dead, limp as a child's stuffed toy. He didn't hear the leaves blowing in the oak trees, didn't hear the occasional car passing along the street out in front. Didn't hear the raucous screaming above him where, atop the fence, six cow birds danced, trying to taunt him. Had he been lightly napping, he would have jerked awake at the first arrogant squawk and leaped up in pointless attack simply for the fun of seeing the stupid birds scatter. But his adventures of the morning, breaking into Stamps's room and his creative concert in the Blankenship fig tree, had left him wrung out. Only if one were to lean close and hear his soft snores, would one detect any sign of life.

He had parted from Dulcie at Ocean Avenue, had stood in the shade of the grassy median watching her trot brightly away toward the courthouse, carrying the photocopy of Stamps's list, the white paper clutched in her teeth as if she were some dotty mother cat carrying a prize kitten; and she'd headed straight for the Molena Point Police Station.

He had to trust she'd get the list to Harper without being seen. When he questioned her, she hadn't been specific.

"There are cops all over, Dulcie. How are you going to do that?"

"Play it by ear," she'd mumbled, smiling around the paper, and trotted away.

And Stamps would never know the list had left his room. What were a few little dents in the paper? Who would imagine toothmarks? Certainly by the time Stamps got home from work the list would be dry, Dulcie's spit evaporated.

And once Dulcie had delivered Stamps's game plan to the authorities, she'd be off for a delightful day of court proceedings.

For himself, a nap had seemed far more inviting. Arriving home famished, he had pushed into the kitchen, waking the assorted pets, had knocked the box of cat kibble from the cupboard, and wolfed the contents. He'd gone out again through the front—there was no cat door from the kitchen; Clyde controlled the other cats' access to the outdoors. Two of the cats were ancient and ought to be kept inside. And the young white female was too cowardly to fend for herself.

And in the backyard, moderately fortified with his dry snack, he had slept until 4 P.M.

He'd awakened hungry again, starved. Slipping back into the house, he had phoned Jolly's. When, twenty minutes later, Jolly's delivery van pulled up in front, he allowed time for the boy to set his order on the porch as he had directed and to drive away. There was no problem about paying—he had put it on Clyde's charge. When the coast was clear he slipped out, checked for nosy neighbors, then dragged the white paper bag around the side yard to the back and up onto the chaise.

Feasting royally, he had left the wrappers scattered around the chaise and gone back to sleep, his stomach distended, his belch loud and satisfied.

But now, suddenly, he was rudely awakened by someone poking him.

He jerked up, startled, then subsided.

Through slitted eyes he took in pant legs, Clyde's reaching hand. He turned over and squeezed his eyes closed.

Clyde poked again, harder. Joe opened one eye, growling softly. Around them, the shadows were lengthening, the sunlight had softened, its long patches of brilliance lower and gentler. The cool breeze that rustled the trees above him smelled of evening. Joe observed his housemate irritably.

Clyde was not only home from work, he had showered and changed. He was wearing a new, soft blue jogging suit. A velvet jogging suit. And brand-new Nikes. Joe opened both eyes, studying him with interest.

Clyde poked again, a real jab. Joe snatched the offending fingers and bit down hard.

Clyde jerked his hand, which was a mistake. "Christ, Joe! Let go of me! I was only petting. What's the matter with you?"

He dropped the offending fingers. "You weren't petting, you were prodding."

"I was only trying to see if you're all right. You were totally limp. You looked dead, like some old fur piece rejected by the Goodwill."

Joe glared.

"I merely wanted to know if you'd like some salmon for dinner." He examined his fingers. "When was your last rabies shot?"

"How the hell should I know? It's your job to keep track of that stuff. Of course I want salmon for dinner."

Clyde studied his wounded appendages, searching for blood.

"I hardly broke the skin. I could have taken the damned fingers off if I'd wanted."

Clyde sighed.

"You jerked me out of an extremely deep sleep. A healing, restful sleep. A much-needed sleep." He slurped on his paw and massaged his violated belly. "In case you've forgotten, cats need more sleep than humans, cats need a higher-quality sleep. Cats . . . "

"Can it, Joe. I said I was sorry. I didn't come out here for a lecture." Clyde's gaze wandered to the deli wrappers scattered beneath the chaise. He knelt and picked up several and sniffed them. "I see you won't want the salmon, that you've already had dinner."

"A midafternoon snack. I said yes, I want salmon."

Clyde sat down on the end of the chaise, nearly tipping it though Joe occupied three-fourths of the pad. "This was a midafternoon snack? I wonder, Joe, if you've glanced, recently, at my deli bill."

Joe stared at him, his yellow eyes wide.

"Ever since you learned how to use the phone, my bill at Jolly's has been unbelievable. It takes a large part of my personal earnings just to . . . "

"Come on, Clyde. A little roast beef once in a while, a few crackers."

Clyde picked up a wrapper. "What is this black smear? Could this be caviar?" He raised his eyes to Joe. "Imported caviar? The beluga, maybe?" He examined a second crumpled sheet of paper. "And these little flecks of pink. These wouldn't be the salmon—Jolly's best smoked Canadian salmon?"

"They were having a special." Joe licked his whiskers. "You really ought to try the smoked salmon; Jolly just got it in from Seattle."

Clyde picked up yet another wrapper and sniffed the faint, creamy smears. "And is this that Brie from France?"

"George Jolly does keep a very nice Brie. Smear it on a soft French bread, it's perfection. They say Brie is good with fresh fruit, but I prefer . . . "

Clyde looked at Joe intently. "Doesn't Jolly's deliveryman wonder, when he brings this stuff and no one answers the door? What do you tell him when you call?"

"I tell him to leave it on the porch. What else would I tell him? To shove it through the cat door? I can manage that myself. Though this evening I carried it around here, it's so nice and sunny. I had a delightful snack."

"That, as far as I'm concerned, was your supper."

"You might call it high tea."

"And where's Dulcie? How come you didn't share with her? She loves smoked salmon and Brie."

"She planned to spend the afternoon at the courthouse. She said she was going home afterward, for some quality time with Wilma. Dulcie is a very dutiful cat."

Clyde wadded up the deli wrappers. "You were taking a nap pretty early in the day, so I presume you're planning a big night."

Joe shrugged. "Maybe an early hunt, nothing elaborate." He had no intention of sharing his plans for the evening. This proposed break-and-enter into the Aronson Gallery was none of Clyde's business. It would only upset him. He looked Clyde over with interest. "And what about you? Looks like you have big plans. Is that a new jogging suit? And new Nikes? They have to be, they're still clean. And you just had a haircut. What gives? You going walking with Charleston?"

Clyde stared.

Joe bent this head and licked his hind paw. "Simple deduction," he said modestly. "I know that Charlie likes to walk; Dulcie says she's learning the lay of the village, learning the names of the streets. And you told me yourself, she doesn't like fancy restaurants and doesn't hang out in bars. And a movie date is so juvenile. Ergo, you're going walking, and then for dinner either to the Fish Market or the Bakery."

"I don't know why I bother to plan anything about my life. I could just ask you what I'm going to do for the day. It would be so much easier."

Joe lifted a white paw, extended his claws, and began to clean between them.

Clyde glanced at his watch and rose. In a few minutes Joe could hear him in the kitchen opening cans, could hear the two old dogs' nails scrabbling on the kitchen floor in Pavlovian response to the growl of the can opener, and the three cats begin to mewl. Annoyed by the fuss, Joe rose, leaped to the top of the fence and up into the eucalyptus tree. There he tucked down into a favorite hollow formed by three converging branches and tried to go back to sleep.

But within minutes of his getting settled and drifting off, the back door burst open and a tangle of dogs and cats poured out into the falling evening. The dumb beasts began to play, driven by inane, friendly barking and snarls and an occasional feline hiss. Joe climbed higher.

He wasn't to meet Dulcie until eight-thirty, but he needed to be fresh. It would take some quick maneuvering to slip into the gallery unseen just before it closed, find an adequate hiding place, and remain concealed until Sicily locked up and went home. He had a bad feeling about tonight. But Dulcie wasn't going to rest until they took that gallery apart looking for Janet's paintings.

He supposed if they didn't find them, she'd want to search Sicily's apartment next, and who knew where else.

What they should do, of course, was inform the police. Let Captain Harper know about the missing paintings—make one simple, anonymous phone call so Harper could start looking for them.

But try to tell Dulcie that. She'd got her claws into this and was determined to do it her way, to come up with the killer unaided, like some ego-driven movie detective.

Yet he knew he was being unfair. The excitement of the hunt stirred his own blood. And he knew Dulcie was driven not so much by ego, as by her powerful hunting instincts and an overwhelming feline curiosity. Her tenacity in tracking the killer was as natural to her as stalking an elusive rabbit.

But now, of course, one crime wasn't enough, now she'd honed in, as well, on Stamps's early-morning burglary scheme.

Harper should be delighted. Why pay all those cops, when he has us?

But, to be honest, his own curiosity nudged him just as sharply. And what the hell? Breaking into Stamps's place had been a gas. He liked nosing around other folks' turf.

Anyway what choice did he have? What else could he do when Dulcie flashed those big green eyes at him, and extended her soft little paw? Might as well relax and enjoy an evening of burglary. What harm—what could go wrong? What could happen?

17

High above the alley, as Dulcie crouched to leap, the oak branch shivered beneath her tensed paws. She gathered herself, staring across to the narrow brick sill of the courthouse window. She sprang suddenly, flying across–hit the sill, scattering pigeons, driving them up in an explosion of thundering wings.

But even as she clung, steadying herself by pressing against the glass, they circled back, dropping down again into the oak, the bravest ones returning to the ledge to strut and eye her sideways with simpleminded bravado. If she hadn't been otherwise engaged, she would have had one for a little snack.

Hunched on the narrow sill, she peered down into the courtroom, wondering why the windows were closed, why the room below was dark. No lights burned, the long rows of mahogany benches were empty, the jury box abandoned, the judge's big leather chair deserted, the shadowed courtroom as lifeless as a time capsule sealed away to be opened a thousand years hence.

Surely they hadn't concluded the case.

Visions of Rob Lake being pronounced guilty and sentenced filled her with panic.

But it was too soon for a verdict, there were still witnesses to be called. There had been no time for a summing up, not nearly enough time for the jury to deliberate. Puzzled, she turned away, leaped back into the oak tree, sending the mindless birds scattering.

She sat among the branches, licking pigeon soil from her paws. In her haste she'd forgotten the hand towel, had left it stuffed high in the tree among the smallest twigs. She had to know why court was closed.

Maybe the *Gazette* was out early. Maybe it would tell her. Sometimes, when there was an unusual event, the evening edition hit the streets around midday. She gave her paws a last disgusted lick, backed down the rough trunk, and headed for the post office, where the nearest paper rack stood chained to a lamppost.

At least she had delivered the list, had deposited her copy of Stamps's itinerary safely at police headquarters. She hoped it was safe. She'd thought of faxing it to Captain Harper, a safe and direct route, but she'd have to use the library fax when no one was watching, a feat nearly impossible. Besides, the fax still unnerved her.

The Molena Point Police Station occupied the southern wing of the courthouse just across the alley from the jail, from Rob Lake's cell. The station's main entrance opened onto Lincoln Street. A second door, inside the police squad room, opened directly into the courthouse. At the back of the building a third entrance, a locked metal door, led to the police parking lot.

She had arrived long after the change of shift. The fenced parking lot was full of officers' personal cars and a few squad cars, but there was no one about, no officer passing through the lot, no pedestrian in sight at that moment. The brick wall of the jail, across the alley, was blank except for very high windows. No prisoner could see out. Certain that no one was watching, she had tucked the list under the metal door, praying that some officer, coming out, wouldn't let it blow away.

Now, leaving the courthouse, she glanced down the alley to the back of the station, looking for the little white folded paper. She couldn't see it beneath the door. Maybe Harper already had it. She had started over to take a look when a squad car pulled in.

Hurrying on by, she left the court building heading

for the post office news rack. Trotting around to Dolores Street, she sprinted north a block, galloping up the warm sidewalk. The day smelled of green gardens and the sea; the shop windows were bright with their expensive wares; the gallery windows brilliant with an assortment of painting styles. Next to the post office, the Swiss House smelled of sweet rolls and freshly brewed coffee. Pink petunias bloomed beside its door, in ceramic pots. She sniffed at the flowers as she passed, approaching the news rack.

But the rack was empty—no early paper. Strange that the court postponement hadn't generated enough excitement for the *Gazette* to make an extra effort. And even if, at home, she were to push the buttons on the TV, there'd be no news this time of day, only the soaps, every channel busy with degrading human melodramas written by disturbed mental patients.

But at least at home there would be something nice to eat while she waited for the paper. Wilma always left a plate for her in the refrigerator. She hadn't had a bite since breakfast with Mama, a disgusting mess of oatmeal, and then that nibble of peach turnover—more peach on her ear than in her stomach. Breaking into a run, swerving around pedestrians, she nearly collided with an old man and an elderly dog wandering along in the sunshine; then, turning the corner, she was almost creamed by a fast-moving bike. She jumped back just in time as its rider swerved, shouting at her. But soon she turned up her own stone walk between Wilma's flower beds. Slipping in through her cat door, she made a round of the house to be sure she was alone. Charlie could be unusually quiet sometimes, not a whisper of sound, not a vibe of her presence.

No one home, the rooms were still and empty. But trotting back through the dining room she caught the scent of Charlie's drawing materials. Maybe she'd left her sketch box on the table.

In the kitchen, crouched on the counter, the instant

she forced the refrigerator open she smelled fresh crab. Leaping down before the door could shut, she snatched the plastic plate in her teeth, set it on the little rug.

Beneath the clear wrap, the soft plastic plate held a generous portion of fresh white crabmeat arranged beside a small cheese biscuit of her favorite brand, and an ounce of Jolly's special vegetable aspic, heavy on asparagus just the way she liked it. For desert Wilma had included a small plastic cup of Jolly's homemade egg custard. She ate slowly, enjoying each small bite, puzzling over why Judge Wesley would have recessed court.

Maybe Mama Blankenship *had* gone to the police, maybe the recess was until they could arrange for her testimony. Maybe what Mama told the police had been important enough to put a whole new face on the trial. Musing over that possibility, she finished her main course, licked her plate clean, and licked the last morsel of crab off her whiskers. As she started on her custard, she knew she had to call Captain Harper, that she wouldn't rest until she was sure he had the list. Why was she so shy of the phone? It couldn't be that hard. Just knock the phone off its cradle and punch in the number.

Finishing her custard, she headed for the living room, for the phone. But crossing the dining room she was aware once more of the scent that didn't belong in that room, the sketching smell—charcoal, eraser crumbs, fixative.

Wilma's guest room had taken on Charlie's personality, overflowing with Charlie's personal tastes and passions, her sketch pads, her easel, her hinged oak sketch box, and a larger oak painting box. Drawings stood propped against the furniture and the walls, stacks of art books crowded every surface and were stacked on the floor. This clutter was a product of Charlie's deep interests, very different from the dead, dormant clutter of the Blankenship house. Charlie Getz might have left the art world to make a living, but her heart hadn't left it.

Now in the dining room, smelling Charlie's drawings, Dulcie reared up to sniff at the buffet, then leaped up.

Landing on the polished surface she slammed hard into a large drawing, nearly knocked it off where it leaned against the wall. Backing away, she paused, balanced on the edge of the buffet.

There were three drawings. Her heart raced. They were of *her*. Life-size portraits so bold and real that she seemed ready to step right off the page.

The studies were done with charcoal on white paper, and neatly matted with pebbly white board. When had Charlie done these? She hadn't seen Charlie drawing her. She leaped away to the dining table to get a longer view. Looking across at the drawings, she could almost be looking into a mirror, except that these reflections were far more exciting than any mirror image. Charlie's flattery made her giddy. Her tail began to lash, her skin rippled with excitement.

She'd had no notion Charlie was drawing her. And who had known Charlie could draw like this? *What is Charlie doing cleaning houses and grubbing out roof gutters, with this kind of talent?*

She did a little tail chase on the dining room table, spinning in circles, and for a moment she let ego swamp her, she imagined these images of herself hanging in galleries or museums, saw herself in those full-color glossy art magazines, the kind the library displayed on a special rack. She saw newspaper reviews of Charlie's work in which the beauty of Charlie's feline model was remarked upon. But then, amused at her own vanity, she jumped down and headed for the living room. Her mind was still filled with Charlie's powerful art work, but she had to take care of unfinished business.

Leaping to Wilma's desk, she attacked the phone. Joe did this stuff all the time. Lifting a paw, she knocked the headset off.

The little buzz unnerved her. She backed away, then approached again and punched in the police number. But as she waited for the dispatcher to answer she grew shaky, her paws began to sweat. She was about to press the disconnect when a crisp female voice answered, a voice obviously used to quick response.

Her own voice was so unsteady she could hardly ask for Harper. She waited, shivering, for him to come on the line. She waited a long time; he wasn't coming. She'd sounded too strange to the dispatcher; maybe the woman thought her call was some kind of hoax. She was easing away to leap off the desk, abandon the phone, when Harper answered.

When she explained to him about the list which she had tucked under the back door, Harper said he already had it. She told Harper the list had been made by James Stamps, under the direction of Varnie Blankenship, and she gave both men's addresses, not by street number, which she hadn't even thought to look at, but by the street names and by descriptions of the two houses, the ugly brown Blankenship house, and the old gray cottage with the addition at the back.

She told Harper that Stamps walked his dog every morning, watching when people left for work, when children left for school. She said she didn't know when the two men planned the burglaries, that she knew no more than was on the list. Except that Stamps was on parole. This interested Harper considerably. He asked whether it was state or federal parole, but she didn't know. He asked if she was a friend of Stamps, and how she had gotten her information. She panicked then, reached out her paw ready to press the disconnect button.

But after a moment, she said, "I can't tell you that. Only that they're planning seven burglaries, Captain Harper. I thought—I supposed you'd need witnesses, maybe a stakeout."

She'd watched enough TV to know that if Harper didn't have eyewitnesses, or serial numbers for the stolen items, his men couldn't search Stamps's room and Varnie's house. Even if the stolen items were there, she didn't think the police could get inside without probable cause.

She knew it was expecting a lot to imagine that Harper

would set up a stakeout every morning until the burglaries were committed, that he would do that guided only by the word of an unfamiliar informant. Her heart was thudding, she was afraid she'd blown this. "Those are expensive homes, up there. It would be terrible, all of them broken into in one morning. I don't know what vehicle they'll use, but maybe the old truck in Varnie's garage. It would carry a lot." She was so shaky she didn't wait for him to respond. In a sudden panic she pressed the disconnect and sat staring at the headset as the dial tone resumed.

Then, embarrassed, she leaped to the couch and curled up tight on her blue afghan. *I blew it. Absolutely blew it. Harper won't pay any attention. I didn't half convince him.* She thought about what she could have said differently. Thought about calling him back. She did nothing; she only huddled miserably, disappointed in herself.

How was she going to tell Joe that she had failed, that she hadn't convinced Harper, that she couldn't even use the phone without panicking?

She wasn't like this when she hunted; Joe said she was fearless. It was that disembodied voice coming through the wire that put her off. Feeling stupid and inept, she squeezed her eyes closed and tucked her nose under her paw.

She slept deeply, and soon the dream pulled her in, spun her away into that world where the white cat waited.

He stood high above her on the crest of the hills. He beckoned, flicking his tail. And this time he didn't vanish; he turned and trotted away, and she followed. High up the hills, where the grass blew wild, he turned again to face her, his blue eyes burning bright as summer sky. Above him rose three miniature hills. Two were rounded, the third was sliced off along one side, sharp as if a knife had cut down through it. The white cat stood imperiously before it, his eyes glowing with a fierce light.

But as she approached him, a damp chill crept beneath her paws. She was suddenly in darkness, felt cold mud oozing beneath her paws, sour-smelling. They were in a cave or tunnel—blackness closed around them, and a heavy weight pressed in.

A thud jerked her from sleep. She leaped up in terror that the walls had collapsed on her.

But the dark walls were gone, and she was in her own living room, standing on her own blue afghan.

Glancing up at the windows, at the change of light, she realized she had slept for hours. She yawned, made a halfhearted attempt to wash. She felt lost, groggy. It was hard to wake fully. She thought the noise she'd heard might have been the evening *Gazette* hitting the curb.

Trying to collect herself, she trotted into the kitchen.

Pushing under the plastic flap of her cat door, she saw the paper out on the curb. Trotting down the steps, fetching the *Gazette* from among the flowers, she dragged it back, bumping up the short stair, and pulled it endwise through her cat door. And why would any neighbor find her actions strange? She had always carried things home, had stolen clothes from everyone in the neighborhood at one time or another, had stolen not only from their houses but from their porches and their clotheslines and their open cars.

Dragging the paper into the living room, onto the thick rag rug, she nosed it open to the front page. She read quickly; her tail began to lash.

SURPRISE WITNESS IN LAKE TRIAL

Observers predict that new evidence which has come to light in the trial of Rob Lake may be so important that Judge Wesley will call a new trial. A new and unidentified witness is scheduled to testify this week. Neither defense attorney Deonne Baron nor the county attorney would release the witness's name. Neither would speculate as to the nature of the impending testimony. Ms. Baron was not available for comment . . .

Dulcie rolled over, laughing. *Mama did it, that old lady did it. Mama really came through—even if she was scared into testifying by the sudden interference of attorney Joe Grey.*

She wondered if Joe had seen the paper.

The article speculated endlessly about the identity of the new witness, and recapped old facts just to make copy. A blurred photo of Rob Lake and a larger picture of Janet took up half the page.

Maybe I blew it with Harper, but we pulled this off. And maybe—maybe Mama's testimony can free Rob.

And maybe after tonight there would be more evidence, maybe there would be forty-six of Janet's paintings for evidence.

Carefully she folded the paper, carried it back through the kitchen, and pushed it out her cat door. She didn't want Charlie to come home before Wilma and wonder how the evening paper got in the house. Quickly dragging it across the garden, she left it at the curb, then slipped back inside, and cuddled up again on her afghan. She'd just have another little nap, then go to meet Joe. *Mama did it. Hope she doesn't change her mind, get cold feet at the last minute.* And she closed her eyes, smiling.

18

Moonlight touched Jolly's alley; a little breeze fingered between the small shops, stirring leafy shadows; the potted trees shivered; the glow from a wrought-iron lamp mingled with moonlight washing across the many-paned shop windows, brightening the rainbow colors of a stained-glass door. The brick paving was warm beneath the cats' hurrying paws.

Intent on their destination, neither cat spoke. Dulcie was all nerves. Joe was edgy with a need to run—to climb—to fight. They found it hard to stay focused, their spirits, their cat souls, wanted to be elsewhere. This was not a good night for measured discipline. The windy moonlight pulled at them, sought mightily to draw them away. They were filled with ancient hungers, with the moon's wild power, with mysteries surfacing from a vanished past.

Just as the hills above them, so ordinary in daylight, changed under the moon to dangerous veldts and tangled black jungles, so the cats' souls were changed. Ancient yearnings rode with them, drawing them like addicts toward lost times where medieval shadows fled.

Dulcie glanced at Joe and shuttered her eyes, trying to keep her thoughts on their mission. Slowing her pace, she padded demurely beside him. Leaving the alley, turning up the sidewalk, they put on civilized faces. Bland, kitty faces. With effort they returned to the domestic, became simple wandering pets, idle, dawdling.

Curving gently around planters and benches, duly
sniffing at the shop walls, they stopped to investigate a
bit of paper dropped at the curb. They scented mindlessly along a row of flowerpots. They meandered, working their way aimlessly in the direction of the Aronson
Gallery, pretending vague inattention—but watching
intently the gallery's broad bay windows and glass door.
The Aronson, occupying a quarter square block, was the
most prestigious of Molena Point's fifty galleries.

At the curb opposite the wide, low windows, Joe nosed
at one of four huge ceramic pots planted with pink flower-
ing oleander trees. Leaping up, he stretched out on the
warm, potted earth; below him, Dulcie rolled on the sidewalk, both cats feigning empty-minded boredom as they
studied the brightly lit interior, a montage of angled white
walls and jagged, multicolored reflections more familiar to
Dulcie than to Joe. A medley of colliding surfaces as intricate as the interior of a kaleidoscope, its maze of short,
angled walls provided dozens of pristine white recesses
flowing from one to another. Each niche accommodated a
single painting, much as a jeweler displays one perfect
emerald or ruby on a bed of velvet. The viewer could see
each canvas or watercolor in isolation, yet had only to
turn, perhaps take a step, to be immersed in the next
offering. The snowy spaces blended so smoothly that
gallery patrons seemed to wander in an open and airy
world, surprised at each turn by a new and bright vista.

Now from deep within, three figures moved,
approaching the front, their progress broken into crooked
shadows. They seemed to be the gallery's only occupants.
Sicily floated theatrically toward the door, her loose, drifting garments almost ethereal beside the staid figures of
the couple who accompanied her. The middle-aged man
was nicely attired in a raw silk sport coat and pale slacks,
the thin woman elegant in a sleek black cocktail suit, her
shining black hair pinned into a chignon, her huge silver
earrings dangling and flashing in the gleam of gallery
lights. The three paused in the open doorway, stood dis-

cussing painting prices. The cats listened and watched narrowly, pretending to nap, but tensed for the moment when backs would be turned, and they could dart inside. The couple seemed undeterred by the cash sums Sicily was mentioning, money enough to keep the entire cat population of Molena Point in gourmet abundance for the next century. One of the paintings they were discussing was Janet's, a canvas the cats could see inside on the gallery wall, a painting of dark, rainswept hills.

But at last the man and woman stepped onto the street, and as Sicily turned back into the gallery the cats streaked through behind her. Racing for the shadows, they crouched between the zigzag walls. Looking out, they could just see Sicily as she moved away toward the back, unaware of intruders. Above them in the alcove hung a stark painting of a tilting San Francisco street, a work too austere for Dulcie's tastes, and seeming to Joe hard and ugly.

And now, though Dulcie knew the gallery well, confusion touched her. As she peered away among the alcoves, searching for a better place to hide, she was riven with uncertainty. The gallery spaces seemed different tonight, the vibrant colors of the paintings seeming to shatter and converge in strange new convolutions beneath the dizzying lights.

They heard Sicily pick up the phone and punch in a number, listened to her arrange late dinner reservations for four at the Windborne, Molena Point's most luxurious restaurant. This distracted Dulcie. She was able to calm herself with visions of a lovely, leisurely meal at a linen appointed table, waited on by liveried servers as she gazed down through the glass wall to the rolling sea below. Dreaming, she began to relax.

And at last she licked her paw and smoothed her whiskers, preparing for the night's work.

As they crouched in the shadows, Sicily returned to the front wearing a wrap, an African-looking shawl thrown over her shoulders, and jingling her keys. She swept past them, carrying a briefcase and a string hand-bag, pausing at the door to turn out the lights.

The gallery dimmed to a soft glow from the street-lamps. Through the open door a cool breeze fingered in, then abated as Sicily pulled the door closed.

She locked the door with her key and swept away down the street; in a moment they saw her white van go by, and realized they had passed it a block away.

She was gone; the gallery was theirs. They came out from the shadows to prowl the pale recesses, studying each canvas, each glassed and matted watercolor, search-ing for Janet's work, but by the time they reached the back of the gallery they had found only five of her paint-ings. And none of these was new; Dulcie had seen them all in the gallery, long before the fire. In the dim light, the life and color of the work was nearly lost. Only the strong dark and light patterns remained, as if the paint-ings had turned into photographs of themselves.

Deep in the interior, beyond Sicily's desk, four closed doors were half-hidden among the oblique walls. They pawed each open. One led to a rest room smelling powerfully of Pine Sol, one to a closet with a red sweater dangling among a row of empty hangers. The third door opened on a cleaning closet: broom, mop, various cleaning chemicals in assorted spray bottles. The fourth door, to the storeroom, was open, as if per-haps Sicily left it ajar for air circulation.

And at the very back a fifth door, a broad, metal-sheathed loading door leading to the alley, was sealed by a bar and a padlock. Uneasily, Joe looked up at it.

This door was impassable. And Sicily had locked the front door with a key. There was no other way out of the gallery. The realization that they were trapped made him feel as helpless as when, as a kitten, he'd been chased into San Francisco's dead-end alleys by packs of roaming dogs or by nasty little street boys.

He shivered as they slipped into the storeroom. "You said there were no windows?"

"None. If we can throw the light, it won't be seen. The switch is there . . ." She peered up, then pawed the door closed behind them, so light wouldn't be seen from the street.

Joe paced, tightening muscles, staring up. He leaped.

On his third try, scaling up the wall, his paw hit the switch. The lights blazed, three sets of long fluorescent bulbs burning in a white, blinding glow.

Four rows of open racks marched away, bins made of slats to allow for air circulation, and filled with standing paintings. But Joe, shut in, felt his paws grow damp. His brain kept playing the same theme. No way out of the storeroom except this one door. No way to escape the gallery. And this storeroom was like a coffin. In his heart, he was four months old again, cowering away from attacking boys, clawing up restraining walls.

He turned away, so Dulcie wouldn't see his fear.

Hey, get a grip. This is not the behavior of a macho tom-cat. But his paws were really sweaty, and he was beginning to pant.

He got himself in hand sufficiently to move with Dulcie up one corridor and down the next, looking at each canvas, searching for Janet's work. They couldn't move the big canvases out of the racks, but each group of paintings leaned against a slatted divider. As Joe pulled a painting back, Dulcie could slip in between, take a look. Their paws were soon abraded, scraped nearly raw by the rough linen canvas and cut where the raw ends of picture wire had nicked them. They found only four of Janet's paintings, all without frames, the raw edges stapled. No thumbtacks. Two were of village streets done from some high vantage.

"From the tower of the courthouse," Dulcie said. "That's Monte Verde Street below, those red blooming trees and the red roofs. And this other one, that's the Molena Point Inn. Look, she's put in a little cat asleep on the inn roof, a little black cat."

She sighed. "You should come up the tower with me,

it's lovely. Up the outside steps to the second-floor balcony, then along the open corridor and up into the
tower."

Her eyes glowed. "You can pull the tower door open,
they don't lock it. Up the tower stairs to that open place
near the top and there you are, a little jump up onto the
stone rail, you can see all the town below, see the hills
in one direction and the sea in the other. You can . . . "

"Could we hurry this a bit?" Her description of those
seductive open spaces wasn't helping; he hungered for
space and air. "It's about time for the patrol."

The Molena Point police not only conducted tight
street patrols, but they carried passkeys to most of the
shops. Joe had seen, as he prowled the night-dark
rooftops, uniformed officers entering restaurants and
galleries, perhaps because they heard some noise or saw
an unfamiliar light. The department provided a high
degree of security for the small village; you wouldn't
find this kind of attention in San Francisco.

When they found no more of Janet's work, when
they had flipped off the light and fought the door open,
Joe sat in the middle of the open gallery calming himself, getting himself together again; but only slowly did
his heartbeat gear down. Beside him, Dulcie sat
dejected. "I was so sure the paintings would be here."

He washed diligently, soothing his tight muscles and
shaky nerves, he'd never felt so edgy. The phrase *nervous as a cat* had taken on sudden new meaning. "Maybe
they're in a warehouse, maybe one of those around the
docks."

"Possible. There are plenty of warehouses down
there. Remember the fuss in the paper about turning
them into restaurants and tourist shops? That's what
defeated the last mayor. No one wants Molena Point to
be so commercial." She rubbed her face against his
shoulder. "Yes, we can go down to the wharves, take a
look. Sicily . . . "

She stopped speaking, her eyes widening. "Or a storage locker." She stared at him, her eyes black as polished obsidian. "There are storage lockers north of the village. Charlie keeps her tools and ladders there, all her repair and cleaning stuff. Wouldn't the paintings be safer in a locker than in a warehouse? And at two in the morning, would Sicily go down into that warehouse area alone?"

"If Sicily has them."

"If they're in a locker, there should be some kind of receipt. Charlie got a receipt for her locker. I saw it on her dresser, stuck into her checkbook."

"You just happened to be passing."

"Actually, I was looking at her art books. She doesn't care if I prowl."

Trotting across the gallery, she leaped to Sicily's desk, began to nose through the papers in an in-box, then through a little basket containing a tangle of small, handwritten notes and postcards.

She clawed open the file drawer. And as she searched, Joe prowled the perimeters of the gallery, nosing along the bay windows, hoping one would open.

When he turned, all he could see of Dulcie were her hindquarters and tail as she peered down inside the files. "Look for a duplicate key, a spare for the front door."

She raised her head, watching him. His kittenhood must have been terrible. He couldn't bear to be trapped though he would seldom talk about it.

Sicily's files were filled with brochures and announcements of one-man exhibits, with newspaper clippings and reviews. Some contained, as well, glossy, full-color offprints of magazine articles featuring the artist's work. In the front of each file was clipped an inventory listing by title, the medium and size of each painting received by the gallery, the date received, the dates of exhibits entered, and whether the work was accepted or rejected. There were notations of awards won, and of reviews.

The listing also contained the date a painting was sold, the price, and the name and address of the buyer. All the inventories were handwritten in small, neat script. There were three J folders.

Janet's folder contained a list of her work taken by the gallery, but the dates were all months old. Two-thirds of the works had been sold. Dulcie could find no indication that a large number of paintings had suddenly been added to Sicily's inventory—unless the dates had been altered. And when she clawed open the smaller desk drawers she found only office supplies—a stapler, pens, blank labels, stationery, and envelopes—and in one drawer, beside boxes of paper clips, a tangle of bracelets and a lipstick.

She was patting some restaurant receipts back into order when suddenly the burglar alarm screamed.

She shot off the desk straight into Joe, the siren vibrating in waves, exploding, shaking them.

Joe pushed her toward the back, into darkness away from the windows. Her fur felt straight out, her heart pounding.

"They'll send a patrol car," he said. "I was looking for an escape route and I broke the beam." They stiffened as police sirens screamed up the street and Dulcie spun around toward the storeroom.

"No," Joe hissed, "not there. There's not even a window. Come on—under the desk."

"But . . . "

Lights blazed in the street as a squad car slid to the curb. Its doors flew open. Two officers emerged, shining their lights in through the glass, and the cats shrank back beneath the desk. "Keep your face down," Dulcie whispered. "Your white markings are like neon. Hide your paws."

Joe ducked his head over his paws, turning himself into a solid gray ball. From the alley behind the gallery, a second siren screamed.

"If they see us," Dulcie said, "try to look cute."

"You think this is a joke."

"Relax. What can they do? If they shine their lights under here, roll over and smile. You're a gallery cat. Try to look the part."

· "Dulcie, those cops'll know Sicily doesn't have gallery cats. When they open the door, run for it."

"How would they know she doesn't have cats? And what if they do? So they think we got shut in here accidentally. What else would they think? What are they going to do, arrest us?"

"You left the desk drawer open."

"Oh . . ." She tensed to leap up.

He grabbed her, his teeth in the nape of her neck. "They'll see us."

She shrugged, her dark eyes wide and amused. "What are you afraid of?" she said softly.

He was ready to fight, to claw any hand that reached for them, but he was scared, too. "They'll think we're strays and call the pound." The pound had cages, locked cages. Having grown up in city alleys, he was far more aware of the terrors of the pound than was Dulcie. Far more wary of the powers of the police. Who could outfight a trained police officer? A cop knew all the tricks, knew to grab you by the tail and the back of the neck, putting you at an extreme disadvantage.

Those two cops were going to get some heavy claws if they tried that trick.

"They won't hurt us," she said gently. "We're not criminals, we're just little village cats."

"Village cats don't get locked in the stores; they have better sense." He gave her a long look. "Get real, Dulcie. In here, we classify as a nuisance, and a nuisance goes to the pound. You think, at the pound, they allow you to call your attorney?"

He didn't know what was wrong with him tonight; he was acting like a total wimp. Maybe he was sickening with something. He dug his claws into the carpet, watching the two officers let themselves in the front door, shivering as their spotlights swept the angled walls—and trying to talk sense to himself.

So they see us. Dulcie's right, no big deal. We're not strays, we're respected village cats. People know us. Certainly most of the cops know us.

And if some of the cops knew them too well, so what? Though he had to admit, Captain Harper had enough questions about them already without provoking him further.

Harper was, in fact, too damn suspicious. And when Harper asked questions of Clyde, Clyde got upset. And Clyde lit into him.

No, if we're going to snoop into police business, play PI and maybe step on a few police toes, then secrecy is our best weapon—our only weapon.

The cops' lights glanced and paused, illuminating paintings, then running on across the zigzag walls, illuminating a sculpture stand holding a bronze head, flashing across a huge seascape, then onto the desk, blazing inches from their noses.

19

Spotlights hit the desk, focusing on the open drawer above Joe and Dulcie, and an officer approached. Black trouser legs and black shoes filled their vision. He smelled of shoe polish and gun oil, stood above them as if looking into the drawer and studying its contents. The cats barely breathed. But Dulcie's dark eyes were slitted with amusement. She had that devilish look, as if any second she'd trot out from under the desk and wind around the officer's ankles. Joe glared until she quit grinning and settled back into the blackness of the desk's cubbyhole.

But at last the officer turned away, directing his beam on across the gallery, the officers' two lights washing away each shadow, illuminating each niche. And talk about a small world. Lieutenant Brennan and Officer Wendell had been present up at the car agency when Captain Harper found the counterfeit money. The cats, wandering among the officers' feet, had watched the result of their clandestine efforts with great satisfaction. Brennan was the hefty one. It was hard to tell whether his snug uniform concealed fat or muscle. Wendell was skinny, pale, his narrow face too serious. Joe could not remember ever seeing Wendell smile.

As the officers moved toward the back of the gallery, throwing the desk into darkness, Dulcie shifted her position, easing her tension. At the back, the flashlight beams picked out, one by one, the storeroom door, the three closed doors, the loading door.

But suddenly Brennan's beam swung around, returned to Janet's desk, and dropped beneath it. Hit them square in the face. They were pinned in the glare like moths against a window.

Brennan's gun was drawn. When he saw them he lowered it, laughing. "Cats! Only a couple of cats."

"Cats, for Christ sake," Wendell said. "Could cats trip the alarm?"

"It's at floor level. Anything moving could trip it." Brennan approached the desk, but still scanning the room, keeping his back to the wall. He knelt, reached under. "Come on out, you two. Come on out of there." He reached for Joe, gentle but authoritative.

Joe snarled.

Brennan drew his hand back.

"Okay, don't come out. How did you two get in here—you don't belong here. Sicily doesn't have cats." He rose. "We'll let them be, maybe they'll come out on their own." He started away, then looked back. "You better not have left a mess."

The two officers checked the padlock on the loading door, opened each of the other doors, then moved into the storeroom. Switching on the lights, they covered each other as they searched the three narrow aisles. Only when they had cleared the premises, had found no human intruder and nothing else that seemed disturbed except for the open desk drawer, did they return to rout the cats. And, of course, the cats were gone.

Crouched in a dark angle of wall near the front, Joe and Dulcie waited, hoping to escape, hoping one of the officers would open the door. But before they could streak away to freedom Brennan's roving light found them again. Joe snarled into the dazzle. Dulcie gave Brennan an innocent smile, her eyes wide and loving, and raised a soft paw, all sleepy-eyed sweetness. As Brennan knelt to pet her, only Joe saw, only another cat would detect deep within her green gaze, a wicked feline guile.

Behind Brennan, Wendell frowned. "Could those be

the two cats from Beckwhite's? The cats that were hanging around when we found the counterfeit bills?"

"Looks like the same two. That gray one, that looks like Clyde Damen's cat."

Wendell nodded. "Maybe they wandered in before Ms. Aronson locked up—or when someone else came in, or left. That stripy one, I've seen a cat like that over around the dress shops on Dolores."

Brennan shrugged. "Go call Sicily Aronson, use the phone on the desk. See if she'll come down and check the place out before we lock up. Use your handkerchief, don't smear any prints." He knelt again and reached for Joe.

Joe raised a bladed paw, but didn't strike; he studied the officer, considering.

Stupid move, really stupid. Bloody the hand of the law, Bucko, and you're in big trouble.

He drew back his claws.

Brennan touched Joe's ear with a gentle, unthreatening finger. He was reaching to stroke Joe's back when a shout from the street sent the officer spinning around, his hand on his revolver.

The glass door rattled, shook under pounding fists. "What are you doing. That's my cat!" Clyde beat harder, and Joe thought he'd shatter the glass. "That's my cat, Brennan! Let me in."

Brennan rose, unlocked the door, and switched on the gallery lights, illuminating Clyde and Charlie.

"What the hell is this? Put down the damned gun, Brennan. How did my cat—our cats—get in here?"

Joe sat very straight, his ears erect. He was mighty relieved to see Clyde. But he wasn't going to let him know it. As Clyde moved into the gallery, Charlie stood in the doorway regarding the scene, looking from the officers to the cats with a puzzled, crooked little grin. Caught in a deliberate breaking and entering, Dulcie gave her a wide stare, then began to wash, as if all this fuss was unspeakably boring.

Clyde scooped Joe up. "How the hell did you get in here?"

Joe regarded him coldly. Clyde clutched him with unnecessary firmness, gave him a deep, penetrating stare, then glared down at Dulcie. "What the hell were you two doing?" But he looked as if he didn't want to know.

"They set off the alarm," Brennan said, "there below the glass. Must have gotten shut in by mistsake—no harm done."

Charlie knelt and gathered up Dulcie, cuddling her. Dulcie lay softly against Charlie's shoulder, cutting her eyes at Joe, highly amused.

Brennan had holstered his pistol. "Sicily's on her way down to check the place out." He nodded toward the open desk drawer. "Maybe someone was in here and left—but they must have had a key, no sign of forced entry."

Clyde stared at the open drawer. He looked at Joe. He said nothing. His eyes said plenty. He took a firmer grip on the nape of Joe's neck, his fist almost pulsing with anger.

"Sorry they made trouble, Brennan," he said pleasantly. "Damn cats, always into something."

But out on the street again, scowling into Joe's face, he said, "What the hell were you two doing in there? Can't you stay out of anything. Now what am I going to do with you? Turn you loose, you'll be right back in there.

"And I didn't plan to spend the evening baby-sitting a couple of snooping cats. I don't know why you two can't stay out of trouble. I don't see why you can't behave with some sense."

Charlie studied Clyde, puzzled. "Aren't you overreacting, maybe?"

Clyde glared.

She looked at Clyde and Joe, frowning, as if she were missing something. "We can take them over to Wilma's, shut them in the house, then we can have dinner. I'm starved."

Shifting Dulcie to a more comfortable position, she set off up the street, glancing back at Clyde. "You can't expect a cat to think what might happen if he wanders into a shop. How were they to know they couldn't get out?"

Clyde did not reply. Joe could imagine what he was thinking. Joe had a few things he'd like to say in return. He hated when he had to remain mute. It was grossly unfair for Clyde to read him off when he couldn't answer back. He dug his claws into Clyde's shoulder until Clyde drew in his breath.

As Clyde forced his finger under Joe's pads to release the offending needles, a pale blue Mercedes turned onto the street and the driver waved. Clyde lifted his hand in greeting; just one of his customers. Then he pressed Joe's pads, rotating the claws inward, releasing Joe's lethal grip, and shifted Joe away from his shoulder. The tomcat was getting out of hand. It was going to be interesting to hear Joe's explanation for this little escapade. Of course it had to do with the murder trial, he knew the single-minded compulsion of these two.

Whatever they were doing in the gallery, their adventure hadn't helped his own evening. Half an hour ago he and Charlie had been walking along holding hands like kids, joking, laughing, discussing where to have dinner. He hadn't intended to finish off the night playing free taxi to a couple of disaster-prone felines.

Having left his car at Wilma's, he and Charlie had walked up through the village into the hills as the sun set, had climbed above the last scattered houses toward the eastern mountains gleaming gold in the falling light. High up the face of a steep hill among an outcropping of boulders they sat looking down on the village spread below them, watching the sky slowly darken, watching the cottage lights blink on in sudden bursts of illumination, the village quickly coming alive, preparing for evening. They could smell wood fires; the breeze was cool, their mood peaceful and compliant. Their mellow warmth, which had lasted all the way down the hills again and into the village, was shattered suddenly by sirens. They quickened their pace, curious, heading up the street to where the squad cars had careened by . . .

They saw the squad car parked in front of the Aronson, spotlights sweeping the dim gallery as they approached. Then they saw the harsh beams of light fix suddenly on the two cats, catching their eyes in a blaze of fire—and Joe and Dulcie looking as guilty as any two human thieves.

He supposed, overreacting, he'd roused Charlie's curiosity, but it didn't matter. Charlie was as ignorant of the cats' true nature as the two officers.

Joe crept up Clyde's shoulder to a more comfortable position, watched Dulcie cuddling in Charlie's arms happy as a nesting bird. He kept his claws sheathed, and tentatively he rubbed his face against Clyde's ear. Clyde ignored him. Clyde sometimes had an unreasonably sour disposition.

Charlie said, "We'll drop these two off, then grab a quick hamburger. Five o'clock comes early, and tomorrow will be twelve hours or more, without Stamps. When he gets back from his little jaunt, he gets the ax; he's out of here."

Dulcie's head had come up, and, her ears up, she turned on Charlie's shoulder to stare across at Joe, her eyes wide with interest.

"Settle down," Charlie said, stroking her. "We're nearly home." She looked across to Clyde. "Did you decide what to do with Janet's diary?"

Both cats jerked to alert. Charlie frowned at Dulcie and shifted her to a more comfortable position. Clyde looked down at Joe, his grip tightening, his eyes narrowing to sudden realization.

Joe looked back innocently. *So you found the diary. So now you know how it got under Janet's deck. So do you have to look so righteous?*

But at least Clyde had the decency to offer some information. "We'll have to give it to Harper. Good thing you went up to Janet's after work to leave food for her cat. Good thing the kibble box was ripped and empty, and the bowl shoved on under the deck, or you'd never have seen that plastic package."

"I still don't see why someone would hide her diary like that. Why not just steal it? If that's what they intended, why not take it with them?" She stroked Dulcie absently. "It had to be Stamps's dog that ate the food. No other dog would leave pawprints that huge.

"Do you suppose Stamps took the diary from the house? But why would he want it? And why leave it there? I'll be glad when I'm rid of Stamps. He makes me nervous."

"You need workers pretty bad to be firing Stamps just because he's taking a day off—and because his dog growls at you."

"That dog's growled at Mavity a dozen times. If he bites her, or bites anyone at work, I'm the one who gets sued. What if he bit a client? Stamps encourages that mean streak—he laughs when the dog snarls at me. Mavity's terrified of it."

Charlie sighed. "Until today Stamps has been tolerable, but today tore it. To wait until quitting time, then tell me he's taking tomorrow off, just like that, no warning. No time to find someone else. He didn't even have the decency to lie to me, to say he felt sick, just all of a sudden he had to run over to Stockton."

Joe looked across at Dulcie. Her ears were back, her tail lashing, her eyes blazed.

This was it, tomorrow was hit day. Had to be. Burglary day for seven hillside residences. Stamps was taking the day off to tend to his real business. Joe licked a whisker, watching Dulcie. She was clinging tensely to

Charlie, totally wired. Charlie looked down, frowning, and began to stroke her.

"What's the matter, Dulcie? There's nothing to be afraid of. You weren't afraid in the gallery, not afraid of the police and their spotlights. Now all of a sudden . . . What's gotten into you?"

But Dulcie's tension wasn't fear. She was primed. Every muscle twitched, her tail lashed and trembled. The little brindle cat was all nervous energy, set to explode, burning with predatory hunger to nail those two creeps—to see cold justice overtake Stamps and Varnie.

20

The cars that were parked along the curb hulked black in the predawn dark. Their bodies were beaded with dew, breathing out an icy breath radiating the night's chill. Beneath the cats' paws, the sidewalk was damp and cold. Only an occasional house shone with light. Most of the hillside residents still slept. A thin breeze nipped along the sidewalk, teasing the cats as they hurried upward toward the highest houses. Staying close to the curb, to the parked cars, they were tensed to dodge under if a marauding dog appeared out of the dark. The chill of the vehicles they passed made them shiver, but then, coming alongside a Chevy sedan, they were treated to warmth, sudden and welcome. They looked at each other and grinned. They sniffed at the rear wheel.

The metal was dry, the tire dry, the wheel so warm that when Joe touched his nose to the hubcap he drew back. The car smelled of exhaust and fresh coffee. They reared up, trying to look in.

The dark interior appeared empty, but they caught the faint scent of shaving lotion, too. Moving away into the bushes beside a stucco cottage, looking back, they could observe the Chevy's windows at a better angle.

Two figures sat within, unmoving silhouettes poised in blackness. Stakeout car. Dulcie smiled and began to purr. Captain Harper had believed her. Harper had acted on her phone call. Just a few feet from them, two

of Harper's officers sat in their unmarked vehicle waiting for Varnie and Stamps to go into action.

They thought the time must be about five-fifty. The
first mark would leave his house at six-fifteen. Trotting
up across the dew-sodden lawns, soon they could see
above them the steeply peaked roof of the first mark,
the last house on Cypress, number 3920, a handsome
white frame dwelling. Lights were on in what looked
like a bedroom and bath, and as they hurried upward
lights came on in the kitchen. They could hear a radio
playing, an announcer's voice; it sounded like the morning weather report. The human need for weather
reports always amused them. A cat could smell the rain
coming, could feel the change of wind. A cat knows
immediately when the barometric pressure changes, by
the state of his nerves. High pressure, zowie. Low pressure, nap time. The human paucity of senses was really
too bad.

Drawing nearer to 3920, they could hear the faint
rumble of water pipes as if someone were taking a
shower. And they could smell coffee now, then could
smell eggs frying and cigarette smoke.

According to Stamps's list, Tim Hamry would leave
the house in about ten minutes, in a white Toyota. His
wife, June, should depart five to ten minutes later in an
old black Ford sedan. The Hamry's had no children.
They had no dogs, and no electronic alarm system.

The cats entered the yard next door, trotting
through a bed of dew-laden chrysanthemums, and
skinned up a rose trellis to the roof, where they could
observe the impending drama. Lying up along the peak,
they commanded an unbroken view of 3920 and the
surrounding streets. The narrow lanes were lit faintly by
residential streetlights, a soft glow at each corner.

The Hamry's bathroom light went out, soon they
could hear cutlery on plates.

And as Tim and June Hamry enjoyed breakfast, four
blocks down the hill a lone figure leading a large dog

appeared, walking up toward the Hamry house. Stamps and the monster.

"Why would he bring the dog?" Dulcie said.

"I don't know. Maybe they use him as a lookout? He barks loud enough." Joe sat taller on the steep shingles, watching Stamps. "They're headed right for the stakeout car. That dog will pitch a fit."

"Oh, no. That will finish it."

They held their breath.

The dog paused at the stakeout car jerking his lead, sniffing at the Chevy. Stamps swore and pulled him along, but the dog, sniffing at the car, let out a roar loud enough to wake the hillside.

Dulcie moaned. It was over. Stamps would see the cops and take off out of there.

But no, the dog stuck his nose to the sidewalk. He huffed and barked, and took off uphill, jerking Stamps along—following not Harper's men but their own trail. He was headed straight for the house on which they sat.

Joe almost fell off the roof laughing, clawing at the shingles. They watched the beast jerk Stamps along for half a block before Stamps got him stopped. Then Stamps slapped him and whipped him with the end of the lead. The beast cowered and snapped at him, but he came to heel on a short lead, and Stamps led him across the street, not approaching 3920, but heading for Varnie's.

No light burned in the brown house. The Blankenship dwelling was dark, but as Stamps approached, the garage door swung open. He moved quickly inside. They heard him speak to the dog, saw it leap into the truck bed. Stamps moved deeper in, toward the front of the truck, out of their sight.

They heard the truck door open and close. A movement in the darkened garage, beside the window, indicated that Varnie was looking up the hill, watching the Hamry house.

The darkened truck waited. The two men would be

marking time until the Hamrys left for work. Dulcie yawned and settled more comfortably on the sloping roof. The predawn sky was beginning to gray, black tree branches to appear out of the night. Up beyond the black hills, the taller mountains of the coastal range stood dark against the steely sky.

The garage door of 3920 opened. Tim Hamry appeared, wearing a tan suit and black shoes. He turned away within the lit interior and slid into the white Toyota. They heard the engine start.

He backed out, leaving the garage door open, and headed down the hill, his lights picking out parked cars, flashing across the windows of the stakeout car. Its glass shone blank and empty, as if the officers had ducked down.

Joe studied the faintly lit streets, wondering if there might be a second police unit. Every dark, silent vehicle seemed totally abandoned; he could detect no movement within, no red glow of a cigarette—though no cop would smoke on stakeout. They'd chew, maybe, and spit into a paper cup. The officers would be sipping coffee, hunkered down against the chill, yawning as they watched 3920—and watched Varnie's dark, open garage. Stakeout must be like any hunt. Wait for the prey to make a move, be sure you had him cornered, then nail him.

From within the Hamry's lit garage they heard a door close. A woman in a dark suit appeared, slid into the black Ford, and started the engine. She let it idle for a moment, then backed out.

In the drive she left the car running while she went to turn off the light and close the overhead door. Interesting that they didn't have an electric door. Maybe they had cats—automatic doors were death on cats.

The moment June Hamry drove away, her taillights disappearing down the hill, over at the Blankenships' Varnie started his engine. He didn't turn on his headlights. The motor rumbled unevenly, belching white exhaust. He backed out without lights, the truck's slat sides rattling; its open rear end gaped. In the center of the truck bed, the dog balanced himself heavily, lurching as the truck turned uphill.

Beside the dog reclined four plastic garbage bags, heavily filled, and tied shut. "What's with the bags?" Dulcie hunched lower against the rough shingles, looking.

The truck moved up the hill. Pausing before 3920, it backed into the Hamry's drive as bold as if it belonged there, sat idling as, presumably, the two men watched the windows, making certain the house was indeed empty. Varnie had attached a hand-lettered sign to the side of the truck: *Save our earth. Help recycle.*

Who would suspect a couple of guys donating their time to collect recyclables? Maybe the bags contained beer cans for a touch of authenticity. The quickening morning breeze picked up a breath of old fish. Scanning the street, Joe saw a second stakeout car.

"There, across the street and down three doors. That old station wagon."

Dulcie looked, wriggling lower against the shingles. "How can you tell? I don't see a soul."

"I saw a little movement behind the glass, just a shifting in the shadows."

Stamps got out of the truck to open the Hamry garage door, and Varnie backed on in. Leaving the garage door open, the two men disappeared inside. The dog remained in the truck bed.

"I'm surprised he'd stay there," Dulcie said. "Stamps didn't tie him."

"Maybe he's not as useless as we thought."

They heard a faint click from within the garage, then the sound of a door softly closing. In a moment a faint light swung across the kitchen windows, jiggling and darting, then disappeared.

"Come on," Dulcie said. "Those windowsills are wide. We can see right in."

"Hold on a minute. I saw car lights way down the hill, then they went out."

The sky was paling toward dawn, the houses beginning to take on dimension, the bushes silhouetted stark
and black. Down the street within the stakeout car a
shadow moved again, then was still. The cats' paws and
ears were freezing. Their early-morning meal of fresh-
killed rabbit, which had warmed them nicely for a while,
had lost its battle with the chill. And then, glancing
down the street below Janet's house, they saw a third
car moving without lights. It parked below her house,
beneath a row of eucalyptus trees, under the low-hanging
leaves.

They glimpsed something shiny through a back window, then the window went blank, reflecting the tree's
sword-sharp leaves. They could see, within the leafy
reflections, only a hint of the driver's profile. The car
had parked just above the second mark, where the officers could look down into the backyard. "Harper's
doing it up fancy," Joe said. "Three stakeout cars."

"I can hardly believe he's done this just on the list
and phone call. Maybe it's because Stamps is on parole."

"Who knows? Maybe Varnie has a record, too."

"Wouldn't surprise me." She licked a whisker, studying the arrangement of the three cars. "They can see
every house on Stamps's list."

The burglars would have to move up and down the
hill as they followed the homeowners' individual sched-
ules of departure. By the time they had finished, if the
cops let them finish, they would be working in full daylight, in full view of the neighborhood. But what neighbor, seeing Varnie's signs and perceiving the old truck's
altruistic mission to collect cans and newspapers for
recycling, would question its presence?

Now, on the street below Janet's, the car doors
opened without sound. Two officers emerged and
started down the hill into the backyard of the second
mark. "They're going to make the arrest down there,"
Dulcie said. "After the second burglary."

"Maybe."

"Let's beat it down there. I want to see them nail those two."

"If they make the arrest here, we'll miss it. Once they have the evidence here, why would they let Varnie and Stamps trash another house?" Joe said.

"To make a better case? You go down. If we split up, one of us will get to see how it ends."

He looked at her warily. "Will you stay on the roof, not go nosing around the windows?"

She smiled.

"Come on, Dulcie. It's stupid to go over there."

"Promise," she said sullenly.

He studied her.

"I promise." She lashed her tail and hissed at him.

He growled, cuffed her lightly, and left the roof, backing down the rose trellis. But she worried him. If she did go over there, and if the police moved in fast, she could get creamed.

But he couldn't baby-sit her. He sped down the hill across the brightening yards, down past Janet's. As he neared the second mark he glanced back to where Dulcie crouched. Yes, she had stayed put. He breathed easier. On the peak of the roof she was a small dark lump, a little gargoyle against the paling sky. He moved on, toward the stakeout.

The minute Joe disappeared down past Janet's, into the yard of the second house, Dulcie crept to the edge of the roof. Crouching with her paws on the gutter, intently she watched the Hamry house, following the swinging glow of the burglars' flashlight behind the dark windows. The men were taking their time. But why not? They had half an hour before the next house would be empty. Their flitting light was as erratic as a drunken moth. She could imagine them in there pulling open drawers and cupboards, collecting small, valuable items, maybe jewelry or guns or cash.

The shadowed bushes in the Hamry yard would

make excellent cover. She was about to swarm down the trellis when she saw, in the bushes at the far side of the Hamry drive, a dark figure crouching. A man knelt there. She hunched lower over the gutter, watching.

His clothes were dark, but when he turned she saw the flash of something shiny. A gun? She watched intently until the gleam came again.

The object was round, very bright. Maybe it was a camera lens, reflecting light from the paling sky. The man half rose, moving forward in a crouch. He must not have made a sound, the dog didn't turn—the mutt stood in the truck watching the house as if listening to the sounds of his master diligently at work.

From the bushes, the officer would have a perfect camera shot of the truck, and of the inside of the garage as the burglars emerged.

She wondered if this might not be considered entrapment. But Judge Wesley and Judge Sanderson were both old-fashioned jurists, strong-willed and not easily coerced into dismissing for such legal niceties. If a man was guilty, he was guilty.

Watching the photographer, she backed down the trellis, fled across a stretch of open lawn to the Hamry lawn and into the bushes, pausing only a few feet from the crouching officer. She hadn't made a sound.

From this vantage, she could see deeper inside the garage, could see the door into the house, could hear from within, intermittent soft thuds, as if heavy objects were being moved. She heard Varnie swear softly, then the inner door opened.

The two men came out, Stamps carrying a television set, Varnie clutching a CD player and two speakers. Across the drive, the hidden officer raised his camera.

The photographer followed every move with his lens as the men loaded the truck. The soft click of the shutter was hardly audible above the men's whispers and above the creaks of the truck springs. They returned to the house for a second TV, a microwave, and for several cardboard boxes and two plastic bags sagging heavy with unidentifiable objects. Watching, she crept out of the bushes.

The dog snarled. Dulcie froze. He came flying off the truck, straight at her.

But he flew past, leaped at the photographer. Knocked him backward, sent the camera flying. Before the officer could roll away, the dog was at his face. The officer beat at him and fought; the dog was all over him, it would kill him. Dulcie launched in a flying leap onto the dog's back and dug in. Raking and clawing, she grabbed a floppy ear and clamped down.

The dog whirled shaking his head. Loosing the officer, he plunged and bucked, snapping at her. She clung, raking. His teeth gnashed so close she smelled his meaty breath. One more twist and he'd have her. Clawing his face, she leaped away, ran.

Speeding up the hill with the dog behind her, she heard Stamps shout, "Get back here, get the hell back in this truck."

And Varnie screamed, "Leave the damn dog."

The dog was gaining. *Why did I do that?* She fled in panic toward a stand of thick brambles, dived beneath the matted growth. *What the hell did I do back there? Beg to be eaten alive. That young cop could have shot the damn dog.*

Except the dog had knocked him off-balance, was at his throat, could have severed the jugular before the man drew his gun.

The dog plunged into the brambles behind her. She streaked away beneath the branches, and he crashed behind, breaking through—he couldn't see her, but he could smell her. She ran, dodging.

The bushes ended.

She crouched, panting, at the edge of the open hill. He was nearly on her, panting, seeking.

There was nothing above her but a vast plain of short grass. No building, no real tree, only a few spindly saplings.

She bolted out and up the hill, racing for her life.

21

Her paws hardly touched the ground, skimming over the matted grass. Fear sent her flying uphill. There was no shelter above her, only a few tiny trees, hardly more than tall weeds. And behind her the dog gave a burst of speed, snatching at her tail. She jerked away, the tip of her tail blazing with pain. Scorched by terror, she desperately angled toward the nearest sapling, wondering if it would hold her. Leaping for the thin trunk, she swarmed up.

She was hardly above him when the dog hit the tree, bending it. She clung only inches above his snatching mouth, and the tree snapped back and forth under his weight, the little trunk whipping as if it would break. She tried to climb higher but the thin branches bent. The bark was slick, the trunk too small to grip securely. The tree heaved. Its dry pods rattled, and the smell of bruised eucalyptus filled the wind. The dog leaped so high his face exploded at her, teeth snapping inches from her nose, and she could not back away.

She slashed him again, bloodied him good—his muzzle streamed blood, his ear was torn.

But she couldn't stay here. And if she leaped away, out of the tree, there was nowhere to run. All was open grass. Except, up the hill, maybe fifty feet above her, a drainpipe protruded from the hill. She could see its open end, oozing mud. She couldn't see inside very far, just the mouth of the drain, the slick-looking mud, the three smaller hills which clustered above it, probably grass-covered leavings of earth from when the drain was dug. The opening was plenty big enough for her, but maybe big enough for the dog as well. If she was caught in there with the dog crowding in behind her . . . Not a pleasant thought.

But she had no choice. The tree was going to break or bend to the ground under the beast's lunging weight. Assessing the distance, she scrabbled among the thin branches to get purchase, praying she could hit the hill far enough ahead for a successful fifty-foot sprint.

She crouched, every muscle taut, adrenaline pumping her heart like a jackhammer.

She shot over his head out of the tree, hit the ground running. He was on her, lunging to grab her. She spun and raked his face and rolled clear. Streaking for the pipe, she bolted in inches ahead of him and kept running, didn't look back, fled deep into the blackness, slipping in the mud, terrified he'd squeeze in behind her.

Deep in, when she didn't hear him behind her, she turned around in the narrow tunnel to look back.

The end of the pipe was blocked. The dog had his head in and one leg. He was trying to roll his shoulder in.

But he wasn't going to fit. If he pushed harder, he'd be stuck for sure. Smiling, she trotted back down the pipe toward him.

The sight of her sent him into a frenzy. He fought to push inside, his bloodied mouth slavering, his eyes blazing with rage.

She ran at him, hissing, raked him in the face, brought fresh blood flowing. Uselessly he fought to get at her, as she backed away. She turned, switched her tail at him, and moved deeper into the pipe.

Something was bothering her, a picture in her mind kept nudging for attention, she kept seeing the three mounds above at the base of the larger hill, two of them round, the third hill clipped off sharply, as if sliced straight down by a gigantic ax.

She shivered. Touched by images impossible to understand, she sat down in the mud, staring away into the darkness, seeing the hills from her dream.

Everything was the same, the dark tunnel, the sense of tight walls pressing in, threatening to crush her. Even the slime beneath her was the same, turgid and sour-smelling, just like the mud in her dream.

Drawing a shaky breath, she padded deeper in, drawn on shivering into the darkness.

Moving warily, ears tight against her head, tail low, she crept deep into the confining pipe, pulled in, swept by a powerful chill. And something lay ahead, something waited for her within the tunnel's black reach.

Far ahead something pale lay in the mud. She could see it now, and she wanted to turn and run.

As she drew closer, trying to understand what she was seeing, the pale form began to take shape. It was absolutely still, a vague scattering in the mud. She smelled death. She drew nearer.

Before her lay a little heap of bones.

Thin little bones, frail fragments.

The little skeleton lay on a mound of silt that had gathered against a stone. The bones were gnawed clean, the legs and ribs disarranged as if rats had been at them. A few hanks of pale fur clung to the shoulder blade. The skull was bare of flesh. The curved cranium, the huge eye sockets, the brief insert of the nose were readily identifiable. Within its mouth the tiny incisors and daggerlike canines were unmistakably feline.

She stretched closer, studying the small, nearly hidden object which lay beneath the cat's skull attached to its gaping collar.

The collar stood up like a hoop, circling the tiny vertebrae of the dead cat's frail neck, a collar that had once been blue but was now faded nearly to the color of mud. Attached to it was a small brass plate, the three words engraved on it were smeared over by mud. With a shaking paw, she wiped the mud away. She read the cat's name, and the name of its owner. Crouching over the skeleton, she studied the other object lying in the slime. As she leaned to look, her whiskers brushed across the cat's skull.

A wristwatch had been buckled securely around the cat's collar.

Even through the coating of mud she could see how heavy and ornate it was, could see a portion of the gold case flanked by two gold emblems like the wings of a soaring bird. She sniffed at it and backed away, stood looking at the pitiful remains of the white cat and at the last link in the puzzle of Janet Jeannot's death.

She shivered, but not with chill. She was hardly aware of the tunnel and the slime and the dog that still fought to crawl in, struggling to snatch her. All her attention, all her amazement, was fixed on the white cat. He had led her here, to the last clue.

And not only had the white cat sought to show her this final evidence; he had, in coming to her in dream, told her far more.

He had reached out to her from beyond a vast barrier. From somewhere beyond death he had spoken to her. When she dreamed of the white cat she had touched an incredible wonder, had sensed for a little while a small part of a dimension closed to ordinary vision. She had glimpsed what lay beyond death.

She was so engrossed she didn't realize the light in the tunnel had brightened. When she turned to look, the mouth of the culvert was empty. The dog had freed himself and had gone—or he was crouched outside licking blood from his face, waiting for her.

Feeling strong, almost invincible, she headed for the mouth of the tunnel.

Stepping from the pipe, she studied the bushes, the hills falling away below her. She reared up to look above.

The dog was gone.

She sat down just inside the mouth of the pipe, wondering. Strange that he would give up so easily. She cleaned herself up, sleeking her fur, thinking about the white cat. About Janet's death. And about the wrist-watch—Kendrick Mahl's watch—that ostentatious piece of jewelry which matched exactly the watch in Mahl's newspaper picture.

How did the watch get fixed to the white cat's collar? Did Janet put it there, maybe just before she died?

The picture was taken only days before the opening; Mahl had the watch then. Did he lose it the morning of the fire? Was he waiting in the studio when Janet came upstairs? Did he let himself in as she prepared her work, laying out her welding equipment, filling the coffeemaker?

Or had he been there already, perhaps the day before, losing his watch then?

She licked the wounded tip of her tail, removing the congealing blood, smoothing the raw skin where hair had been pulled out—and puzzling over Mahl's watch. He would not deliberately have left it in Janet's studio; he had no business there.

Licking her tail, she found that none of her little verte-brae was broken. She was lucky, the way that dog grabbed her, that half her tail wasn't missing, like poor Joe's—though he seemed to get along fine with a docked tail, seemed as proud of that short appendage as if he were some kind of fancy retriever, an elegant feline bird dog.

For herself, she would be lost without her tail. She took great pride in that dark, mink-colored, silky, tabby-striped extremity. Before ever she could speak human language, she had talked with her tail as much as with her eyes and her twitching ears. Her repertoire of tail dances could convey a whole world of needs and emotions to a perceptive viewer. She'd detest some debilitating injury to that elegant appurtenance.

Well her dear tail was intact, her wound was only a scratch. It would heal, the hair would grow back.

Mahl killed her, she thought nervously. *Janet's last act on this earth was to buckle Mahl's watch around Binky's collar and somehow chase him away, make him run away from the burning building.*

She thought about the white cat's appearing to her in dreams long after he was dead, showing her things she could not know in any other way—extending to her a heady promise. The promise there would be something else, another life after her own small bones had shed their earthly flesh. Promise of *Joy*, as Wilma had read to her once, *Joy, different from ordinary pleasure. The brightness of another kind of light . . . from within another dimension.*

She rose, stepped out of the pipe to the fresh green grass, sat down in the thin wash of sun fingering down across the hills behind her. Wrapping her tail around herself, she sat looking down the falling hills and up to the mysterious sky, and a deep, pure happiness sang through her, pulsing and shaking her.

It was there that Joe found her, sitting happily in the sun rumbling with purrs.

22

Under the hill, deep within the dark and slimy drainpipe, Joe crowded beside Dulcie, looking down at the little pile of bones, the frail skull, the faded collar and its metal plate, the mud-caked watch—Mahl's watch.

He looked for a long time, said nothing. Then, "Too bad. Really too bad it can't be used as evidence."

"Of course it can." Her green eyes blazed. "Why couldn't it? Why else would it be on Binky's collar unless Janet put it there before she died, unless she buckled it on during the fire, chased Binky away when she couldn't get out herself. It has to prove Mahl set the fire, why else . . . "

"But Dulcie—

"If Mahl stole the paintings, he could have lost the watch then. He was in a hurry, he didn't know it was gone."

"But this is all conjecture."

"That Monday morning when Janet found the watch, she knew Mahl had been there. She had to wonder what he was doing in her studio, but maybe she saw nothing disturbed. The racks were filled with paintings. Easy not to notice the edges had thumbtacks instead of staples. It was early, she wanted to finish the fish sculpture, was anxious to start work. Maybe she dropped the watch in her pocket, meaning to find out later what Mahl had been doing there."

"But even if . . . "

"Let me finish. She made coffee and drank some. As she stood looking at the sculpture, she began reacting to the aspirin that Mahl had put in the pot. She didn't know what was wrong, maybe she thought she was just sleepy. Maybe she drank some more coffee, trying to wake up. She turned on her tanks to get to work.

"The minute she turned on her oxygen, it exploded. By now she was dizzy and confused. As the fire blazed up, Binky ran to her, frightened."

"But even if that's the way it happened, we can't . . . "

"She was weak, faint. Maybe she tried to crawl away. Maybe Binky came to her, he must have been terrified, confused by the fire. They clung together."

"Dulcie . . . "

"Then she remembered the watch—Mahl had been there, he was responsible for the explosion. She was so dizzy, sick, maybe hurt by the explosion, too. She dug in her pocket, buckled the watch on Binky's collar. With a last effort she chased Binky away; he fled out the window."

She paused, searched his face, lifted a paw. "It could have happened that way."

"But even if it did, we can't tell that to the police."

"Why ever not? There's no reason . . . "

He laid his white paw on her small, brindle paw. "How does a human informant, talking to Captain Harper on the phone, tell him that the evidence is fifteen feet inside a drainpipe—a pipe no human could get into, or could see into?"

"But I . . . But we can't move Binky's bones and move the watch, we'd destroy evidence."

She turned to lick her shoulder. "I could say I was walking my poodle, that he stuck his nose in the pipe and I . . . "

"And you—the human informant—could clearly see fifteen feet back in the dark, could see this little pile of bones."

"Maybe I had a flashlight."

"So with your light, you saw the bones. And you deduced from what you saw that this was Janet Jeannot's cat. That it was wearing the killer's watch attached to its collar, a watch invisible from the mouth of the pipe.

"With her flashlight, this human informant read the plate on the collar that isn't visible. So of course she knew it was the skeleton of Janet's lost cat.

"Don't you see, Dulcie? There's no way you can tell Harper this."

"But we have to tell him. This is the only conclusive evidence that Rob didn't kill her."

Joe glanced away toward the mouth of the tunnel. Dulcie's theory did make sense. What other explanation was there for the presence of the watch buckled around Binky's collar?

"Maybe," Dulcie said, "maybe if we could find the missing paintings, Mahl's fingerprints would be on them. Maybe then we wouldn't need the watch. But," she said, "if the watch isn't important, if it can't be used for evidence, then why did Binky bring me here?"

He didn't want to talk about that. The idea of a cat beyond the grave leading them here shook him; such thoughts thrust him head-over-tail into speculations far too unsettling.

Dulcie rose. "Come on, let's go sit in the sun, I'm sick of mud and stink and of having to look at poor Binky."

But at the mouth of the drainpipe she paused, looking out warily.

"No danger," Joe said, pushing on out. "He's gone. By now that mutt's locked in the pound." He stretched out in the hot grass. "I was hoping one of those cops would shoot the beast, but no such luck."

"So what happened? Tell me what happened."

"I just got settled above the second mark, up in that eucalyptus tree beside the stakeout car, when I heard shouting up the hill.

"I could see out through the branches some kind of disturbance, and I figured you were in trouble, or soon would be. I took off for the Hamry house.

"When I got there, Varnie was in the truck, goosing the engine, and Stamps was running up the hill, chasing the dog.

"Varnie took off in the truck—it looked like he was going to leave Stamps to take the rap. But the other two surveillance cars were already moving. They whipped in from both ends of the street to block him. Cops jerked him out of the truck, there was a lot of confusion. They handcuffed him and locked him in a police car, and three cops took off running after Stamps.

"The young photographer was torn up pretty bad, his face and throat bleeding. Two cops were patching him up, trying to stop the bleeding. I didn't hang around, I caught your scent mixed with the dog's scent going up the hill, and I took off again.

"All the way up the hill his scent was mixed with yours, and I smelled blood. And then I found the grass all torn up, around that little tree, and the smell of you and the dog and the blood, and I thought the worst.

"I kept running, following his track, then way above me I saw that the cops had cornered Stamps and were cuffing him. There was no sign of the dog.

"I had nearly reached them, trying to stay out of sight, when down they came, forcing Stamps ahead of them and dragging the mutt by its collar. I heard one of them say something about rabies, about locking up the mutt for observation. Of course they'd do that after he mutilated one of their finest.

"There was so much blood on its muzzle I was sure you were dead meat. The higher I got up the hills, the more certain I was.

"But then I came up the next rise and here you were. Sitting in the sun purring like you didn't have a care."

She smiled, and licked his face. "So they're all in the slammer. Varnie. Stamps. The dog."

He grinned. "You did a number on the mutt."

She smiled modestly, gave him a speculative look. "Joe, even if we could find the paintings and prove that Mahl took them, that doesn't prove he killed Janet. Only Mahl's watch, if Janet's fingerprints are on it, could . . . "

"Mahl could say he'd given her the watch, maybe the night of the reception."

"Why would he give her his watch? He hated Janet."

Joe sighed. "There's no point in talking about it, there's no way we can get that evidence to Harper. Even if we could, what would he tell the court? He just happened to find a dead cat, and this watch was buckled to its collar? He just happened to look up that drainpipe?

"And why, if she was conscious enough to buckle the watch around the cat's collar, couldn't she get herself out of the burning studio?"

"You don't want to see how it might have happened," she said irritably.

"I'm just looking at it the way the police would, Dulcie. And the way an attorney would. Janet wasn't trapped under anything heavy, and she had no broken bones. If she could buckle the watch on Binky, why couldn't she get out—crawl through the window?"

"Don't forget that when her van exploded, it turned that fire into an inferno." She licked her paw. "Janet was weak from the aspirin, sick and weak, trying not to faint. Her doctor's testimony—he said aspirin would make her pass out. She was just able to move her hands, buckle on the watch."

"Maybe," he said doubtfully. "But another thing—would Janet be welding, with Binky in the studio? Would she light her torch with her cat so close? His long fur . . . "

"I'm guessing she usually made him leave before she actually got to work. Maybe she'd taught him to go on outside, out the open window. But that morning he didn't go out, he was there when the fire started. She was disoriented, maybe didn't realize he hadn't gone out until he ran to her after the explosion."

She shivered. "Janet sent Binky to safety with the evidence. And Binky—Binky came to me. Now," she said softly, "now we have to help."

The morning had grown bright, the sun warm on their backs. "If we can find the paintings," she said, "then Harper will pay attention to the rest of the evidence."

Joe just looked at her. She was so hardheaded. "And where are we going to look for the paintings? Don't you think Mahl would have taken them back to the city that night?"

"He had to be in a hurry, he had only a few hours to get down here, switch paintings, load up Janet's canvases, stash them somewhere, and get back to San Francisco, to the hotel. San Francisco is huge," she said. "Would he have time to hide them somewhere in the city? Don't forget he lives miles north, across the bridge." She gave him a clear green look. "Maybe it would have been faster to hide them in the village."

"Sure. Right here in his Molena Point condo."

Mahl had kept the condo after he and Janet were divorced; he used it on weekends, and had seemed to enjoy running into her in the small village.

"If we can get into the condo," she said patiently, "maybe we can find some receipt for a warehouse or locker. The receipt for Charlie's rental locker has the name and the locker number on it. Coast City Lockers, up on Highway One." She nuzzled his neck. "We could try. We got into the gallery, that wasn't hard. So we can get into Mahl's condo."

Joe looked at her a long time, then rose and prowled up the hill above the buried drainpipe. Pausing on the tallest of the three little hills, he cocked his head, studying the mound and the way it nestled up against the big hill behind.

Below at the mouth of the pipe she sat in the sun

watching him, curious—she had no idea what he was up to, but she could almost see the tomcat's wily mind ticking away, turning over some wild idea.

From the little hill, Joe smiled. "Go up the tunnel, Dulcie. Stand beside Binky and yowl—scream like the devil himself is tickling you."

"Do what?"

"Sing, baby. Make a ruckus, scream and wail—sing like I sang to the Blankenships."

She cocked her head, let her eyes widen. She smiled. She vanished within the tunnel, running.

And atop the little hill, Joe bellied down, his ear to the earth, listening.

He heard her, her voice louder than he'd imagined. Down there her yowling song echoing along the pipe must be loud enough, even, to wake poor Binky. He followed the sound beyond the little mound, where the earth curved down again, against the larger hill. Pausing to listen, he soon pinpointed her exact location, and there he clawed the grass away, inscribing a large ragged X.

When she joined him, racing up out of the tunnel, he was still picking up little stones from among the grass, carrying them in his teeth to drop them into the X. She helped him, pressing the stones down with her paw deep into the earth, constructing a sturdy hieroglyph.

And then, finished, they headed down the hills to pay an unannounced visit to the weekend apartment of Kendrick Mahl.

23

Kendrick Mahl's apartment occupied the third and highest floor of a casual Mediterranean condominium three blocks above the ocean, on the west side of Molena Point. The complex did not have a locked security door as Joe had envisioned, but was a structure of open, sprawling design, with gardens tucked between its rambling wings. Against the pale stucco walls, flowers bloomed all year in blazes of orange and pink and reds, and at occasional junctures, trellises of bougainvillea climbed to the roof, heavy with red blossoms.

Each first-floor unit opened to a terrace, and the glass doors of the upper apartments gave onto walled balconies set about with redwood chairs and potted plants. At one end of Mahl's veranda, a bougainvillea vine clung to the rail, providing from the ground below a comfortable vertical highway, an access tailored to the use of any inquisitive feline.

Joe and Dulcie, having checked the mailboxes in the open, tiled entry patio, headed for apartment 3C. Two floors straight up from 1C, Mahl's balcony was an easy climb. There was no one on the surrounding balconies to notice them, no one in the gardens below. The condo compound, this late afternoon, seemed to provide no visible witness.

From high up the vine they could see a small parking area, down between the buildings, surrounded by trees and flowers. But as they dropped down from the vine onto Mahl's balcony, they drew back. Classical music was playing softly, and the glass door stood wide-open. Deep within the bright living room, Mahl sat at a large, richly carved desk.

He was talking on the phone. They could not hear much of his conversation above the soothing music, something about delivering a painting. He seemed to be trying to arrange a suitable hour for his truck to arrive.

A skylight brightened the room, sending a cascade of sunlight down the white walls and across the whitewashed, polished oak floors. The room's furnishings were a combination of white leather and chrome set off by several dark, carved antique tables and chests, and half a dozen small potted trees. The pillows tossed on the long white sofa were deep-colored antique weavings. A Khirman rug in soft shades of red and rust graced the sitting area, nicely mirroring the fall of red bougainvillea on the balcony. And on the pristine walls, seven large paintings provided brilliant pools of color. None, of course, was by Janet Jeannot. Nor were any of the works by Rob Lake.

As the cats watched, peering in through the glass, Mahl hung up the phone and bent to some paperwork. In the instant that he turned to pull a file from the desk drawer they slipped in and fled, swift as winging moths, across to a white leather couch and behind it. Crouching in the dark between couch and wall, they looked out, assessing Janet's ex-husband.

Mahl was dressed in immaculate ivory slacks and a blue silk shirt, but the sleek clothes seemed too fine for his sour, owlish face, for shoulders hunched forward in an owlish manner. The cats grinned at each other, watching him, amused by his big, round, blank glasses. Even Mahl's nose was too much like a beak; Dulcie found him so humorous she had to hold her breath to keep from laughing aloud. And though Mahl was large and wide-shouldered, he did not look strong. His oversize form seemed put together carelessly, perhaps in haste. One had the impression of a creature that might be nearly hollow inside, of a thin, frail, loosely connected bone structure without strength.

They waited impatiently for Mahl to finish whatever work occupied him. At last he rose and retired to the kitchen; they heard the refrigerator door open and close, the sounds of metal cutlery on a plate. As Dulcie leaped to the desk, Joe slid behind a planter, where he could keep an eye on Mahl. From his leafy cover Joe watched Mahl make a roast beef sandwich, piling on thin, rare slices from a white deli wrapper. The rye bread and beef smelled so good he had to lick drool from his chin. But soon the smell was spoiled by the sharp scent of mustard. He never would get used to humans spreading all that smelly goo on good red meat.

Atop the desk Dulcie pawed through Mahl's in-box and stacks of papers, looking for some record of a rented locker or warehouse space. Most of the papers were letters, some about painting sales. She scanned them, but did not find them useful. None mentioned any kind of storage facility. None, of course, mentioned Janet's work. She left a few cat hairs clinging to the papers, but one could not help shedding. Mahl used as paperweights a small bronze bust of a child, a piece of jade as round and large as a goose egg, and a small pair of binoculars. All were hard to move as she perused the papers, all were hard to put back again. She had just moved the binoculars back into position and was fighting open the top desk drawer when Joe hissed.

She leaped off the desk, leaving the drawer open four inches, and slid underneath into the dark kneehole. The desk was a heavy mahogany piece with ball-shaped, carved feet that left a three-inch space beneath the back and sides. If she had to, she could just squeeze under.

Mahl came to the desk, but didn't sit down. His feet, inches from her face, were clad in soft leather slippers and cream-colored argyle socks below the creamy slacks. He grunted with mild surprise, and she heard him shut the drawer—the drawer she had worked so hard to open. She heard a paper rattle as if he had retrieved something from atop the desk, then he turned away, returned to the kitchen. She heard a chair scrape as if he had sat down at the kitchen table.

Leaping back to the top of the desk, again she worked the drawer open.

But it contained only a few desk supplies—pencils, pens, a plastic box filled with paper clips, a checkbook. She pulled out the checkbook and nosed it open. If Mahl found toothmarks in the leather, how would he know what they were?

Inside, besides the checks and check register, was a long, thin notepad. On the cover of the pad Mahl had written several phone numbers, an address, and on the lower left corner, in faint pencil, the numbers L24 62 97. The sequence looked familiar; this could be a padlock combination. It was the same pattern of numbers as Charlie's padlock.

Joe would make some comment about her rooting into Charlie's private possessions, but if Charlie didn't want cats nosing in her stuff, she should put it away. And Charlie had never rebuked her for jumping on the dresser.

Of course the numbers on Mahl's notepad could mean anything. There was no name of a locker complex, no number for the locker itself. She repeated the combination to herself twice, and then again. She could hear Mahl rinsing his plate. She searched the other drawers and looked beneath the blotter. She was down again, beneath the desk, searching up underneath in the best detective fashion, when Joe hissed once more, and she heard the soft scuff of Mahl's slippers. Sliding out under the end of the desk, she crouched behind a white leather chair. The music had increased in volume and intensity, until it was very military. She was not well hidden by the chair's chrome legs, but it was too late to move. Maybe he wouldn't look in her direction. Crouching behind the cold, shiny metal, she considered the task ahead.

They'd have to check every locker facility in Molena

Point and, once inside, have to try their combination on every lock. And how were they going to turn the dial of every combination lock in every locker complex, when, probably, they couldn't even reach the stupid locks? She'd never seen a door for humans with a latch she could reach.

Crouching in Mahl's apartment behind the chrome chair, the task seemed impossible. They had no proof the numbers were a lock combination, and no proof what a locker might contain—maybe nothing more exciting than old worn-out furniture or tax files. How many locker complexes were there on the outskirts of Molena Point? How many lockers in each one?

It would be no use to try phoning the locker complexes, making up some story to get information: *This is Kendrick Mahl, I've lost the number of my locker, I need to send it to a friend* . . . because certainly Mahl would not have put the locker in his own name.

When Mahl turned away she slipped out from under the chair and slid behind the couch, beside Joe. He lay stretched full-length, half-asleep, as if without a care. She crouched beside him, depressed.

But when the music on the CD player grew stormy, she began to fidget, her thoughts circling. There had to be an easier way to find the locker.

Joe woke and glared at her. "Cool it," he whispered. "He's bound to leave sooner or later. Curl up, have a nap. A few hours—then we can take this place apart." He rolled over, closed his eyes, and went to sleep. She stared at him, unbelieving. Oh, tomcats could be maddening.

But she curled up against him, trying to think of a plan. The music progressed to the more powerful strains of Stravinsky, she knew that one from home. She could still smell that nice roast beef. Why did humans have to spoil everything with mustard?

She listened as Mahl made several phone calls. He ordered a grocery delivery of lettuce, some frozen breakfasts, a case of imported ale, and a loaf of French bread. He called his San Francisco gallery twice and talked to his assistant about some sales and about taxes. He made a date for an early dinner, before the local Art Association meeting. *The Firebird* finished, and Schoenberg's *Transfigured Night* lulled Dulcie into a little nap. The more familiar music eased her, soothed her jittery nerves. At five o'clock, Mahl put on a recording of the *New World Symphony*, and went to take a shower. Dulcie could hear the water pounding. She heard, from the bedroom, drawers being pulled out, and hangers sliding in the closet.

The discs had finished when he returned to the living room. He was dressed in dark slacks, a white, turtleneck pullover, and a suede sport coat. And though his clothes were handsome, Mahl still looked like a bad-tempered owl. He turned off the CD player, locked the sliding door to the balcony, and left the apartment. Joe woke as Dulcie raced to the balcony and leaped to unlock the door again, slapping at the latch.

Outside, they jumped to the rail to look down, watched him cross the parking lot, get into a white BMW, and head out. Beyond the parking lot and beyond the red tile roofs of the condo complex, the hills and the mountains were burnished gold in the late-afternoon light. They could not see the ocean, to the west, or the setting sun. But off to their right, beyond the village rooftops, the bay looked like melted gold. Along the bay sprawled the warehouses and wharves.

"Rob's studio is there," Dulcie said. "I bet, if Mahl had binoculars, he could see it from right here."

"And if he could?"

"I don't know—a funny feeling." She lay down on the concrete rail, batted at a bougainvillea flower. "Rob got home from San Francisco the morning of the fire around four. That's what he told the court. He said he partied late, drove home tired, and went to bed.

"But then a phone call woke him around four-thirty. He said he answered and he guessed it was a wrong number, no one was there."

"What are you getting at?"

She licked her paw. "It would probably have been easy for Mahl to get hold of Rob's car keys, maybe when Rob was in the gallery unloading paintings. Pick them up, step out for a few minutes, have them copied."

He waited, ears forward.

"Just assume Mahl did take the paintings. He might even have used Janet's own van, taken it out of the St. Francis parking garage late Saturday night. Say he drove down to Molena Point, used his key to her studio, loaded up the paintings. Hid them in that locker . . . "

"If there is a locker."

She flicked her ears impatiently. "He hid the paintings, drove back to the city, arrived before dawn Sunday morning. Put her car back in the garage . . . "

"So what did he use for a ticket, to get her van out in the first place?"

"Used his own parking ticket, for the BMW. Then when he drove her van back in Sunday morning, he got another ticket. Used that to take the BMW out, Sunday night.

"But somewhere along the way he realized he'd lost his watch.

"He couldn't turn around and drive back to Molena Point—it was nearly dawn. He had to be seen having breakfast in the hotel, that was part of his alibi."

"And then," Joe said, "it was daylight, he didn't want to be seen going into Janet's studio in broad daylight. And that night, Sunday night, was the opening, he had to be seen there."

Mahl had testified that after the opening he did not return to his home in Mill Valley, but had driven down to the Molena Point condo, intending to meet with two buyers on Monday morning. Both buyers, one a well-known collector, had testified that they did meet with Mahl late that Monday morning.

Dulcie leaped down and began to pace the balcony. "He must have been panicked about the watch. He wanted it back; he didn't dare let it be found in Janet's studio."

She smiled, smoothed her whiskers. "He got here to the condo sometime after midnight. All he could think of was the watch. Maybe he sat here on the balcony, with the binoculars, watching the warehouse area, watching for a light to come on in Rob's studio."

"But when a light did come on," Joe said, "maybe he couldn't be really sure it was Rob's studio. So he picked up the phone. That's what the phone call was."

"Yes. When Rob answered, Mahl hung up. Got in his car, drove down there, took Rob's Suburban, and hightailed it up to Janet's to get his watch."

Joe nodded. "But Janet was already up, lights were on in the studio, he didn't dare go in. All he could do was hope the watch would be destroyed in the fire, melted beyond recognition."

"And when the watch didn't turn up as part of the evidence, and when no one had testified to seeing him take Rob's Suburban or return it, he thought he was home free."

"Right. Except that this is all supposition."

"It won't be supposition if we find the paintings," she said.

Joe sighed. "You're imagining a lot. Talk about a needle in a haystack." He scratched a flea, then rose, trotted back inside across the thick oriental rug toward the kitchen. "But first things first. I'm not going to search two or three locker complexes, all those miles of buildings, on an empty stomach."

In Mahl's kitchen they polished off half of the remaining roast beef, hoping Mahl would assume that was all he'd left when he made his sandwich. They enjoyed a hunk of Camembert, but left the remains suspiciously ragged. They smoothed it out as best they could with neat little nibbles. They split the last yogurt and hid the empty container in the bottom of the trash can. Who would guess cats had been at the refrigerator? They licked up a few stray cat hairs and then, strengthened, searched the condo.

Looking into the cupboards, the dresser drawers, the

closet, and the nightstand, they found nothing of interest. But when Dulcie pulled out a briefcase from behind
Mahl's Ballys, they hit pay dirt.

The closet was neatly arranged. The hanging garments
were sorted as to type and color with the help of one of
those intricate modular systems designed for optimum
space utilization. The white, wire mesh shelves beneath
his slacks and suit coats held twelve pairs of perfectly
arranged dress shoes and loafers, a leather overnight bag,
a pair of golf shoes, and a small metal tool box. In the corner leaning against the wall was an expensive-looking golf
bag and a three-foot-long pair of heavy-duty bolt cutters.
The briefcase was on the bottom rack behind the shoes.
They dragged it out, sliding the shoes aside.

The combination lock wasn't engaged. The briefcase
contained a stack of letters, and a sheaf of paid bills and
receipts secured by a rubber band. Dulcie pulled off the
elastic with her teeth, and they began to nose through.

"I don't believe this," Joe said when, halfway
through, they found a receipt from Shorebird Storage,
for locker K20. Dulcie said nothing. She only smiled.
The locker had been rented four months ago, for an
annual fee of twelve hundred dollars.

They put the bills back as they had found them, closed
the briefcase, and slid it behind the shoes, straightening
the Ballys to perfect symmetry, as Mahl had left them.
And within minutes they were down the bougainvillea
vine and headed for Highway One, the locker combination firmly engraved on their furtive cat minds.

The golden October evening was deepening, the sky
streaked with indigo. As they trotted up Sixth Street,
enjoying the warmth of the sidewalk beneath their paws,
they sniffed the good village smells of fresh-cut grass,
crushed eucalyptus leaves, and the salty, iodine smell of
the sea. And at this hour the air was filled, too, with the
aromas of suppers cooking in the houses they passed,
the scents of baking ham, of hot cheese and beef stew.
That snack at Mahl's had been a nice first course; but

who knew if there was anything edible in a concrete locker complex? Who knew how long they'd be occupied? Cats, as Joe had pointed out to Clyde on more than one occasion, needed frequent sustenance.

In an overgrown flower garden they stalked and caught a starling. The bird was tough, not tender and sweet like a robin or a dove, but it was filling. They finished their supper quickly, washed up with a few hasty licks, and trotted on into the deepening evening.

Crossing over the top of Highway One, where it tunneled under Sixth, they turned north. Traveling along through a string of cottage gardens, leaping through flower beds and watching for sudden dogs, Joe looked ahead lustily, his yellow eyes burning. Dulcie, watching him with a sideways glance, had to smile. He was all aggression now, hot for the kill—as if nothing would keep them from Mahl's locker even if he had to claw through solid wood.

And now they could see, a quarter mile ahead where the highway came up out of the tunnel, the Shorebird Storage Lockers sign, its red neon glowing brighter than fresh blood against the gathering evening.

Their plan was to slip into the complex before it closed, wait inside until the caretaker locked up and went home, until they had Shorebird Lockers to themselves. And Dulcie shivered with anticipation. They could be coming down, tonight, on some heavy stuff. If the paintings were there, this would blow Rob's trial wide-open. Detective Marritt's sloppy investigation, his lack of investigation, would be clear for everyone to see.

She would not even consider, now, that they might be disappointed, that the locker might contain something very different from Janet's paintings, she had put that unworthy idea aside. Dulcie felt success in her bones; she was afire with the same surge of blood, the same deep, sure excitement as when they trotted up into the hills on a fine hunting night—on a night she knew would be laced with some pure, hot victory.

24

Shorebird Lockers was a complex of twelve concrete buildings, each a hundred feet long, with wide aisles between. The roofs were of corrugated metal, and a six-foot chain-link fence enclosed the compound, its posts and bottom edge set securely into cement. The facility had all the charm of a concentration camp as seen in some old World War II movie, barren, chill to the spirit, hard to escape.

But there were no prisoners here, this camp was empty of humanity. The only life visible was the two cats trotting quickly up a wide concrete alley beneath the yellow glow cast by security lamps rising at regular intervals from the corners of the buildings. The cats avoided the center of the alley, where metal grids covered a six-inch gutter littered with refuse, scraps of paper, muddy leaves, bobby pins, an occasional lost key. The corrugated metal doors above them reflected their swift shadows flashing through shafts of harsh light. Some of the doors were narrow, some as wide as a double garage. Locker K20 was halfway up the last alley. The time was eight-fifteen. The complex had been closed for fifteen minutes.

Earlier, slipping inside the open gate, they had hidden behind a Dumpster, watching for the caretaker to come out of the office, lock up, and go home. The office occupied the far end of the building nearest the gate, and the lights were still on. They presumed the caretaker's car was parked beyond the fence on the street, one of several at the curb in front of the adjoining hardware and tool rental stores. Both those shops were closed.

Soon the man appeared, heading for the gate, a small, silver-haired old fellow. They watched him pull the chain-link gate closed from inside, snap the padlock, and turn back into the complex. He made no move to leave. Entering the little office, soon those lights went out and lights at the back came on, in the room behind, accompanied by the sound of a television, the unmistakable canned laughter of a sitcom.

"He's in for the night," Dulcie said. "I hadn't thought he might live here. But maybe the TV will hide whatever noise we make."

"I'm not planning to make any noise." He trotted away toward the back, following the numbers.

But when they had located locker K20, in the building nearest the back fence, they found there would be two locks to open.

One communal door led to a group of inner rooms, apparently small lockers sharing an inner hall. The outer door to lockers K17 through K28 was secured with a combination lock. This might be the lock Mahl's combination opened, or it might not. There was bound to be another lock inside at his individual door. Maybe a keyed lock, maybe another combination. There was also the question of the keyed padlock on the front gate. Mahl, at three in the morning, had to have a key for that. And he would have had to be very quiet loading and unloading the paintings, with the old man asleep so nearby.

They looked up at the communal padlock, its tiny silver numbers etched into a black circle. Crouching, Dulcie leaped at the heavy lock, clawing at the dial, grasping at it ineffectually with her paws.

She jumped six times and fell back. It would take both paws to turn the dial and would take a steady stance—she couldn't do it, jumping. She tried balancing on Joe's back but still she needed both paws and couldn't stay steady without bracing herself against the door. "Stop shifting around. Can't you stand still? Can't you hold your back flatter?"

"My back is not flat. I can't balance you unless I move around. This isn't going to work."

This was totally frustrating. Cats were masters at the art of balancing; any scruffy stray could trot casually along the thinnest fence. But trying to stand on Joe's back she felt as clumsy as a two-legged dog.

Irritated, she began to pace. Joe hardly noticed her as he stared high above, toward the roof.

"There's a vent up there." He crouched. "Maybe I can get through the screen."

Before she could comment he gave a powerful spring, hit the top of the metal door, clawing, digging into the wood frame. Hanging from the frame, fighting, reaching up, he was just able to hook his claws into the screen of the small, high vent. The screen ripped under his weight, and with one powerful heave he pulled himself in. Hanging in the rectangular hole, half in and half out, his belly over the sill, he kicked again and disappeared inside.

She crouched, wiggled her butt, and sprang after him up the side of the wall—and fell back, her claws screeching down the steel door so loudly she was sure the watchman would hear.

She tried again. And again. At the third leap she caught the bottom of the vent, clawing, scrabbling to hang on. Kicking hard, she pulled herself up through the screen, felt its torn, ragged edges tearing out hanks of fur.

Inside she stood in darkness, perched above the lockers just beneath the metal roof. It was warm against her back, the day's accumulation of heat still radiating from the metal. The tops of the locker walls formed an open grid stretching away. The only light was from the vent opening behind her and a matching vent maybe forty feet away, at the back. In the locker directly below her, she could make out stacked furniture, tables, chairs, bedsprings, suitcases. Peering along above the walls, she could not see Joe. She didn't call to him, she mewled softly.

"Come over the walls." His voice sounded hollow. "The fourth locker."

She crept along the top of the wall, brushing under cobwebs. The second locker smelled of mildewed clothes and was piled with cardboard boxes. Two bicycles hung on its wall beside several car parts: bumpers, fenders, a hood. The third locker was empty, emitting a chill breath that smelled of concrete. She found it mildly amusing that humans accumulated so many possessions they had to rent lockers to store them—or clutter the house to distraction, like Mama.

But why should she be amused? Was she any different, with her box of stolen sweaters and silk stockings and lacy teddies? Who knew, maybe if she was a human person she might have every closet and dresser crammed full, a compulsive shopper mindlessly dragging home everything that took her fancy.

But then, peering down into the fourth locker, she forgot human foibles, forgot her own acquisitive weakness. Looking, crouching forward, she caught her breath.

The locker was filled with paintings. Not a foot below her marched a row of big canvases, standing upright in a wooden rack.

Oh, the lovely smell of canvas and dried oil paints. Shivering, her heart pounding, she reached down her paw to pat their rough edges.

And the canvas was stapled. She could not feel any thumbtacks.

Then she saw, on the floor beyond the painting rack, Joe's white face, white chest and paws, the rest of him lost in darkness. "Be careful," he said, as she bunched to leap down, "there's some . . . "

Too late. She landed on something hard that flew from under her, crashing to the floor loud as an explosion.

"Some wooden crates," Joe finished. "Are you okay?"

"Damn. I'll bet the guard heard that."

"Maybe not, with the TV on. His room is clear across the complex. Maybe the crates contain Janet's sculpture; that one rattled like metal when it fell." The six wooden crates had no markings, but they were heavy and solid, securely nailed.

She reared up to look at the paintings, then hopped up into the rack between them, looked closely at a big landscape.

Yes, it was Janet's, a splashy study of the Baytowne wharves, stormy sky, crashing sea. She pushed the painting back, to reveal the next, looked up at blowing white cumulus and red rooftops. She wanted to shout, turn flips. Pushing several more canvases to lean against their mates, she feasted on blowing trees, reflective shop windows, a view uphill of dark roofs against seething cloud, the rich colors dulled in the darkness, but the movement and bold shapes were unmistakably Janet's.

They counted forty-six paintings.

"Then Stamps and Varnie didn't take any, they're all here." She frowned. "But the way they talked, they must know where the canvases are hidden."

"Maybe they plan to come back when things die down, maybe with bolt cutters."

"Why would they think the paintings would still be here? That Mahl—if he wasn't caught—wouldn't move them?"

"I don't know, Dulcie. I guess that's why Stamps said, 'Get ours while we can, and get out.' Mahl had nerve," he said, "stashing them nearly on top of the murder scene."

"Maybe he thought this was the last place anyone would look, maybe . . . "

"Shhh. Listen." He backed away from the door.

Footsteps approached down the wide alley beyond the communal door.

Metal rattled as the outer door rolled up. They leaped to the top of the crates, to the top of the standing paintings balancing on their edges. They were poised to spring up to the top of the wall when lights blazed on, the bare bulb on the wall of their unit nearly blinding them. And the yellow glare above, washing across the ceiling, told them the lights in all the units had come on, ignited by a master switch.

Footsteps entered the inner corridor, sending them flying to the top of the wall and away toward the back, through light as bright as day.

Below them from the hall the old man shouted, "Come out of there. You're in the complex illegally." His voice was raspy, very loud for such a small man. "Come out now, or I call the cops." He began to pound on doors. "You won't be arrested if you come out now."

"How can he think anyone's here?" Dulcie whispered. "The doors are locked from outside."

"The empty ones wouldn't be locked."

"But . . ."

They heard him open one of the lockers, then another, heard him rattling padlocks; and warily they moved away again, along the top of the wall. "Let's get out," Dulcie said softly.

"Be still. He'll be gone in a minute. If we go out the vent now . . ."

"What if he has keys?"

"He can't see us; he'd have to climb to see us. And what if he did?"

She shivered.

"We're cats, Dulcie. He'd just chase us out. I've never seen you so jumpy."

She leaned against him. "I've never been afraid quite like this. I don't know why."

"Nerves," he said unhelpfully. But then, as they crouched atop the wall, the lights went out and the footsteps headed away again. The outer door rattled as it was pulled down and they heard the padlock snap closed.

Alone again in the warm dark they relaxed, basking in the heat from the roof, feeling their thudding hearts slow, breathing more easily.

"He didn't waste any time getting out," Joe said. Stretching, he trotted away around the top of the wall, heading toward the vent. There he waited, listening. Dulcie followed. They heard a light scuffing along the alley as if the old man was shuffling away, but then silence, as if he had stopped.

"He's up to something," Joe said.

She moved to look out through the vent, but he pulled her back.

"Now who's acting nervous?"

"Keep your voice down. He didn't walk away—unless he took his shoes off."

"We could go out the back vent." But suddenly from below came the hush of tires on concrete, the soft rolling sound of a car pulling down between the buildings.

The engine stopped. They heard a second car, then the static of a police radio.

"He called the cops," Joe said incredulously. "Before he ever came out here, he called the cops."

"That crash, when I knocked the crate off. He called them then. Who knows how long he was standing out there—who knows what he heard."

They listened to car doors opening, men's voices mixed with the harsh radio voices. Again the outer door rattled up, and the overhead lights flared on like a gigantic third degree. Quickly they slipped away along the top of the wall toward the back. They heard the cops enter the little hall, hard shoes on concrete.

"Police. Come out now."

Doors were flung open as officers checked the empty lockers. Locks rattled. But then at last, silence. A softer voice. "There's no one in here, sir. The locks and hasps are all in place, nothing looks tampered with. You must have . . . "

"I heard someone talking. Not my imagination. Maybe they got locked in from outside. Maybe someone's sleeping in here, got locked in . . . "

"If there's anyone trapped here, they're mighty quiet about it."

The footfalls receded, the men's voices became fainter. But the lights remained on, and the officers left the outer door open. The cats listened to a long silence broken only by the rasping crackle of the police radio.

Joe said, "They're waiting for something. Or planning something."

Dulcie had started on toward the back when a new sound froze them. The scrape of wood on concrete. Then a little click. They crept up to the front, to look.

Below them in the hall the watchman had set up a wooden stepladder, and an officer was climbing. They backed away and ran, heading for the back vent.

They were crouched by the vent when the officer rose above the wall of the first locker. Tilting his head sideways, pressing his forehead against a rafter, he managed to look over into the first little room, peering down through the six-inch gap.

"This one's empty, some furniture but nothing to hide under."

The minute he vanished again, presumably to move the ladder, they clawed a hole in the screen and pressed through. Poised on the sill, they stared down at the concrete walk nine feet below. They leaped together, landed hard, jolting every bone. And they ran, skirting along beside the fence. They were crouched to swarm up the six feet of chain link when Joe stopped and turned back.

"What?" She remained poised to leap.

"Idea," he said, briefly trotting away around the far end of the building. She followed him, puzzled and excited, toward the alley where the patrol cars were parked. When Joe was silent, some wild plan was unfolding.

He crouched at the corner, listening to the police radio. Carefully he peered around, down the alley toward the patrol cars.

"They're still inside. Come on."

She sped beside him toward the two squad cars. The drivers' doors stood open, maybe to give quick access to the radios. They slipped beneath the first car.

"Keep watch," he said, and slid up into the driver's seat, sleek and quick, a vanishing shadow.

She pictured him inside, stepping delicately among the cops' field books and gloves and radio equipment, then she heard him talking, his voice soft.

But when he pressed the button to talk, the voices and static were silent. Those cops would hear him, they'd come charging out. She crouched shivering beneath the car's open door, ready to hiss at Joe, ready to run like hell.

But the caretaker's raspy voice filled the air, steady and loud, as he told the three officers some long involved story. No one glanced toward the squad car.

Joe went silent, slid out and from the patrol car, a swift shadow, and they streaked away up the alley. Around the corner they sat down and made themselves comfortable beside the wall, to wait.

The third patrol car parked beside Mahl's locker. Not ten minutes had passed. They watched Captain Harper emerge. He was not in uniform but dressed in jeans and a Western shirt. Detective Marritt was with him, fully in uniform, his expression sour. As the two men moved inside, the cats approached, slipping down the alley close to the wall, crouching just outside the big open door, to listen.

Harper was puzzled, then angry. He went up the ladder for a look. Which officer had called in? No one had. Well why hadn't they? Didn't anyone wonder about those paintings? Didn't anyone look at them? What was the ladder for, if you didn't look at what was there? You could see two of the paintings clearly. Didn't anyone wonder about those big splashy landscapes? Didn't anyone recognize them?

When Harper sent the watchman to get a pole, the cats crouched under a squad car out of sight. The small, wiry man trotted by, looking half-afraid. He returned quickly, carrying a six-foot length of door molding.

They watched Harper climb the ladder and reach his pole to move the leaning paintings; he would be gently flipping them back one at a time, looking. Soon his voice, always dry, took on a quality of both excitement and rage.

"Didn't any of you connect this locker to Janet? Did you forget there's a case in court involving her death? Didn't you think it strange that so many of her paintings are here?

"Don't tell me that not one of you three recognized her work, after all the damned fuss and publicity. Didn't any of you remember the Aronson testimony, that there are only a few of her paintings left?"

Dulcie and Joe glanced at each other. Harper was really steamed.

"Didn't you think when you saw this stuff that it was worth checking out? What were you doing in here?

"And who called into the station, which one of you?"

None of the three had called.

Harper centered on the caretaker. "Did you use the police radio? Did you call in when you went to get the ladder?"

The old man swore he hadn't. Harper said if none of them had called, then who did? Why did he have to rely on some anonymous informant, and how the hell did an informant get hold of a police radio? The cats could tell he was itching to get back to the station and get to the bottom of the puzzle.

When Harper began on the watchman, boring in, the cats felt sorry for the old fellow. Little Mr. Lent said the man who had rented the locker was a Leonard Brill, Brill had given a San Francisco address. Mr. Brill was, Lent said, extremely nice and helpful. When the compound had been broken into a few weeks ago and the outer gate padlock cut off, it was Mr. Brill who saved the day, he had happened by shortly after the occurrence.

One of the officers remembered the incident. Lent had put in a call when he had found the lock cut off, but nothing had seemed disturbed inside the complex. They thought the break-in had been an aborted attempt, that perhaps the burglar had run off when the watchman showed up, had never actually gotten inside.

"And then Mr. Brill happened along," Mr. Lent said. "Just after the officers left. He'd seen the police cars, and wondered if there was trouble.

"Well it was dark, and most of the stores were closed. I didn't know where I was going to get a lock for the night, and I didn't want to leave the place open. Mr. Brill had a lock in his car, a brand-new heavy-duty padlock. He said I could use it. I told him I'd return it, soon as I got a new one, but he said, no need. Said he'd bought it for his garage down in Santa Barbara but then he'd changed his mind, had decided to put in a remote door opener. More secure, he said. Said he was always losing keys." Lent laughed. "I know about losing keys. If I didn't keep 'em chained to my belt, I wouldn't have a key to my name.

"I had to argue with him before he'd let me pay him. But after all, the lock had never been used, it was still sealed in its plastic bubble, still in the hardware store bag with the receipt. So of course I paid him. Management reimbursed me later. Nice man, Mr. Brill, a real gentleman."

Lent's description of Brill was large, hunched, and rather owl-like in appearance but handsomely dressed, a fine camel hair sport coat, and a nice car, a red sports coupe of some kind.

"Maybe a rental," Joe said. This explained the bolt

cutters in Mahl's closet. Explained nicely how, at three in the morning, Mahl was able to get into the complex. No problem, before ever he gave Lent the "new" lock, to carefully open the sealed package, have the key copied, then seal it up again with its keys.

The men stopped talking, the ladder rattled. The cats nipped back up the alley, they were crouched below the chain-link fence when they heard car doors slam, heard the first car start. One big leap and they were up, clinging to the wire. Scrambling over, within seconds they were headed home, Dulcie purring so loud she sounded like a sports car slipping down the street.

"I'm glad her paintings are safe. I told you we'd find them."

He brushed against her, licked her ear. "Without you, Mahl would have gotten away with it."

"And," he said, "Rob Lake *might* have burned for Janet's murder." And trotting along through the night, Joe grinned.

So Clyde thinks we don't have any business messing around with a murder case. So we ought to be chasing little mousies or playing with catnip toys. He could hardly wait to say a few words to Clyde.

25

Moreno's Bar and Grill was a small, secluded establishment tucked along one of the village's less decorative alleys, a narrow lane two blocks above the beach. The carved oak door was softly lit by a pair of stained-glass lanterns, the interior carpet was thick, plain, expensive. The music was nonthreatening, tasteful, and soft. A patron entering Moreno's felt the stress of the day begin to ease, could feel himself begin to slow, to relax, to recall with deeper appreciation the small and overlooked details of an otherwise unpleasant afternoon. Moreno's offered fine beers and ale on draft and a deep emotional restorative to soften the rough edges of life.

The interior of Moreno's was comfortably dim, the walls, paneled in golden oak, were hung with an assortment of etchings and reproductions highlighting the history of California, scenes dating from the time of the first Spanish settlements through the gold rush days. Max Harper sat alone in a booth at the back, sinking comfortably into the soft, quilted leather.

He was not in uniform but dressed in worn Levi's, plain Western boots, and a dull-colored Western shirt. The old, unpretentious clothes seemed to belong perfectly to Harper's long, lean frame and dry, weathered face. He smelled of clean, well-kept horses; he had spent a leisurely afternoon riding through the Molena Valley, giving both himself and his buckskin gelding some much needed exercise. He tried to ride twice a week, but that wasn't always possible. He was smoking his third cigarette and sipping a nonalcoholic O'Doul's when Clyde swung in through the carved front doors, stopped to speak to the bartender, then made his way to the back. As he slid into the booth the waiter appeared behind him, carrying two menus and a Killian's Red draft.

Harper was not in a hurry to order. He accepted a menu and waved the waiter away with a brief jerk of his head. He had chosen the most secluded booth, and at this early hour there were only five other customers in Moreno's, three at the bar and a couple of tourists in a booth at the other end of the room. The dinner crowd would be moderate; the bar would begin to fill up around eight.

Clyde sat waiting, fingering his beer mug, watching Max. Despite the bar's soothing atmosphere, the police chief was wound tight, the lines which webbed his face drawn into a half scowl. His shoulders looked tight, and he kept fidgeting with his cigarette.

Harper eased deeper into the booth, glanced around the nearly empty room out of habit. Normally he wouldn't share this particular kind of unease with Clyde or with anyone. He sure wouldn't share this specific distress with another cop. He would have told Millie; they had shared everything. Two cops under one roof lived on shop talk, on angry complaints and on a crude humor geared to emotional survival. But Millie was dead. He didn't talk easily to anyone else.

He had told Clyde earlier in the day about finding Janet's paintings in the storage locker up near Highway One. Now he studied Clyde, trying to sort out several nagging thoughts. "I didn't tell you how we knew the paintings were in the locker."

Clyde settled back, sipping his beer. "Isn't there a watchman? Did he find them?"

"Watchman made the first call, asking for a patrol car. He'd heard a noise in one of the lockers, like something heavy fell.

"But it was after the two units arrived, that the second call came in, about the paintings. That call was made from a unit radio."

Clyde looked puzzled, sipped his beer.

Harper watched him with interest. "Caller told the dispatcher that there were some paintings I ought to see, that they had to do with Janet's murder. Said I might like to go on over there, take a look for myself. Said the evidence was crucial, that the locker had been rented by Kendrick Mahl."

He stubbed out his cigarette. "An anonymous call, from a unit radio. There is no way to identify which car the call was made from, dispatcher has no way to tell. I've been over this with every man on duty that night."

He fiddled with his half-empty cigarette pack, tearing off the cellophane. "No one in the department will admit to making the call, and no one left his unit unattended except my men up at the locker, and they were right there, not ten feet away, with the big locker door wide-open. Anyone moved out in the alley, they would have seen him."

"Sounds like one of your men is lying, that one of your own had to have made the call. Unless there's some sophisticated electronic tap on the police line?"

"Not likely, in a case like this. What would be the purpose?"

"Could the caretaker have slipped out to the squad cars, and lied about it? But why?"

"The caretaker didn't make the call. Only time he left my officers was when he went to get a ladder, and I told you, they were watching their cars." He crumpled the cellophane, dropped it in the ashtray. "After we impounded the paintings we searched the locker complex. Found no one, nothing disturbed."

He shook his head. "I trust my people; I don't believe there's one of them would lie to me. Except Marritt, and he's accounted for. And those paintings have blown Marritt's investigation, so why would he make the call?"

"Well," Clyde said, "whoever made the call did the department a good turn. And the paintings are safe in the locker?"

"We put new padlocks on the two doors and the gate, cordoned off that part of the complex, and left an officer on duty. It will leave us short, but we'll keep a guard there until the guard Sicily hired comes on duty, and until the canvases can be moved. Forty-six of Janet's paintings, worth . . ."

"Well over a million," Clyde said. "But weren't painting fragments found in the fire?"

"Lots of fragments—all with thumbtacks in the stretcher bars. We know, now, that Janet used staples. That's the kind of investigation we got out of Marritt. He had no clue that Mahl substituted some other artist's work. Sicily suggested Mahl might have used students' paintings, bought them cheap at art school sales."

"But wouldn't Mahl have known about the thumbtacks? He knew Janet's work too well to . . ."

Harper smiled. "When Janet and Mahl were married, Janet stretched her canvases with thumbtacks. It wasn't until after she left him, when her thumbs began to bother her from pressing in the tacks, that she started stapling her canvases." He fingered his menu, then laid it down. "But there's something else."

Clyde waited, trying to look relaxed, not to telegraph a twinge of unease.

"I told you we found Mahl's watch, and that it could be conclusive evidence," Harper said.

"That was when you said we needed to talk. I thought . . . What about the watch?"

Harper turned his O'Doul's bottle, making rings on the table. "The prosecuting attorney examined the new evidence this morning. Took a look at the paintings and talked to Sicily about them. Mahl's prints aren't on them, surely he used gloves. We sent his watch to the lab, and we've had two men searching out photographs of Mahl that show the watch."

Harper peeled the wet label from his beer bottle. "Late this afternoon, Judge Wesley dismissed charges against Lake." He spread the label on the table, smoothing it. "And it looks like we might get a confession from Mahl. He's lost some of his arrogance; he doesn't like being behind bars, and he's nervous. Shaky. If he does confess," Max said, "it'll be thanks to our informant."

Clyde kept his hands still, tried to keep his face bland.

"It's the informant that troubles me," Harper said. "We don't get many informants calling in cold, without previous contact. You know it takes time to develop a good snitch, and this woman—I don't know what to make of her."

Clyde eased himself deeper into the soft leather of the booth, wishing he were somewhere else.

"She has a quiet voice, but with a strange little tinge of sarcasm." Harper sipped his beer. "A peculiarly soft way of speaking, and yet that little nudging edge to it.

"Her first calls seemed to have nothing to do with the Lake trial. She called to tell me she'd slipped a list under the station door, and to explain about it. I had the list on my desk when she called." With his thumbnail he began to press on the wet beer label he'd stuck to the table, pressing at its edges. "It was her list that led us to that burglary up on Cypress.

"We made two arrests, caught them red-handed, impounded a truck full of stolen TVs, videos, some antiques and jewelry, ski equipment, a mink coat.

"The list of residences to be hit was very detailed, showed the times each householder left for work, kind of car, times the kids left for school, time the school bus stops. Right down to if the family kept a dog.

"But no indication of what day the burglaries would come down. She said she didn't know, suggested I set up a stakeout, was almost bossy about it. She put me off, and I almost tossed the list." Harper looked uncomfortable, as if the room was too hot.

"But then she called back, later that same night. Gave

me the hit date, said she'd just found out." Harper abandoned the label, lit a cigarette. He had shaped the O'Doul's label into a long oval with a lump at one end. "That second call came maybe an hour after that fuss up at Sicily's gallery, the night those cats got locked inside."

Clyde grinned. "The night my stupid cat got shut in. You saying this woman made the call from the gallery? That the cats got in when she entered?"

"No, I'm not saying that," Harper snapped. He stubbed out his cigarette and fingered the half-empty pack, then laid it aside, started in on the label again, working at it absently with his thumbnail. "I'm not saying that at all. Simply stating the sequence of events.

"And it was that same day," he said, "midafternoon, when the new witness turned up. The one who saw the white van in Janet's drive."

Clyde watched the beer label taking shape, Harper's thumb forming a crude, lumpy head.

Harper finished his beer, draining the glass. "You know I don't believe in coincidence. But the strange thing is—that witness who saw the white van, she turned out to be the mother of one of the burglars."

Clyde frowned, shook his head as if trying to sort that out. He had to swallow back a belly laugh. Despite Harper's obvious distress, this was the biggest joke of all time on his good friend. And he couldn't say a word.

Harper still hadn't told him about the watch. It was the watch that was really bugging Harper.

"Yesterday the informant called, asked if we'd found Janet's paintings. She seemed pleased that we had.

"She told me that when we found Kendrick Mahl's watch, that could wrap up the case. She said it was in a drainpipe up in the hills, that we'd have to dig down and cut through the pipe. She thought if we cut straight down into the pipe, we wouldn't disturb the evidence, could still photograph it before we moved it. She gave me the location of the marker where we were to dig, a little pile of rocks, up the hill from the mouth of the drain."

He looked a long time at Clyde. "The drainpipe turned out to be just up beyond the burglarized house, and not fifty yards from where we arrested James Stamps. He'd run up the hill chasing his dog. Dog bit Thompson real bad."

Harper grinned. "Thompson was crawling around in the bushes taking pictures of these two perps, and the dog jumps him.

"We got Thompson to the hospital, took the dog to the pound for observation. Don't know what it got mixed up with, but its face was one bloody mess, Thompson didn't think he did that. Long scratches down the dog's nose and ear."

Harper gave the head on the O'Doul's label two pointed ears, pushed the wet paper again, starting to form a tail. "No one," he said, "could have known what was in that drain. You couldn't see a thing from the opening, not even with a flashlight. The watch was maybe fifteen feet back inside.

"But my informant knew. Knew where the watch was, knew whose watch it was. She described the stone marker exactly. Little pile of rocks pressed into the earth in the form of an X, where the grass had been scraped away."

"Pretty strange," Clyde said. "Makes you wonder. You don't think she's a psychic or something?"

"You know I don't believe in that stuff. It was some job digging down into the drainpipe, and I didn't believe for a minute we'd find anything. I thought this would end up a big department joke."

"Then why did you do it?"

"There's always that chance. Better to be the butt of a joke than miss something. We dug down seven feet to the metal pipe, then cut through the metal with an acetylene torch, kept the flame small as we could.

"Broke down into the pipe two feet above the skeleton of a dead cat."

Clyde wiped his mouth with the back of his hand.

"The cat had a collar around its neck with Janet Jeannot's name on it." Harper was very still, looking at Clyde. "Kendrick Mahl's watch was buckled to the collar."

Clyde shook his head, did his best to look amazed. He'd had to listen half the night to Joe bragging about the damned watch, and about the paintings.

"We photographed the watch and got it and the skeleton to the lab. Lab found Mahl's prints on the watch, underneath Janet's prints.

"We have photographs of Mahl wearing the watch a week before Janet was killed. And a shot of him the night of the museum opening wearing a different watch, a new Rolex.

"We found the store where he bought the Rolex, a place on the other side of San Francisco from the St. Francis, little hole in the wall. They sold it the day of the opening. The customer fit Mahl's description. He paid cash." Harper grew still as the waiter brought another round of beers, the round little man moving quietly, leaving quickly.

"After we arrested Mahl we searched his apartment. Found the bolt cutters he used to cut the lock off at the storage complex. Found the keys to Janet's studio and to her van, under the liner of his overnight bag. And he had a set of keys to Rob's Suburban. The way we see Mahl's moves, he had already brought the substitute paintings down to Molena Point, sometime before that weekend, and put them in the locker. On Saturday he checks into the St. Francis and puts his car in the underground parking.

"Saturday night he uses his parking ticket to take out Janet's van—he knew she was out to dinner with friends, probably had a good idea she'd make an early evening of it. He drives down to the village, gets the fake paintings, switches them for Janet's, rigs Janet's oxygen tank, and drops some aspirin in her coffeemaker. Stashes her paintings in the locker and hightails it back to the city before daylight.

"He puts Janet's van back in the parking garage, uses that entry ticket later to retrieve his own car. He'd have had to put the van back in the same slot. Probably he pulled his own car into her slot, to reserve it while he was gone. Counted on Janet's not coming down at some late hour; he knew she didn't like to party.

"Who knows when he missed his watch? We're guessing he didn't miss it until he was back in the city, and then it was too late to turn around and go back. He had to be seen at the St. Francis for breakfast, be seen around town that weekend, and, of course, at the opening Sunday night.

"But when he gets back to Molena Point after the opening late Sunday night he takes Rob's Suburban while Rob's asleep, goes to get his watch."

"But he's too late," Clyde said. "Janet's already up in the studio. And no one saw him switch the paintings, no one saw him around the locker?"

"Caretaker says there were two men nosing around outside the fence a couple of nights earlier. He didn't see them clearly, didn't see their car." Harper opened his menu, looked it over. "There were some pieces of sculpture in the locker with the paintings, probably he'd put them in some time before. Early work that, Sicily said, Janet hadn't liked much, that she'd left behind when she split from Mahl and moved out. Maybe Mahl thought they'd be worth something now."

He closed the menu. "Think I'll have the filet and fries."

Clyde grinned. This was Max's standard order, filet medium rare, fries crisp, no salad. "It's a weird story, Max. Don't know what to make of it."

Max shaped the wet label more carefully, its front paws tucked under, its long tail curved. "Informant sees a watch where it's impossible to see it. Night watchman hears voices, but no one there. Call comes over a unit radio, and no trace of the caller.

"But we've got a positive ID of the handwriting on

the locker file card and lifted a nice set of Mahl's prints from it."

"Then you've wrapped up the case," Clyde said. "Mahl's in jail. You have solid evidence. And you told me Marritt is off the case and in a bad light with the mayor."

"You bet he is."

"And a new trial pending. Sounds like you're in good shape."

"That watchman can't have heard voices."

"So if no one was there, was the old man lying?"

"One theory is, he was nosing around the lockers for his own purposes, maybe stealing. That when he looked over the wall into K20—or maybe picked the lock to K20—he realized the paintings were Janet's and knew he'd better report it to avoid trouble, so he dreamed up the voices routine.

"Good theory."

"But I don't buy it. I've known old Mr. Lent for years. That old man wouldn't steal if he was starving. And he was really upset by what he thought was a break-in.

"And there's the vent," Harper said. "Vent screen above those lockers was torn."

"A vent screen?"

"Vent about four inches by eight inches."

"So what does that mean? He hears voices through the vent and thinks they're in a locker?" Clyde thought he was getting good at this, at playing dumb—it was little different than lying. Though he didn't much like that skill in himself.

"First thing the watchman heard was a thud, when he was making his rounds. Said it sounded as if something heavy fell. He'd gone around to where he heard it, was standing beneath the vent listening, when he heard the voices, couldn't quite make out what they were saying. A man and a woman, he said, talking real soft."

Harper frowned. "That vent—Lent says the screen

wasn't torn when he inspected the buildings earlier that day. Said he always looks along the roofline under the eaves, checking for any signs of leaks."

He settled back sipping a fresh O'Doul's, watching Clyde. "There were hairs clinging to the torn screen. Dark gray hairs, very short. And some white hairs and some pale orange."

"Whose hair was it?"

"It was cat hair."

"Cat hair? I thought you were going to say you had a make on someone besides Mahl. Why would a cat go into a storage locker? Mice? Remind me not to store anything up there. And how could a cat—how high was the vent?"

The waiter brought their napkins and silverware, and the condiments, and a complimentary bowl of french friend onions, and took their order. When he had gone, the two men sat quietly, looking at each other.

Max said, "Millie told me once, a couple of years before she died, 'Don't fool around with the far-out stuff, Max. It can put you right around the bend.'"

Max's wife Millie had been a special investigator. She had spent much of her time checking out odd reports, saucer sightings, nutcases, relatives returned from the dead. Once in a while she'd get one that wouldn't add up, that didn't seem to be a nutcase, and that upset her.

"That stuff she worked on, it always did give me the creeps."

A police officer's training made it hard to deal with the unexplainable. Cops were trained to remember every fact, see and remember every small detail, trained to smell a scam a mile away. A cop was totally fact-oriented, a good officer didn't go for the crazy stuff. So when the facts added up to the impossible, that could really be upsetting.

Harper wiped beer rings from the table with a paper napkin, wiped away the misshapen O'Doul's label from the oak surface. "Now I know how she felt. How easy it could be, given certain circumstances, to wander right over the edge."

"I don't know anything that would put you over the edge," Clyde said. "Hell, Max, be happy with what you have, a case wrapped up, solid evidence—take it and enjoy."

Harper wadded the O'Doul's label into a little ball and dropped it in the ashtray, watched the waiter approaching with their steaks.

26

The county animal pound stunk of dog doo and cat urine and strong disinfectant. Dulcie could smell it long before Wilma carried her inside. The barking and high-keyed yapping, the cacophony which had been triggered by the sound of their car pulling up in front on the gravel drive, deafened her.

The cement block building was located five miles south of Molena Point, isolated among the hills near a water treatment plant. A small patch of lawn surrounded it, neatly clipped. Beyond the lawn rose a tangle of weeds. Dulcie had never been inside an animal pound; it wasn't an experience she had anticipated with any great joy. But now, riding over Wilma's shoulder, she let herself be carried inside.

The office was small, the cement block walls painted a nauseating shade of pale green. Once the door was closed, the frenzied barking began to subside. Behind the counter a young, heavy, pear-shaped woman shook back her dark hair, looked at Wilma expectantly, and held out her hands to relieve Wilma of the cat.

Wilma drew back, held Dulcie against her. "I'm not bringing her to you. I'm not giving her to you. We—I want to look at your kittens. I brought her along to see if any of the kittens appeal to her." Wilma smiled winningly. "If she's going to have a companion, I want to be sure they're compatible."

The young clerk looked amused, as if she were used

to patronizing the addle-brained elderly. As she led them back into the feline portion of the facility, the barking exploded again beyond the block wall.

She left them in the cat room among the rows of wire cages, abandoning Wilma to her own devices, but cautioning her that though she could wander at her leisure, she mustn't open any of the cage doors, and she gave Wilma a stern, proprietary look to make sure she would comply.

The abandoned kittens and cats crouched on cold metal floors, some looking unwell, some dirty, some very thin. But their cages and boxes were clean, and they had food and clean water. Dulcie supposed the sick ones, which were isolated at one end, were being treated. But she didn't like peering in at the hopeless, mute beasts. She had never been in a cage, she had never had any of the experiences that these strays had encountered, and though she wasn't particularly proud of the fact, she was grateful. Once, when Joe told her she was a hothouse flower, she had belted him so hard she drew blood.

She knew that the caged kittens were better off here, where they could be fed and cared for, than starving and alone, but it hurt her to see any cat confined. And the only stray cats she was familiar with were those few who lived beneath the beachside boardwalk and wharf, surviving on fish offal from the pier above, and fed by one or two villagers. Those cats were given shots by the local vet, her own Dr. Firreti; the cats were captured, treated, and turned loose again.

As she and Wilma moved along among the cages, she saw no cat like herself and Joe, no cat who brightened unnaturally at her appraising look. Just dear, homeless cats and kittens, mute and frightened.

And though she and Wilma spent an hour at the pound, Wilma talking to the kittens and making a fuss over them, Dulcie found none that suited her. None seemed bold enough, healthy enough, pushy and strong enough for her purpose.

She felt a twisting guilt at leaving the homeless kits, and she knew Wilma would bring one or several home if she wanted, but it was a big job raising kittens, and Wilma did not seem eager to be responsible for another cat. And Dulcie herself hardly knew yet what her own life was about. As they turned away, she prayed the youngsters would find someone to love them. It was not until they had driven back to the village and gone to see Dr. Firreti, that they found the right kitten.

The black-and-white kitten was from a litter of seven that had been left on the clinic doorstep. Too often unwanted animals were dumped on Dr. Firreti. He found homes for a surprising number of orphans.

He had already given this kitten his shots, and the little male was wildly healthy, a big, strong youngster with a black mustache beneath his nose, big floppy paws, a broad head. This was a kitten who would grow into a big, powerful cat, a cat who could hold his own against Varnie Blankenship. By the time Varnie got out of prison, the kitten would be maybe two years old and quite able to stand up for himself.

But the youngster was cuddly and sweet-tempered, too, and when Dulcie licked and snuggled him, he was delightfully huggable. She played with the kit for a long time, teasing him, testing him, learning about him. Her antics amused Dr. Firreti, but he was a tolerant man. He said animals never ceased to amaze him.

When she slapped at the kitten and prodded him, he came right up at her, spitting and snarling, sank in his teeth, showing more than enough spunk to take care of himself in the Blankenship household. She just hoped that when he got older he would remain a lap sitter and not go rampaging off on his own, leaving the old lady lonely. She was surprised at how much she had grown to care for old Mrs. Blankenship.

Leaving Dr. Firreti's, they drove straight up into the hills toward the Blankenship house. The kitten sat on the seat beside Dulcie, erect and observant, looking up through the windows at the treetops and sky with a wide, delighted gaze, lifting a paw now and then as branches whizzed past.

Wilma parked a block from the brown house and waited in the car while Dulcie directed her charge down the sidewalk beside her. He seemed thrilled with the warm wind and the fresh smells, with the blowing leaves and the tender grass, but he stayed close. Though six months was a silly, defiant age, he minded her very well. He gamboled and pranced, but he didn't bolt away on his own. She led him up to the shabby brown house, straight to the old woman's window.

Leaping to the sill she found the window open as if, all this long time, day after day, Mama had continued to wait for her. Inside, Mama sat dozing in her chair.

Dulcie looked down at the kitten, and mewled.

He tried to jump up to her, made a tremendous leap, and fell back. Tried again, then tried to scramble up the wall. After his third fall she jumped down and took him by the nape of his neck.

The kitten was heavy, she hardly made it herself carrying the big youngster. She landed clumsily on the sill to find Mama awake.

Mama's face registered joy, surprise, confusion. She stared at the kitten with a strange uncertainty.

Dulcie nosed the kitten toward her, urging him on over the sill. He looked up at Dulcie, puzzled, then stepped right on in, waded across the cluttered table, placing his big paws with care among the bottles and china beasties, stood at the edge of the table looking intently into Mama's face.

Mama scooped him up and cuddled him against her flowered bosom—but she was watching Dulcie. "I missed you, sweet kitty." She frowned, her pale old eyes looked sad. Holding the kitten, she reached to the table, began absently to rearrange the little china animals. When she looked back at Dulcie, she said, "He wasn't as strong a son as I'd hoped, my son Varnie." She shook her head. "He won't like it in jail. He was real mad when I went to the police, when I did what Frances wanted, what that attorney wanted. Varnie was real mad. And then," she said sadly, "this other thing happened, and he got arrested." Mama sighed. "I guess, kitty, that I didn't do a very good job with Varnie.

"But that young man in jail, he's free now. That Rob Lake. And he didn't do anything wrong. Strange how things turn out." She cuddled and stroked the purring kitten, and looked hard at Dulcie.

"You're not going to stay, are you, kitty?

"But you've brought me a kitten who will—maybe a kitten who needs me?" She looked carefully at Dulcie, then looked into the youngster's pansy face. "A little black-and-white kitten. Black mustache and blue eyes." Unceremoniously she turned the kit over on his back and looked between his hind legs.

"Little male cat. Well, that's fine. He should be a match for Varnie—when Varnie gets out." Righting the kit, she cuddled him again, looking deep into his eyes. "I'll call you Chappie. I had a cat once named Chappie—for Charlie Chaplin. Chappie stayed with me for fifteen years. Funny," she said, looking at Dulcie, "I never did give you a name, did I, kitty?

"Maybe I knew," she said, and her old voice trembled. "Maybe I knew, all the time, that it was just a visit.

"But Chappie," she said, stroking him, "Chappie's come to stay, hasn't he?" She cocked her head, watching Dulcie. "Strange thing for a little cat to do, to bring me another kitty, someone to take your place.

"But then," she said, "cats are strange little folk. Aren't they, sweet kitty?" Reaching across the table, she stroked Dulcie gently.

Dulcie nudged her head beneath Mrs. Blankenship's hand, and gave her a long, happy purr. She let the old woman pet her for a while, but at last she turned away. Crouched on the windowsill, she gave the old woman one last look, then leaped to the lawn.

And she ran, racing down the street to Wilma's car and in through the open door.

She did not take her usual place on the seat. She slipped under the steering wheel into Wilma's lap and stayed there, close, as Wilma drove home.

27

Leaving her old van parked in front of the Aronson Gallery, Charlie walked down to Jolly's Deli to take delivery of the picnic hamper Wilma had ordered earlier in the day. She liked the deli, with its clean, whitewashed and polished woodwork, its tile floors of huge handmade tiles glazed pale as eggshells, its hand-painted tile counters decorated in flower patterns; she loved the smell of the deli, a combination of herbs and spices and baking so delicious it was like a little bit of heaven reaching out into the street, pulling in passersby. The tiny round tables set before the windows were always full as villagers enjoyed Jolly's imported meats and cheeses, homemade breads and delectable salads.

She liked old George Jolly, too. He was always happy, seeming sublimely satisfied with the world. She imagined him in his old truck making early-morning trips to Salinas to buy the best produce, imagined trips to some exclusive specialty wholesaler for his fine imported meats and cheeses. She wondered if he did all the baking, at perhaps three in the morning, or if he delegated that task to one of his efficient assistants. She knew Jolly did his own roasting of hams and sides of beef, in a large brick room behind the deli kitchen. She wondered if he had grown up consciously striving to live up to the name of Jolly, or if his name was only coincidental. Too bad he couldn't dish out to others some of his optimism, dish out helpings of cheerfulness as he dished up Greek salad and salmon quiche.

Too bad George Jolly couldn't sell a pound or two of happiness to Beverly Jeannot. That bad-tempered woman could use it.

Beverly had been at the gallery when Charlie left. She'd seen Beverly come in as she sat at the back, at a card table, preparing a work proposal, bidding for the gallery's cleaning account. When she looked toward the front windows, Beverly was coming in, pausing for a moment just inside the glass door as if for maximum effect, before making her way to Sicily's desk.

She was dressed in a pink suit reminiscent of a bowl of strawberry ice cream. Pink shoes. Her hair in perfect marcel waves. Of course Beverly would be coming to the gallery, Sicily was her sales agent now, Sicily would be marketing—for fabulous prices—the last of Janet's canvases.

Sitting down opposite Sicily, Beverly spied Charlie at the back and beckoned imperiously.

Summoned like a servant, Charlie stood waiting beside the desk while Beverly made herself comfortable, settling securely into her chair, arranging her pink handbag carefully in her lap. She didn't waste time on social niceties. "Your cleanup work, Miss Getz, still cannot begin. The police have not released the house. I find this delay intolerable. I presume there is no help for it."

What was she supposed to say? That she'd clean illegally after midnight?

"Now, with this case dismissed and with a second trial pending, I have no idea when the work can start." She looked Charlie over. "I presume that when the police do give me a release, you still intend to perform the work immediately."

"Whenever that occurs," Charlie said. She wanted to tell the woman to stuff her damned job. Beverly didn't seem to care about the trial itself, or that the man who really murdered Janet would now be punished. Didn't seem to give a damn that an innocent man had been freed. What an insufferable woman. How could she be Janet's sister?

"If you will call me, I'll have my crew there as soon as possible." Of course she'd given Beverly no hint that her crew had consisted of three people including herself—or that now she'd lost a third of that staff. With James Stamps in jail, she'd have to hustle to find enough help to do a decent job—or any job. What a joke that one person made up a third of her entire work force.

Returning to the back, she had filled in, for Sicily, a multiple-copy work proposal for weekly maintenance of the gallery, number of hours per week she would give Sicily, exactly what that would include; and her weekly fee and what items, such as repairs, would be charged extra. She could hear clearly the conversation at Sicily's desk.

"I am anxious that the paintings be removed from that locker right away. Such a place does not seem suitable. All this impounding is most inconvenient."

"There are new, heavy-duty locks on the doors and gate," Sicily said. "And there is a guard on duty. The moment the locker is released, the moment the police give me permission, Janet's work will be brought here. My storeroom has a metal-shielded door, fire alarms, and frequent police surveillance. I must admit I'm somewhat surprised."

"Surprised at what?" Beverly said, bristling.

"Surprised and interested that you do not appear to be grieving for your dead sister."

Charlie hid a smile.

Beverly squared her shoulders, dangerously stretching the pink fabric. "Janet and I were not close, not even as children. When our parents were divorced she went with our father, I with Mother. We did not see each other often after that. Were, in fact, like strangers. I would be hypocritical to pretend more distress than I feel."

But you were still related, Charlie thought. *You were sisters*. And she wondered why Janet had left all her assets to Beverly, when they weren't close. But maybe Janet had felt differently about blood relationships, about family.

"I knew Janet so very little, she was more an acquaintance than a sister. I am deeply sorry she died so horribly, and I do feel eased now that the real killer seems to be in custody. I did not think that Rob Lake person was capable of killing anyone, but it was not up to me to decide."

Charlie signed the proposal and tore off her copy. Placing the gallery's copy in a white envelope, she left it at Sicily's desk, not stopping to disturb the two women, and headed for Jolly's.

Now, standing at the counter in the bright deli, she accepted the picnic hamper, wondering, amused, if she was going to be able to carry it. The huge wicker basket, covered with a red-and-white-checkered cloth, looked big enough to supply the entire street with supper.

Signing the tab, she exchanged small talk with Mr. Jolly. She had, as she'd passed the alley, seen two cats scoffing up some delicacy from a paper plate—not Dulcie or Joe. It amused and pleased her that Mr. Jolly fed the village cats. Not that the cats of Molena Point were exactly on welfare status. But they must enjoy those special treats; she thought of Jolly's alley as a sort of feline social club.

Carrying the hamper back to her van, which was parked in front of the gallery, she placed it safely on the floor, where it wouldn't spill, and headed for Clyde's house. Driving slowly across Ocean beneath the lacy filtered shade, breathing deeply the aromatic scent of eucalyptus, she realized how at home she felt in Molena Point after only a few weeks; as if she had lived all her life in the small village. Molena Point just suited her, it was big enough and had enough well-to-do residents to provide her with the means for a thriving business, but was also cozy and friendly.

Clyde was waiting for her on the porch, wearing faded jeans and a padded red jacket. The gray tomcat was draped across his shoulder. As she slid out and came around the van, the big cat watched her intently, his yellow eyes wise and appraising.

This was a first for her, taking cats on a picnic. As she fetched out the deli basket and started up the walk, the tomcat fixed on the basket, nose twitching, his gaze riveted. She supposed to a cat the scents were overwhelming.

Clyde took the basket, stashed it in the backseat of his big antique Packard. They didn't need to discuss which vehicle to take—no one wanted to share her van among the ladders, mops, buckets, and half-empty paint cans. He settled the basket on the floor of the backseat between some folded blankets, the tomcat edging forward off his shoulder.

"Leave the picnic alone, Joe. It's for later."

The cat cut his eyes at Clyde with sly humor, and kneaded his claws in Clyde's shoulder. And as she swung into the passenger's seat, Clyde tossed Joe in next to her. The cat gave her a wide yellow stare and immediately climbed into her lap.

He turned around three times, getting settled, his hard paws bruising her thighs. She was flattered to be honored with his presence. She'd really expected him to jump in the backseat and tear apart the picnic.

When she stroked him, he smiled and purred like some potentate receiving obeisance from his subjects, his attitude insolent, imperious. This cat, Charlie thought, was very full of himself.

Clyde backed out of the drive, swinging up to Ocean, and turned left. Two blocks farther on he pulled into the ten-minute zone in front of the library. A lacework of light and shadows patterned the sidewalk around them, and painted the library's white stucco walls. When Wilma came hurrying out she was carrying a green book bag from which protruded two tabby ears— these two people were obsessed with their cats.

As Wilma slid into the backseat, Dulcie rose up inside the bag and peered over the top, her green eyes gleaming, her paws clutching the top of the bag, kneading softly as if with excitement.

Watching her, Charlie felt like she'd not only fallen into a delightful place to live, but maybe into Alice's wonderland, into a world of smirking cats and what promised to be a mad hatter picnic.

Heading up Ocean to Highway One and turning south, Clyde's old Packard received interested glances. Both villagers and tourists turned to look at the bright red antique touring car.

They drove down Highway One five miles, looking out at the sea, then headed inland a short distance. Turned right again onto a narrow dirt road that led off through a little woods, a deeply shaded stand of close-set saplings.

Parking in the woods where the road ended, they set off walking, carrying the picnic hamper and blankets. The cats surprised Charlie again by trotting along beside them as obedient as a couple of dogs. On the narrow, leafy path alone in the dim woods, the five of them made a strange little procession. They couldn't see the ocean, but they pressed ahead eagerly toward its thunder.

The woods ended at a flat green pasture spreading away like a green tabletop. And that velvet field ended abruptly a quarter mile ahead. Nothing beyond but sky and sea. And a gigantic rock thrusting up out of the sea. They could hear the waves crashing against it, wild and rhythmic.

The pasture grass was damp, soaking Charlie's tennis shoes. The cats raced away, chasing each other, stopping to sniff at rabbit holes. Neither Clyde nor Wilma seemed concerned that they would run away. Charlie had never seen cats who behaved like this. The three of them walked in companionable silence to the edge of the cliff.

Ten feet below, churning breakers foamed against the chimney rock. Directly below them at the foot of the cliff lay a white sand beach tilting down, falling away to a strip of dark, wet sand. Between that strip of sand and the chimney rock seethed a narrow neck of sea, foaming up, sucking back clear as green glass. They descended the cliff and spread the blankets on the warm sand, and the cats immediately settled down on the smaller blanket, expectantly watching the picnic basket.

Tucked into one side of the basket was a good Pinot Blanc and a tray of goose liver canapés. Wilma poured the wine into plastic cups, laid out the canapés. They toasted the sea and each other as the breakers sucked out, lifted, crashed in again wild and foaming.

No one had hinted to Charlie that this picnic was a celebration, but she got the idea that it was. Some secret celebration, not so much a secret from her, perhaps, as simply a very private matter.

But what a strange thought.

Yet there was some odd little mystery here, clinging around Wilma and Clyde and the two cats.

Maybe when she had lived in Molena Point longer she'd learn to understand what it was that they sheltered so carefully. She felt certain it was nothing that would dismay her, she had more a sense of lightness, almost of whimsy. Something that, if she knew, should delight her. Meantime, their silent celebration was nice. She liked knowing people who had secrets.

But the strange thing was, the cats seemed to share in the secret, their eyes were filled with some keen feline satisfaction. Both cats had an after-the-kill look. The kind of look a cat had when he dragged a dead rabbit into the parlor and left it on the rug, the look of the triumphant hunter bestowing a priceless gift.

Puzzled and amused, she helped Wilma unwrap the feast that George Jolly had prepared. In insulated containers, the French bread was still warm from the oven, the large portion of Jolly's best Puget Sound salmon was admirably chilled. The assorted fruits and the big wedge of Brie were room temperature; and there was a pint of thick fresh cream, with two small plastic bowls.

Wilma fixed the cats' plates first, with a little bit of everything but the fruit, and Charlie poured cream into the bowls. And the cats feasted, each with that smug smile. And what cat could be more charming than these two? Even when they were smug, Dulcie's green eyes were laughing, Joe's yellow eyes gleaming with challenge. What cat could be more mysterious and charming?

Get cozy with

CAROLYN HART's

award-winning DEATH ON DEMAND mysteries

APRIL FOOL DEAD
978-0-380-80722-2

A felonious forger has made it appear as if mystery bookstore owner Annie Darling is accusing some of her neighbors of murder. Then the town's body count starts mysteriously increasing.

SUGARPLUM DEAD
978-0-380-80719-2

Annie Darling's yuletide preparations have to be put on hold thanks to several rather inconvenient distractions—including murder, as she has to prove the innocence of her own deadbeat Dad.

WHITE ELEPHANT DEAD
978-0-380-79325-9

Annie's dear friend (and best customer) Henny Brawley stands accused of murdering a Women's Club volunteer-cum-blackmailer. And only Annie and her husband Max can prove the hapless Henny innocent.

YANKEE DOODLE DEAD
978-0-380-79326-6

Annie and Max watch their Fourth of July holiday explode not only with fun and fireworks, but with murder as well, as retired Brigadier General Charlton "Bud" Hatch is shot dead before Annie's eyes.

SRM2 1007